THE EYE STONE

Roberto Tiraboschi

THE EYE STONE

*Translated from the Italian
by Katherine Gregor*

Europa
editions

Europa Editions
214 West 29th Street
New York, N.Y. 10001
www.europaeditions.com
info@europaeditions.com

Translation by Katherine Gregor
Original title: *La pietra per gli occhi. Venetia 1106 d.C.*
Translation copyright © 2015 by Europa Editions

Library of Congress Cataloging in Publication Data is available
ISBN 978-1-60945-265-0

Tiraboschi, Roberto
The Eye Stone

Book design by Emanuele Ragnisco
www.mekkanografici.com
Cover photo by Franco Gatti

Prepress by Grafica Punto Print – Rome

Printed in the USA

To my friends

"Se pareba boves,
alba pratalia araba
et albo versorio teneba
et negro semen seminaba."
(He drove the oxen by himself,
Tilling a white field
Holding a white plow
Sowing black seed.)
8TH–9TH CENTURY VERONESE RIDDLE

"No light, but rather darkness visible."
—JOHN MILTON

CONTENTS

THE EYE STONE

I.
BOBBIO ABBEY

I saw a shadow teetering atop one of the towers. It was mumbling a prayer as it swayed over the abyss, against a night sky black as tar. A winter's night in the year of Our Lord 1106.

The bells had just summoned the monks to Lauds. Ademaro was walking through the cloisters, his head down to protect himself against the icy wind that eddied beneath his habit. Every so often, he glanced at his brothers as they advanced in single file, and searched for Edgardo, whom he had not seen join them. Perhaps he was already inside the church.

Eighty-six prayers. Thirteen for the Blessed Virgin Mary, thirteen for the day, thirty for the living, and thirty more for the dead.

Edgardo had not arrived yet, which was puzzling, since he risked a severe punishment of twenty lashes. An icy whirlwind penetrated the slits in the aisle, raising a cloud of dust. The monks bent double in the pews, withdrawing their heads into their hoods like frightened tortoises.

After Lauds, Ademaro left his brothers, who were on their way to the refectory, and climbed the stairs to the library scriptorium, above the chapter house. It sometimes happened that Edgardo, seized by a kind of frenzy, would spend the night stooped over his parchment, finishing a copying task.

It was still dark, and Ademaro groped his way up, supporting himself against the stone wall of the staircase. His frozen fingers had turned blue. In the library, covered in books and

manuscripts, the outlines of the lecterns looked like the petrified remains of a forest ravaged by ice. He walked into the
scriptorium. It was deserted. He was about to leave when, next
to one of the lecterns, he noticed sheets of parchment scattered
on the floor, as though blown there by a gust of wind. At the
end of the hall, the tiny door leading to the library tower was
open, something which never happened. Nobody ever went up
there. He approached and looked up the winding staircase that
led to the top. A soft lament, like a litany, came from above. He
started to climb the narrow stone steps. The moaning, something between a prayer and a sob, grew louder.

When he reached the bastion, he glimpsed the outline,
wrapped in the night mist, of a shapeless mass swaying on the
parapet like the branch of a tree shaken by the wind, and emitting a low, animal lament. He lunged toward the shadow and
hugged it by the legs.

"Brother, stop! For the love of God, stop!"

The man turned, and in the darkness Ademaro recognized
Edgardo.

"May God forgive you, Edgardo. Come. Hold onto me."

Edgardo dropped into his arms, exhausted and drained of
all strength.

"My God, what were you thinking?"

Edgardo looked pale and was having trouble breathing.

"What happened to you? Why . . . ?"

In whom could he confide, if not in Ademaro, his only
friend? They had grown up together at Bobbio Abbey. All
those endless days spent hunched over manuscripts, studying,
then the long apprenticeship under the tutelage of the oldest
master copyist. Only Ademaro would understand his torment.

When, at dawn on that autumn day in the year of Our Lord
1081, they snatched him from his mother's belly and his father,
proud of having sired a son, lifted him, still covered in blood,

toward the sky, no one noticed that his body was as crooked as the root of a sick olive tree. Together with the other noblemen of the county, the family feasted for three days to celebrate the firstborn, Edgardo d'Arduino, heir to the seigniory.

As he was growing up, however, everyone quickly realized that Edgardo would never become the knight his father hoped for. A rounded, graceful hump on the breastbone and a deformed pelvis that did not quite fit the right leg gave him a skipping, pendulous gait that was more appropriate to a jester than to a knight. Out of deference to his noble origins, he was nicknamed Edgardo the Crooked, instead of just being called the Cripple.

At fourteen, he expressed the wish to retire to Bobbio Abbey as a cleric, in order to devote himself to studying and writing, a decision that made his father happy and relieved not to have to bear the sight of the little monster any longer.

For seven years, he studied the art of the Trivium and the Quadrivium, taught by Benedictine monks, and applied himself to the art of copying.

Edgardo thought this would be his destiny for the rest of his life. God had deprived him of a strong, well-proportioned body but given him a steady hand and sharp eyesight. So why had He abandoned him now?

"I don't want to live anymore, Ademaro. My eyes . . . " he touched his eyelids, "I can't see anymore. I can't make out letters and words, everything is blurred. I'm going blind."

Ademaro hugged him.

"You're probably tired," he said, trying to cheer him up. "You've been working on the copy of *De Consolazione Philosophiae* for months without a day's respite. The waxed canvas over the scriptorium windows only lets in a pale light that's tiring to the eyes . . . "

"No, I started getting the first signs a few months ago, and recently they've become worse. I can't manage more than three or four pages a day and even that's a great effort, whereas before I never did fewer than twelve. Everything I've built over years of study and hard work is disappearing. There's nothing else I can do except copy, copy and copy. Only then does my life acquire a meaning. I'm happy only when I'm bent over a parchment, quill in my hand, surrounded by the pungent smell of goatskin and ink." He drew his face closer to his friend's and stared at him. "What can I do with this crippled body if I can't copy or read? It's pointless carrying on living."

"Calm yourself, I beg you. There must be a way to stop this disease that's eating away at your eyes. I know there are ointments that can restore the sight."

"Our herbalist brother has given me a balm I rubbed on my eyes for days on end, but there's been no improvement."

They leaned against the crenellated parapet to shelter from the wind. Edgardo's face had a deadly pallor.

"I always thought that Our Lord chose to give me a cripple's body in order to distract me from the vanity of the world, and thus show me the path to glorifying Him by passing on the written words of wise men and poets to mankind. Now if my eyes fail, my life has no more meaning, no more purpose. A copyist with no eyes is a joke on God's part. What sin have I committed to provoke Our Lord's wrath and deserve such a terrible punishment? God cannot be so cruel."

"Don't blaspheme, Edgardo," said Ademaro. "Everything has a reason."

"Then tell me what it is," Edgardo implored.

Ademaro knew the love and self-denial with which Edgardo devoted himself to copying. Although he was only twenty-five, he was considered a master among the Bobbio copyists for the precision of his lines, the quality of his lettering, his fidelity to the text, and his ability to memorize the pericope, that part of the text that could be learned by heart, increasing the scribe's speed at transcribing. Ademaro would have liked to find a clear and easy answer to boost his friend's faith. However, all he could say, in a faint voice, was, "The ways of Our Lord are unfathomable."

"I cannot accept that," Edgardo shouted in despair. "I don't believe God would punish me like this. If I have to be blind, then it's better to die."

Ademaro put a hand over his mouth to silence him.

"Enough. Be quiet. There's always a light at the end of even the darkest tunnel. Listen to me . . . " He hesitated before continuing. "I don't know if I'm right in telling you this . . . I don't want to give you false hopes . . . "

"I beg you, tell me."

"Some time ago, during one of my trips in search of manuscripts for the library, I met a merchant who traded with the Orient. He said that a traveler from Alexandria in Egypt had told him he'd seen with his very eyes, in the library there, elderly wise men who used a stone, clear as water and transparent as air, to help them read. He said they used it precisely to heal eye diseases caused by old age."

"A stone for the eyes?" asked Edgardo, anxious to know more. "Is it some kind of amulet? Or a substance to take with medicine?"

"I don't know any more than that. At the time, I didn't think to ask more about it. It sounded like one of those absurd daydreams made up just for fun by travelers from faraway countries."

"And what if it's true? What if the eye stone really exists?"

Ademaro fell silent. The seed of hope had wormed its way into his friend's mind and would now never cease to torment him.

Edgardo insisted. "Do you think a stone that restores eyesight really exists? Have you ever read anything about it in any treatise?"

"Don't delude yourself."

"I am not deluding myself but I don't see any other way, don't you understand? I'd do anything to continue to see." He grasped at his friend's habit. "Ademaro, tell me where this merchant lives."

Ademaro rubbed his face.

"I must go to collect some manuscripts from the Abbey of San Giorgio soon. His shop is nearby."

Edgardo did not hesitate. "Take me with you."

"I'm not sure I'm doing the right thing."

"I beg you, in the name of our friendship." Edgardo sought his hand and gave it a powerful squeeze.

Ademaro bowed his head. He could not deny hope to a friend.

"I'll tell the abbot I need help to choose which manuscripts to buy. And you have a lot of experience."

"It's a good excuse."

"I think it'll be a fruitless attempt," Ademaro added with severity.

Edgardo hugged him. "Let God decide. Is it far to the Abbey of San Giorgio?"

Ademaro's voice grew deeper, softer, but also more uncertain, as though remembering a dream he had had as a boy.

"Two days from here, along the coast of our sea, where several rivers flow together and interweave in an inextricable labyrinth of basins and canals, lakes and pools, a city rises, built on water. Its inhabitants move about only on boats and ride the waves faster than galloping horses. They know the names of all the fish in the ocean, they can govern the winds and are not afraid to push their ships beyond the Pillars of Hercules. The name of this city is Venetia."

II.
MEDOACUS MAIOR

He awoke, hit in the face by the rays of scarlet light peering through the branches of the birches along the bank. Edgardo opened his eyes and saw Ademaro sitting in the bow, examining the sky. He looked around, trying to remember where he was. For years, he had woken in the same place, surrounded by the gray stones of his cell, wrapped in the stench of dank straw that covered the floor. He breathed in deeply the humid river air and felt a shudder of pleasure, as though conscious of having a body for the first time.

Illumined by a red reflection that colored the surface of the river, the *sandolo** glided silently across the water. They had been sailing since Terce, following the course of Medoacus Maior until they had lost track of time.

"Does sunset in this region always have such fiery colors?" Edgardo asked.

Ademaro continued examining the sky. "I've never seen such a display. It's as though the sun's burst."

The boatman bent forward. His oar cut through the water without a splash, like a blade.

"There's a fire," he said, sounding weary. "One of the districts is being destroyed by fire. You'll see it soon, more or less at the last river bend."

Transported by the current and surrounded by purple-red streaks, they were sailing downstream toward unknown places.

---

* The asterisks refer to notes at the back of the book.

A sense of anxiety crept into the initial feeling of pleasant exhilaration. Edgardo had never before left Bobbio Abbey. This was his first journey. His curiosity about visiting unknown lands was mixed with disorientation and the sense of being on the brink of a new world. Fortunately, Ademaro, whom he trusted wholeheartedly, was with him. He had always envied his confident demeanor, his balanced thinking, his sturdy, grounded body, and especially his absolute faith in God's will.

The *sandolo* increased its speed, swept along by a rapid. Pieces of white bark, blown from the beeches by the dry wind, fell on the water like snowflakes. The riverbed grew wider and the despairing shrieks of seagulls reached them from the horizon. A gust of torrid air filled their lungs and their eyes blurred with tears. The monks withdrew their heads into their hoods and the boatman bent forward like a blade of straw licked by the flame of a torch. The vegetation grew scarcer and the riverbanks more distant. As the boat advanced, the waters of the Medoacus started to lose their clarity and became contaminated with putrid, muddy trails followed by floating lumps of green algae. The river, with its cortege of trees, had vanished and the *sandolo* was suddenly surrounded by an endless expanse of grainy, gelatinous liquid with metallic gleams, still and without ripples, which gave off a stench of putrefying flesh.

Scattered around, you could see, peering through the surface of the water, tongues of soft, muddy soil, covered in shells and fragments of crustaceans, and crisscrossed by natural canals. The banks, which were more compact, were overrun by sparse blades of rough, yellow grass. In the middle of the tiny islands, where the action of the salt water was less strong, there was a proliferation of veritable walls of rushes and canes interwoven like an impenetrable canvas.

As the boat advanced, the sky, more purple now, drew closer, and the air became difficult to breathe.

After several turns, they came out into an open space where you could see a deep red glow on the horizon.

The boatman lifted his oar and pointed into the distance. "There's the fire."

"The whole city's burning!" said Ademaro.

"No, it's up north," said the boatman. "Perhaps an island in the muddy sea."

Edgardo leaned cautiously toward the bow. "It's like reaching the gates of Hell," he said.

The boatman gave an amused sneer. "It's no Hell, it's Venetia. Our houses are all made of timber. The soil is too soft and treacherous to support stone. So all it takes is for a spark to fly through the air and everything catches fire, and if the wind is against us then the whole city is swept away. It's already happened many times. Don't worry, though, we'll keep our distance. We're following the Vigano canal and going around Spinalunga, so we'll come in through the back. I don't want two monks in Hell on my conscience . . . " He gave a sharp, sobbing laugh that sounded at odds with his mastiff-like body.

With one stroke of the oar he swung the boat south. Edgardo let himself fall to the floor. The bones in his legs were hurting. He lay down, cradled by the rustling sound of the sparse grass scratching the keel.

They moved forward in a world that was suspended and unreal, in a silence broken only by the distant crackling of the fire. Daylight was rapidly fading and the purple of the sunset blended with the cinnabar glow of the fire. To the east, like a mirage, a thick, luxuriant forest covering a large, protruding island suddenly appeared, and you could see other signs of thriving vegetation in the distance.

They were going along a narrow canal when they hit something with a jolt. The *sandolo* rocked violently and Ademaro grabbed hold of his friend in order to avoid falling into the water.

"A canker on you—what the devil have we hit?"

The boatman pulled out the oar and they all leaned over the edge to examine the surface. In the shadow of the rushes, Edgardo saw a dark mass emerging in front of the bow. With the help of the oar, the boatman tried to push away the obstacle. It was a shiny, slippery substance of an undefined gray. It looked like the back of a large animal, a cow, perhaps. Shells and crabs were clinging to the fur, their feast forming a living, swarming carpet. He pushed again with the oar but the mass, perhaps jammed in the riverbed, would not budge. Edgardo took the other oar and tried to lever the animal, which finally turned on its side with an eerie sucking sound.

"Merciful God!" said Edgardo.

Ademaro leaned forward. "It's disgusting."

Before them, legs up in the air, a cow floated, its belly full of air like a goatskin. Instead of udders, it had a second head sprouting from its intestines. It was a muzzle complete with open mouth, hollow eye sockets and a nose eaten by fish.

"A two-headed beast," said the boatman with detachment.

Edgardo stared at the monster with more compassion than horror, almost as though feeling solidarity with all that was deformed.

"They've found so many others like that, deformed animals, freaks of nature. Pigs with hens' feet, geese with the bodies of dogs, fish with hooves like a stag's, asses with heads instead of backsides. It's the Devil trying to dazzle us with his magic tricks. We must repent—something terrible is about to happen."

"Even creatures that do not follow the golden rules of nature are the work of God and deserve respect," said Ademaro.

"All I know is that anything that's deformed is a sign of the Devil," the boatman grunted confidently and, with a final stroke of the oar, he pushed away the carcass of the animal, which, as a sign of farewell, spewed out of its second open mouth an eel that swam away, undisturbed, through the rushes.

Edgardo was absorbed in his thoughts. He had heard those two words together so often: devil and deformed. So much so that he had started to believe it, too.

The sky was now dark and threads of fog wavered over the shoals. All of a sudden, out of nowhere, a thick row of black pillars that seemed to rise from the water appeared right in front of the bow.

"Here we are," said the boatman. "This is the island of San Giorgio."

The *sandolo* drew up alongside the shore and Edgardo realized that the menacing figures were tall, slender cypresses that covered the entire island.

They disembarked on the *junctorio*,* walked up the wooden steps, then groped their way in the dark across the small stretch of soil that led to the gates of the abbey. They knocked.

After a long wait, the monk who acted as gatekeeper, thin, lanky and wearing a habit that was too short for him, let them in.

"We were expecting you earlier. Compline finished ages ago and all the brothers are already in the dormitory." His tone was gruff but then he looked at them with a compassionate expression.

"You must be hungry. Come with me."

They walked under the portico of a small, rustic cloister in the center of which towered a row of cypresses, slim and oblong like the monk escorting them. As he came out of the first cloister, Edgardo noticed the dark outline of the bell tower that seemed to watch them from above through its triforia and its arches.

The kitchens were beyond the second herb cloister, near the refectory. The beanpole handed them two bowls containing some kind of muddy pulp that stank of rotting fish.

"It's an eel and oat pie. There's wine in that carafe, if you'd like some. You're entitled to it after a long journey, to replenish the blood. You can stay in the guest quarters for tonight—

Ademaro knows the way—and tomorrow we'll allocate you your cells."

Having said that, he handed Edgardo a candle stub and walked away, his steps like a camel's.

There was a long table protruding from the wall, but no sign of stools or chairs, so the monks put their bowls on it and got ready to eat standing up, like horses.

"He treated us like two beggars," said Edgardo, smelling the contents of the pan. "This is nauseating."

Ademaro laughed. "You'll have to get used to it. For people who live on water, fish is like grain to the peasant."

Edgardo stuck two fingers into the mush and lifted some to his lips. "It's not that poisonous after all," he said.

"You're always prejudiced. It's your noble origin that rears its head every so often. You must accept new things with an open mind."

Edgardo bowed his head. Ademaro was right. However, it was not his nobility that gave him that seemingly haughty attitude. Anger smoldered in his soul, a deep resentment that gnawed at him, and prevented him from facing life with the joy and faith appropriate to a Benedictine cleric.

They ate greedily in a hollow silence accompanied only by the gentle rhythm of the lapping water that seemed to be gurgling right under their feet.

When they had finished, exhausted, they went up to the guest quarters on the first floor. At the end of the hall, behind tiny niches upholstered in mold, they found long tables covered with straw. Even though large wooden beams were nailed to the windows, there was a humid, salty draught coming through, which smelled of sun-dried algae. Edgardo lay down, and felt his twisted bones ache.

"Let me give you some advice," Ademaro murmured, sitting up on his pallet. "It would be wiser not to mention to anyone here at the monastery the true reason for your journey."

Edgardo was surprised. "Why not? I see nothing wrong in trying to find a cure for my failing eyesight."

"Abbot Carimanno is a wise and levelheaded man. He's in the process of transforming this abbey into one of the most important study centers in Civitas Rivoalti. He's brought together clerics, translators and highly-reputed copyists. Day by day, the library grows richer in new books. However, he's an old man, tied to tradition and not very well-disposed toward novelties. It's better not to upset him."

"Do you think a stone could throw this holy man into turmoil?"

"Wait," Ademaro interrupted, "I've never told you this stone really exists. What was related to me was the tale of a merchant, and it could be no more than the product of a rich imagination. Let's leave fantasies and dreams outside this sacred place. Let's keep them to ourselves."

They had spent years sitting beside each other in the scriptorium and yet Edgardo had never heard his friend sound so worried.

"Very well, if that's what you want."

Ademaro smiled, relieved. "I'm only asking you to be cautious."

"I'll be cautious, I promise." Edgardo said, and wrapped himself in his cloak, shaken by a slight sense of anxiety.

The word "cautious" could only mean one thing. That in some corner, behind the eyes of a stranger, perhaps even among his brothers, danger might be lurking.

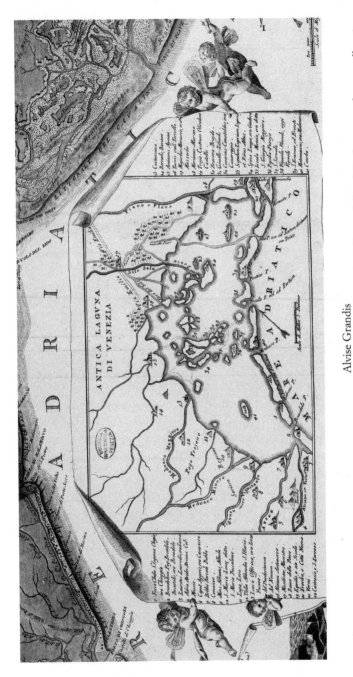

Alvise Grandis

The Venice Lagoon, ancient and modern, newly outlined and distinct with its Islands, Valleys and Canals in the present day, as well as, in comparison, the Lagoon as it was at the time Venice was founded, with both the old and new names.

III.
AMURIANUM

At the first light of dawn, thick soot was still raining down from the sky, spreading a veil of embers over the thatched roofs, the fields of sea lavender, and the waters green with algae. Seagulls and crows flapped their wings, raising clouds of ash, while the first rays of the rising sun struggled to filter through the layers of smoke that drifted over the island of Amurianum.

The fire had been put out during the night but the smell of burning still lingered on the paths, among the huts and in the furrows of the canals.

Angelo Segrado pulled down the cloak that was covering him and, blinded by the glaring morning light, half-closed his eyes. For a moment he thought it had been a terrible nightmare. He inhaled deeply and the smoke filled his lungs, taking his breath away. It had not been a dream, everything really had burned down. In just one night, the fire had swept away his furnace and storehouse, then spread to the neighboring houses. He had nothing left.

They had called him when the first fire had broken out at the start of the night, and he had taken the *scaula** and rowed with all his strength from Metamauco with Kallis, in order to arrive in time. They had fought the flames until Lauds but there was nothing they could do. Exhausted, they had fallen asleep under a fig tree in the *campo** in front of the furnace, in that deserted area behind Santa Maria degli Angeli where nobody wanted to live because it was infested with snakes and malaria.

Segrado stood up. Kallis was still asleep next to him, wrapped in the remnants of a torn sail. He took a step toward that which, only the day before, had been his realm. Everything had burned down: his work bench, the blowpipe, the punty, all the willow and alder used to fuel the fire, as well as the cups, phials, chalices and cruets for the ointments—the high temperature had caused everything to explode. Even the brick furnace was no longer usable. The fireplace had been salvaged, but the central chamber for the cauldrons had collapsed together with the room for annealing. No point in even thinking about starting it up again—it would be far too costly. All that remained of his workshop was ashes, embers and charred beams. He could have screamed like a wounded giant.

He was known in Amuranium as the bald bear because his huge body, covered in dense hair, was dominated by a totally smooth skull. His hands, as large as shovels, he could turn into the delicate fingers of an embroiderer as soon as he handled the pliers and shears he used for shaping lumps of molten glass. They said he had had all his teeth pulled out so that he could blow through the blowpipe with more power and that he lived in Metamauco, like a hermit, alone with Kallis in a hut no one had ever seen.

He approached the bundle lying on the grass and nudged it with his foot.

"Come on, get up!" he ordered. "See if you can at least salvage a few tools."

The sail unrolled as though swelled by a gust of wind and a long, thin figure emerged, wrapped in a tortoiseshell cloak that revealed only a face with Oriental features, tapered fingers and large, knotty feet. Her skin had an amber glow and blended with the cloak fabric in a single-hue brushstroke.

Kallis stood up and with quick, light steps, as though flying over the puddles of mud and ashes, approached what was left of the oven. Like a thread of wool blown by the wind. A delicate and sinuous thread from the hands of a Mongolian weaver. She started rummaging among the ruins, lifting poles, moving bricks and stones so quickly that one naturally wondered how such a small body could conceal such strength.

"Master . . . Master . . . my God, what happened?" Niccolò, the servant boy who stoked and fueled the fire in the furnace, was running toward him, filled with despair. "Merciful God, everything's burned down!"

Segrado lowered his head. "We arrived too late."

Niccolò was shaking, rocking back and forth like a child. "It's not fair! Why has God done this to us?"

"Did you check the fireplace before you left last night?" Segrado asked in a harsh tone.

"Yes, Master, I left it barely lit, like I always do. Besides, there was no wind yesterday, so no danger from the embers. I closed the door and the smoke holes."

"And yet the fire broke out," Segrado said, thoughtfully.

"It's not my fault, Master, I swear on Our Lord."

Segrado looked around. "The fire can come from inside— or from outside. A sly spark from who knows where, carried by the wind or by the hand of a man."

Niccolò did not understand.

"Perhaps here in Amurianum, someone's blood simmered with envy at seeing me have an oven of my own."

On her knees, Kallis was digging with her bare hands, surrounded by blowpipes, steaming ashes, and plumes of smoke, as though she were rummaging in the crater of a volcano.

"What are we going to do now, Master?" Niccolò asked, anxious.

Segrado seized his head, glistening with sweat, in his hands, almost wishing he could split it in two in an attempt to find an answer.

"I don't know . . . Perhaps we can look for another oven,

one we could hire, so that we can continue our work. Although there are very few glassblowers left who own a furnace."

"Master Tàtaro has bought almost all of them."

"A canker on him . . . If he carries on like this, all Amurianum glass will end up coming out of his ovens."

Niccolò took a step forward. "What will become of the experiments, Master?"

Annoyed by Niccolò's words, Segrado tensed up and glared at him. "That's right, the experiments . . . The experiments will end up in the storehouse for my shit!" He patted his behind and shook himself like a wet bear.

Kallis smiled with the satisfaction of a little girl and lifted, like trophies, a shovel, a blowpipe and a pair of tweezers, which was all she had managed to recover.

The bell had just rung for Prime and a new day was beginning on the island of Amurianum. Beggars, lepers and penitents were already crowding beneath the wooden portico at the entrance of the Basilica of Santa Maria Vergine. The façade of the church, which had a nave and two aisles, had just been rebuilt in brickwork. The roof was still covered in reeds and straw.

Along the *rio** of the glassmakers, onto which almost all the glassmakers' ovens gave, the servant boys loaded barges with items in colorful mosaics, beads, phials, glasses, bottles, and chalices, to be transported to the Rivoalto,* ready to be stowed alongside other goods onboard merchant ships bound for the Orient.

A young porter, laden like a mule, staggered out of a storehouse. When he was halfway along the plank that connected the shore and the boat, he started swaying dangerously.

"Be careful, you dimwit!" the owner of the storehouse shouted, running to his aid and grabbing him by the jacket before he could fall into the canal with all the merchandise.

"What's the matter? Are you drunk?"

The porter stared back at him. "There's a man in the canal . . . "

"Where?"

"There, twisted in the rope, between the keel and the shore."

The master bent over and, in the pale light of the winter dawn, saw the body of a man floating upside down.

"It's true, you're right," he said without losing his countenance. "There's a dead man in the canal."

It often happened that during the night a drunk would fall into the water in another quarter, then be carried about by the current for hours and even days before being found. For that reason, the discovery did not cause much stir. People gathered and, with some effort since the bank was slippery, managed to carry the body ashore. It was covered in mud and algae, swollen, and the skin had turned so purple, it must have been in the water for a long time.

"That's Marco Balbo!" someone cried.

"Who's that?"

"A *garzone**from Torcellus. He worked here in Amurianum."

"That's right, it's him. He was an assistant in various foundries."

"He must have drowned."

The owner of the storehouse opened the damaged jacket. "No, he was stabbed."

There was a deep, gaping wound right in the middle of his belly, letting a section of gut protrude.

"He was a good lad, skilled at his trade. God be with him."

The storehouse owner tried to wipe the dead man's face with a rag.

"Holy Mother of God!" he cried out. "Look! Look!"

Through the blotches of slime on his face, the half-opened eyelids revealed an unnatural, whitish sheen that gave the eyes a somewhat artificial, eerie expression. Everyone was dumb-founded, as though those strange eyes possessed some evil power.

The storehouse owner plucked up the courage to lift the eyelids in full, and a gasp of horror rose from the crowd. Marco Balbo's eyes had been gouged out and replaced with two perfectly crafted glass ones. At the center of the opaque, milky glass eyeballs were two ruby-colored pupils, shining like gemstones, which produced a fiery glow and inspired a feeling of torment and fear.

The men looked at one another, terrified.

"These eyes are the color of hell," someone cried out. "It's the work of Beelzebub!" Everyone immediately made the sign of the cross.

No one had ever seen such horror. Gouged-out eyes, cut-off hands, men hanged and women burned at the stake were everyday events, but that fixed gaze and the icy light of the stones penetrated your soul like an omen of death, a curse, the Apocalypse foretold. Who could have done this to the hapless Balbo?

I n one night, Hell has been transformed into Heaven, Edgardo the Crooked thought as his eyes wandered over the surrounding land and water.

With the first light of dawn, after prayers, Ademaro had taken him around the monastery to see the cloisters, the chapter, the refectory, the church and all the way up to the belfry. It was the first time Edgardo had been able let his eyes stray beyond the walls of Bobbio Abbey. He was overcome with a profound emotion, a feeling of insignificance and powerlessness—the feeling of the wretched mortal who would never be able to fathom the secret of Creation.

Sky and water sank into each other, blending in an all-enveloping mother-of-pearl glow. A light northerly wind had swept everything away, and cleaned Venetia of the infernal smoke and fog. The city appeared to him in all its incomprehensible and daring desire to steal land from the waters and build on nothing—churches, convents, towers, and dwelling places—in a defiant array of joists, platforms, bridges, dikes, and stilt houses. The fresh water that descended into the sea from the mouths of the rivers ended in a swamp and mixed with salt water, creating, with soil and mud dragged in by the floods, a labyrinth of small and large canals, streams, pits, ponds and a succession of pools among rises, tidal shallows, and fords.

On some of the islands, there were bursts of luxuriant vegetation, oaks, elms, willows, beeches, and alders, as dense and shady as in forests in the hinterland. These alternated with land cultivated as vegetable gardens and vines.

Some stretches, scattered on the lagoon, reflected a blinding white glare and seemed illuminated by supernatural reflections.

"They're saltworks," said Ademaro. "There are many on the islands around Venetia. With trade and fishing, they are a mainstay for these people." He pointed at a distant corner of the island. "There's also one here in San Giorgio. With the mill, it contributes to making the abbey self-sufficient. The salt is exchanged for other goods. Then there are vegetable gardens, fruit trees, and fish."

Edgardo half closed his eyes to protect himself from the glare which had become more bothersome with the rising of the sun. "This landscape gives you a feeling of peace and soothing languor, as though nature here has the power to protect you from all suffering and harm."

Ademaro cut him short. "Let's go now, I must introduce you to the abbot. You'll see, he's a deeply spiritual man, and witty, too."

They slowly went down the steep spiral staircase. Every step sent an excruciating pain through Edgardo's hip. He was used to living with his crooked bones, which seemed intent on forcing him to slither like an invertebrate insect.

Abbot Carimanno was waiting for them in the library on the ground floor. Edgardo was deeply disappointed by the meager number of manuscripts on the shelves in the small room. He had always imagined that all abbeys had libraries containing at least seven hundred volumes, like their own in Bobbio. Moreover, monks who had traveled south had told of libraries with over a thousand volumes.

"We're building our knowledge step by step. We collect, copy, translate and preserve the knowledge the wise men of the past have bequeathed to us."

Abbot Carimanno had a thin, hoarse voice. Tufts of white

hair sprouting from his nose and ears joined at the top of his skull, like a halo. He reminded Edgardo of a mangy old crane that used to nest on the tower of their castle when he was a child.

"We do the best we can without having the kind of resources you have at Bobbio." He smiled slyly. "Many manuscripts from Constantinople and Alexandria arrive in Venetia and we try to secure them for ourselves . . . even if our Ademaro here sometimes swipes the best morsels from right under our noses." He laughed. "I have confidence that within a few years, thanks to the generosity of our faithful, the library of San Giorgio will become one of the most important in any Benedictine monastery. An abbey with no books is like a stronghold with no provisions." Edgardo nodded reverently. "Ademaro says you've come along to help him choose new manuscripts for your library."

Edgardo lowered his head. "That is so," he said.

"And he also says you're an excellent copyist—the best in Bobbio."

"Ademaro is too kind," Edgardo replied cagily.

The abbot took a few springy steps toward the door leading to the cloister, and suddenly started mumbling, "What a foolish, doltish man I am! One of the most brilliant copyists of our monasteries has come to see us and I'm not even taking him to see our scriptorium . . . Fool. Ass . . . Please, follow me." And he climbed the stairs, skipping from step to step.

The scriptorium, on the first floor, right above the library, gave onto the botanical cloister, where medicinal herbs and spices were grown that were essential for the brother in charge of the sick. The room was not very large but filled with much more light than the one in Bobbio. The windows, in pairs, tall and with pointed arches, took up an entire wall and looked over an open field. An even, vibrant and almost unnatural light filtered through the waxed canvas. Various lecterns were aligned beneath the sources of light, and upon them were the codices to be copied or translated, as well as the smoothed-out parchment bearing lines traced with charcoal sticks.

Seeing his fellow brothers stooped over their papers, focusing on their work, engrossed in writing, he felt deeply sad. He wondered if his own time for writing had gone forever.

Ademaro had stopped to speak to a monk with a ruddy complexion, red as a crab, with bright, darting eyes.

"This brother looks like someone devoted only to the pleasures of the flesh," Ademaro said with a smile, introducing the monk to Edgardo, "but in truth he mainly cultivates the pleasures of the spirit. He's the most illustrious translator of Arabic into Latin I know. His name is Ermanno di Carinzia."

Edgardo bowed his head in a sign of homage. The monk self-consciously shook his entire body like a wet dog trying to shake off the rain. "No, no, Ademaro exaggerates . . . Still, appearances don't lie and I do like wine more than books." He burst out laughing, and the hilarity immediately alarmed the abbot, who quickly approached the trio.

"I would like your opinion," Carimanno said, taking Edgardo by the arm, "on a young copyist I consider to be very promising. He has a firm hand, an extraordinary memory, and very sharp eyesight." He pulled him toward a skinny young man who seemed to be drowning in a habit that was too large for him. He was writing, bent double, curled like a dry leaf, and had the greenish complexion of a sick person.

"His name is Rainardo," said the abbot. "Look, what do you think of his writing?"

For a moment, the light bouncing off the parchment numbed Edgardo's sight, and beads of sweat formed on his forehead. All the words looked out of focus. He turned to look at the abbot and had the impression the old man's dark eyes were searching his soul.

"So, what do you think?" Carimanno insisted.

Edgardo drew closer to the sheet of paper, perhaps too

close, with visible effort, and squinted. "I think it's excellent," he lied. "He has a fine ability for shaping letters."

"We would be honored if you'd now give our disciple an example of your own skill."

"I don't think that's necessary," said Edgardo. "The youth is already on the right path and doesn't need a teacher."

"I beg you, he'll find it useful," Carimanno insisted, handing him a goose quill.

The abbot's face had twisted into a sinister grimace, his lips tight, his curly hairs wriggling like threadworms. Edgardo wished he could hurl into the distance the pen that was dancing before his eyes.

"Writing is an art that requires solitude and silence, and never strives to show off."

"Just one line," Carimanno persevered, sneakily.

Edgardo turned abruptly. Why was he insisting? Did he know everything? Had he detected the impending blindness in his eyes?

"Most Illustrious Father, may I have your permission to postpone the test to another occasion?" Ademaro readily intervened, fearing his friend would grow rude and aggressive, as often happened when he was contradicted. "It's almost Terce and the boatman is waiting for us on the bank to take us to the book merchant. May we take our leave?"

Carimanno made a disappointed grimace. "If your task is so urgent, then you may take your leave." He stared into Edgardo's eyes. "We will have another opportunity to test your art."

Edgardo stared back at the abbot with defiance. Ademaro took him by the arm and pushed him toward the exit.

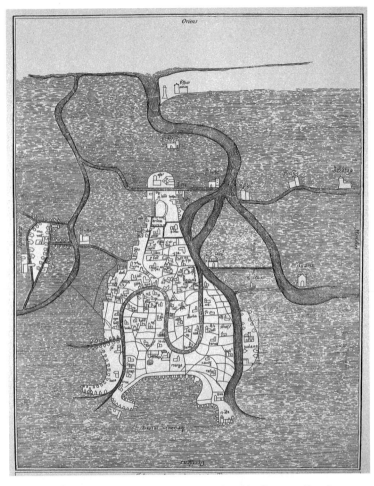

Paolino da Venezia's map (1346), reproduced by Temanza (detail)

V.
SAN MARCO

The water level had risen during the night and flooded the *junctorio* in front of the abbey. There was a gondola waiting for them at the bottom of the steps. The two monks went onboard and the boatman pushed away from the bank with his oar.

Edgardo stared at the greenish water with a dark expression. "What does the old man mean?" he snapped.

Ademaro tried to calm him. "Don't be disrespectful."

"I'm a cleric from a noble family—I've not taken vows. He has no authority over me."

"He just wanted a demonstration of your expertise."

"No, Ademaro. It was more than that. I read suspicion in his eyes. There's something untrustworthy about him."

"He's just curious. Don't worry, he suspects nothing."

Anxiety. A sense of instability. Equilibrium that suddenly vanishes and is replaced by a nervousness full of questioning. What had happened to take away his peace of mind? Edgardo could find no answer but he did not like that feeling. He looked up. "Where are we going?"

"To the shop of the merchant who told me about the stone for the eyes, as I promised."

Edgardo nodded. His agitation and bad mood prevented him from enjoying the amazing spectacle unfolding before him as they approached the dock opposite the Basilica of San Marco.

A wall of white sails swelled by the light breeze obscured the view of the piazza. Masts tall as towers swayed against the sky, almost touching one another. Oars interweaved and crossed. Hawsers flapped on the water surface with a low wheezing sound. The smaller boats maneuvered under cables and ropes, as if through the vines of a forest.

In the front row, chelandions, acazias, and war galleys protected the cogs that were unloading on the shore.

After many turns among those giants, the gondola managed to reach the dock that penetrated deep into the piazza until it lapped at the south entrance of the Basilica, which was mirrored in the water of the lagoon. The two monks got out and pushed their way through the crowd. Edgardo had never seen so many people in such a small space. Sailors, traders, servants, beggars, slaves, monks, whores, and pilgrims thronged in front of San Marco, shouting, negotiating, and complaining. Cries, arguments, calls. A Tower of Babel of languages and races.

The façade of the Basilica was surrounded by scaffolding swarming with men working on mosaics that rose under the narthex. On the opposite side of the piazza a wooden tower was being erected, which, as Ademaro explained, was used for sighting enemy ships or Dalmatian pirates, and for signaling the harbor, with a fire lit on the top, to those navigating at night. On the eastern side, in front of the lagoon, Doge Ordelaffo Falier had rebuilt the Doge's Palace after it had been totally destroyed by the fire of 1105. The towers on all four sides, their crenellated walls with bartizans, machicolations and lookouts, reminded Edgardo of his father's castle, and he felt a momentary twinge of nostalgia. However, the Doge's Palace had no need for a moat to protect it, since it was surrounded on two sides and at the back by a canal, the Rio Palazzo, which isolated it completely.

"Follow me and keep close, or you risk getting lost in this anthill," Ademaro warned.

Leaving the palace behind, they pushed their way through the crowds toward a waterway, the Rio Batario, which flowed at the end of the piazza and cut sharply across the green *campo* the people of Venetia called Brolo, the word suggesting an area dense with grass and trees. In the midst of all this green was a chapel dedicated to San Giminiano.

Carrying on straight ahead, they circumvented a luxuriant elder tree. Here, Edgardo stopped in amazement. Two large purebred piebalds were grazing quietly in the shade of the branches. The presence of the horses seemed extravagant and unreasonable to him, and he wondered how they had ended up here, in this watery landscape, crossing marshes and canals.

Ademaro edged into a narrow *calle** which started from the piazza and was called Calle delle Merzerie. "Mind how you walk," he said. In truth, it was almost impossible to advance through this narrow, crowded alley. Men on horseback traveling in both directions arrogantly pushed their way through a sea of people who relied on their wits to fulfill their daily chores. Along both sides of the clay walkways there were tiny timber houses, one story high at most, with thatched or plank roofs. Some had a small covered loggia on the upper floor. On the ground floor of every building were the workshops of craftsmen, shops with various merchandise, and storehouses crammed with goods. Everybody looked extremely busy and, perhaps unused to city chaos, Edgardo struggled to understand what it was they were doing exactly or in which direction they were going. They went in and out of the shops, laden with stuff, arguing and shouting. A *garzone* was running, pursued by the screams of a man who was probably his master. The horses kept releasing excrement without an ounce of decency. Anonymous arms appeared at first-floor windows and poured out nauseating fluids without any warning. On the roof of a small house, a young man who had just got up was pissing sleepily on the loggia of the neighboring house. Walking ahead without any unpleasant accidents was a difficult enterprise. Everyone skipped as best they could from one clod of earth that was still clean to another, so that one got the impression of a city populated by grasshoppers.

In front of the shops of tailors, doublet-makers, goldsmiths, dyers, boot-makers, and barbers, merchandise of every shape and kind was on display. Exhibited in front of a surgeon's shop, in a row of stuffed exotic animals, there was even a well-preserved Egyptian mummy in its sarcophagus. They struggled to walk through the street, which reminded Edgardo of a miniature, like the ones that adorned the margins of a page. A live drawing interwoven with monstrous beasts, winged horses, and deformed faces immersed in a background of drenched vegetation that gave off a revolting smell.

"Here we are," said Ademaro, sliding into a dark, moldy lair from which rose a wretched little wooden staircase. They went up, making creaking and wheezing sounds, until they reached a large room on the first floor.

In the time it took to turn the page, the miniature completely changed its image. The stench turned into a breathtakingly sweetly scent: cedarwood and amber flavors typical of the shores of the river Nile blended with the camphor fragrance of myrrh and civet. A heavy cloud that impregnated everything and penetrated every nook and cranny.

Edgardo looked around in a daze. They seemed to have entered the shop of a merchant who had lost his mind. A messy heap of objects, fabrics and furniture filled every corner from floor to ceiling. The floor was overloaded with Oriental rugs sporting colorful patterns. On the wall were displayed boar hooves, deer antlers, flags, suits of armor, scimitars, and shields. The shelves, covered in damask cloths, overflowed with dishes full of spices. Finally, as though to crown this treatise on folly, on a canopied bed, a woman lying on her side like an odalisque, covered with nothing more than a sapphire-colored tunic that revealed abundant quantities of a flaccid body brazenly exhibiting folds and crevices of unashamed sensuality.

Edgardo had never seen such a fair, ivory complexion. The round, bloated face barely left room for two small, dark, porcine eyes. Her lips were pale and defenseless, her arms lay abandoned on her flabby belly.

"My respects, Madama Teodora," Ademaro introduced himself.

"Who are you? I don't recognize your voice, come closer so that I can look at you in this semidarkness." She had a sleepy, singsong voice. The two monks drew closer.

That was where that sickly scent came from. From this woman's body.

"Oh, it's you, Brother Ademaro. I beg your pardon, I fell asleep. You've come back, what an honor . . . Come and sit by me, and your friend, too." She motioned to a bench at the foot of the bed. "Unfortunately, I can't move. My legs are at odds with my head, they've been poisoned by bad humors and have turned all blue." She stared at Edgardo. "Is your brother a surgeon, or a herbalist by any chance . . . ?"

"No, I'm a copyist," said Edgardo.

"You as well? God help you. We're expecting a new shipment of codices from Alexandra. The finest stuff, enough to make your mouth water, manuscripts in Arabic, Spanish, Greek . . . but meanwhile," she suddenly dropped her voice, "I have something extraordinary to offer you, God bless you, something only two holy men like yourselves will appreciate for its value and its redemptive significance."

Ademaro did not seem very impressed by the spice trader's words. "I came to see your husband . . . "

"He'll be here any moment . . . Listen to what I'm about to tell you, brothers, but you must swear on all the saints, the angels and archangels, that you will not tell anyone."

"We don't swear on what is holy," said Edgardo.

"Your will be done . . . but I'll tell you anyway, so listen and be amazed . . . " The hag swelled her double chin and began.

"Bloody battles, escapes, dangerous journeys from the East to the West—our knight had to survive all that on his return from Pope Urban's holy crusade in order to safeguard a thing that even now I don't dare name and shiver at the very thought of showing . . . "

"What are you prattling on about?" Edgardo said, impatiently.

The woman made a grimace, closed her eyes, seemed to nod off, then suddenly burst out, "The relic."

Ademaro sighed. "What relic would that be?"

"I don't know that I'm worthy to speak its name."

Edgardo cut her short. "Probably not, but try anyway."

"A relic that would give your church eternal sanctity. This relic alone would summon hordes of faithful from every land . . . May God forgive me if I dare speak his name: John the Baptist."

Ademaro did not stir at the mention of that name but began toying with a bristly beard that looked dark against his pale face.

"Did you hear me? John the Baptist," Teodora repeated, then fell silent for a long time, closed her eyes again, and took a deep breath. "I miraculously came into possession of John the Baptist's foreskin." Having spoken, she took a tiny brocaded box out of a drawer and opened it right under Ademaro's nose.

"Isn't it sublime? Look at how much light it gives off."

Edgardo also came closer, intrigued, and saw, in the box, laid out on a tiny pillow, a shred of dry skin, black and wrinkled, which looked just like the peel of a chewed-up prune.

"It's truly amazing," Ademaro said, without losing his composure.

"To you, holy men, I will give it for a low sum."

At that moment, there was a racket on the stairs, hoarse panting and coughing fits that announced the appearance of a short little man with no neck and a long beard that wavered over a large, pyramid-shaped belly. As soon as she saw him, Teodora quickly closed the box.

"What are you doing? What are you doing?" he shouted. "Daughter of an infidel, put that stuff away in front of these holy men . . . I beg your pardon, my dear brothers, have pity on my wife. She has no restraint. She comes from the Orient, the daughter of a merchant from Constantinople. She'd sell her mother if she still had one."

The clerics stood up and approached him. "May the Lord be with you, Karamago," said Ademaro.

"I'm honored by your presence and happy to see you again. A whole summer's been and gone since your last visit. Come, come," he said, drawing away from the bed. "How can I be of service? Are you still hunting for manuscripts?"

Teodora insinuated herself into the conversation. "We're expecting a prodigious shipment."

Karamago lost his temper. "Silence, silence, infidel's daughter. She knows nothing but tries to stick her nose into everything. As I was saying, I'm expecting a prodigious shipment—"

Ademaro interrupted him. "We'll be happy to see it but right now I need your help with another delicate matter."

"My heart will be full of joyful joy if I can be of service. . ." Karamago always seemed on the point of losing his balance and being dragged forward by an oversized belly that his small body could not support.

"My fellow brother's name is Edgardo. He's a talented scribe, one of the best at Bobbio Abbey. Unfortunately, despite his youth, his eyes have been growing weaker for some time now and his eyesight is failing. As you can appreciate, this is a terrible misfortune for one who has chosen to devote his life to writing."

"It would be like depriving a Venetian of the sea," Karamago said in a cutting tone.

"During my last trip," Ademaro continued, "I remember

you told me about a merchant back from the Orient who'd seen elderly scholars in those countries use stones that help cure ailing eyesight."

"A stone for ailing eyes," Karamago repeated. "Let me just recall my recollections."

"Of course, yes, don't you remember?" Teodora butted in, her flesh wobbling and spreading wafts of civet.

"Silence! Keep silent."

"It was Bartolomeo Ziani, just after he returned from Alexandria," Teodora continued, unperturbed.

Karamago darted a peeved glance at his wife. "Oh, yes, that's right."

"And where can we find this Bartolomeo?" Edgardo asked, on cue.

"In the sea," Teodora promptly answered, "probably being eaten by fish."

Karamago nodded. "That's right, he was abducted, dismembered, cut into pieces, and thrown into the sea by Dalmatian pirates. But our beloved Doge Falier promptly responded to the outrage by sending out five galleys that destroyed their entire accursed fleet."

"Was there anyone else who knew what Bartolomeo had seen?" Edgardo insisted.

"I don't know. I remember he told me about a transparent stone, a crystal maybe, yes, a miracle crystal that restored the sight . . . but he never told me how it worked, whether it had to be finely crushed and applied like an ointment or else diluted in a liquid and drunk."

It was over. It had been just a brief illusion. Ademaro looked at his friend.

A high-pitched sound rose from the bed of spices. "Still, if it concerns crystals, then perhaps Jacopo Zoto* knows something about it."

"Who's Zoto?"

"They call him that because he limps. He's a crystal-maker, he works with many different polished crystals and knows their every secret. He was in touch with Bartolomeo because the latter obtained precious stones for him for his trade."

"Where can we find him?" Edgardo asked.

"In San Giacomo di Luprio. Go to Rivoalto and ask there. Everybody knows him."

"Many thanks, Karamago, you've given us a precious piece of information."

"I'll send for you when I receive a new shipment of manuscripts." Karamago drew his beard closer to Ademaro's ear. "Would you like me to set some special morsel aside for you?" He gave a complicit smile. "*Ars amatoria* by Pubes Ovidius Naso?"

Edgardo approached Teodora. "Thank you, and may God watch over you."

"So what about that foreskin?" she hissed, leaning forward. "Will you think about it?"

Edgardo smiled and nodded. They said goodbye to Karamago and went down the stairs. A cloud of spices and fragrances pursued them as far as the door.

"We stink like that odalisque," said Edgardo, nauseated.

Ademaro smelt his habit. "This way we'll corrupt the entire abbey. Won't Carimanno be pleased!"

They laughed and dived into the crush of Calle delle Merzerie.

VI.
FOUNDRIES

They spoke of nothing but Marco Balbo's horrific death. The Doge's gastald had arrived with two soldiers, asked questions, and examined the body in an attempt to establish when the glassmaker had been killed. The purple skin tone and flabby flesh suggested the body had been in the water for several days, so he could have been stabbed anywhere. What nobody could understand and everybody found worrying was the chisel job the murderer had done on the eyeballs, which had been carved out with expertise, like peach kernels, then filled with perfectly crafted glass castings. If all this had been inflicted on the man while he was still alive, he would have suffered the torments of hell, truly sublime torture worthy of a pain artist. If, however, the murderer had spared him by ripping him open before the extraction, then one wondered as to the meaning of those glass eyes with fiery irises. Was it a warning? A curse? An omen? Many were already grumbling about the unease Marco's ghost would cause in the city, wandering in search of his torturer, staggering about angrily because his vision had been distorted by those two pieces of glass. Those who worked in foundries claimed that only a master glassmaker could have performed such a precise operation, while others were saying that gouging eyes out was common practice these days, since it was the penalty for thieves and murderers, so anybody could do it. As for the glass, you didn't need to be an expert: all you had to do was go to the *garzone* of any shop.

Opinions differed, but nobody could put a face or a name to "the eye murderer," as the residents of Amurianum promptly christened him.

The *rio* of the glassmakers was still crowded with people discussing the event when Segrado arrived, followed by Niccolò and Kallis, who was buckling under the weight of the bundle in which she had gathered all the equipment salvaged from the fire.

"What happened?" Segrado asked a glassmaker he knew well.

"They killed one of our own, someone called Marco Balbo, and shat molten glass into his eyes."

Segrado gave a start and bent over as if someone had just torn out his guts, then forced himself to take a deep breath to clear his head.

"God almighty, Marco . . . he was my *garzone* until just recently. He suddenly disappeared, so I thought he'd gone to set up his own business, as *garzoni* often do . . . Poor Marco. He was a good assistant . . . Do they know who did it?"

"Some say it's the devil . . . and they're right, but it's a devil who lives here in Amurianum."

Segrado's face grew even darker. "But why did they have to work him over like that?"

The glassmaker smiled. "Who knows? Maybe his eyes were as dull as a boiled fish when he was alive, so at least he might be happier now." Then he added, "Didn't your oven burn down last night?"

"We've lost everything," said Segrado.

"God doesn't love you anymore . . . Your furnace destroyed . . . your *garzone* murdered . . . " The glassmaker looked sad. "You must repent—"

"Listen," Segrado interrupted, "I can't work without fire, so I'm looking for a foundry owner who can hire an oven out to me."

The glassmaker smiled. "And who's got an oven of his own anymore? You know Tàtaro has gobbled them all up, by hook or by crook. The few who've still got one are working for him . . . He's got us all by the balls."

"So what are we supposed to do—starve to death?" Segardo glanced at Niccolò and Kallis, who was sitting quietly on the bank, staring at the green surface of the water.

"I'm telling you, Segrado, it won't be easy to find an oven. Nobody wants to upset Tàtaro, they're all scared." Then he winked with a sly expression. "You can always go to him. Maybe he'll give an oven to you, since you're one of the best . . . You never know."

Segrado chewed saliva with his toothless gums, ruminating like a cow, then spat on the ground. Even though the sun was not high yet, drops of sweat ran down his shiny skull, marking his dark face like slug mucus. He turned and motioned to Kallis. The girl did not budge. Her hood had fallen to her shoulders, revealing glossy black hair like an obsidian casting that ran thick and smooth and framed a high forehead, pronounced cheekbones, and eyes as narrow as the sliver of a waning moon.

"Move. Get the stuff," Segrado grumbled.

She gave him a cold, piercing look, then slinked to her feet, stretched her thin arms, and, as though picking up a bundle of wool, lifted the load on her shoulders and followed him. Niccolò looked at her with compassion but said nothing.

Tàtaro's oven was the most important in the lagoon. It was right at the beginning of the *rio*, just beyond the lighthouse: a wooden tower on top of which burned a fire like the one at San Marco and which, through a mirror trick, could be seen from all the islands in the north: Burianum, Majurbium, Torcellus, Costanciacum, and Aymanas.

The consortium of Master Tàtaro's foundry was the largest

in the city. There were four of them working there: Master Tàtaro, the senior assistant, the junior assistant, and the boy, plus the occasional craftsman who came from outside the consortium, an apprentice aspiring to become a *maestro*.

Segrado arrived at the shop and was immediately enveloped by a heatwave that made him feel as if he were on fire. The center of the workshop was dominated by an enormous furnace, circular, dome-shaped, and divided into three levels. In the largest chamber, at the bottom, four loading mouths opened up so that the fire could be fed with alder and willow wood. The central mouth was for the production of molten glass, a mixture of beechwood ash and purified sand. The combusted gases went from the first level through a hole in the middle of the shelf where the crucibles were heated, from which molten glass was then collected so that it could be blown through a blowing pipe. On the top level of the oven the glass objects that had been manufactured were placed for gradual cooling. Maestro Tàtaro's assistants moved around the furnace with expert, fluid gestures. Their naked bodies, drenched in sweat, reflected the quiver of the incandescent paste, which bathed everything in a vermillion light shot through at times by pearly thunderbolts and by explosions of sparks that floated through the air like incandescent snowflakes. To the eyes of someone unfamiliar with the world of glassmakers, this would have appeared like a scene from hell. Bodies with burned skin twisting among the flames, blinded by the glare. Yet to Segrado this was a vision of heaven, an example of universal harmony, of man's mastery over the elements, and of his ability to turn stone into a substance that was pure, transparent, malleable, and essential—a manifestation of divine perfection.

Maestro Tàtaro had just collected a little ball of vitreous paste from the crucible and was about to blow it into the form of a chalice. It was amazing to watch the transformation— almost a miracle—of that body. Unlike Segrado, Maestro

Tàtaro was slender, bony, with nerves pushing up under his skin at the slightest effort.

The same way many birds, in the act of courting, swell, increase in size, and alter their color, shining in their splendor, the same way Tàtaro, in the act of blowing, seemed to gather in his miserable little lungs the wind contained in the sails of a thousand chelandions, and in his arms the power of all the waves in all the world's oceans, thus transforming his gaunt body into a Greek statue.

Segrado approached, leaving Niccolò and Kallis at the door. Totally absorbed by his art, Tàtaro did not notice him at first; then he turned and saw him. Segrado thought he glimpsed a sneer in the blown chalice.

They had known each other for many years, too many to remember the exact number. They had started off together as *garzoni*, when there were still few people molding glass in Amurianum, and had grown up observing one another with a certain detachment, albeit with respect. That was until the different paths their spirits had chosen became evident. Tàtaro had decided to pursue what he called his "art": objects manufactured out of top-quality glass, which he knew how to sell to noblemen and merchants, and which had earned him success, wealth and power. In just a few years his operations had expanded to include every field of production and he had even become the largest supplier of mosaics to the Basilica of San Marco, thus establishing a monopoly on glass production in Venetia.

Segrado had ventured along different, more winding, and hidden paths. He had never spoken of art, preferred instead to follow his inspiration. His inventions and his pieces were prized not only throughout the city but also by inland merchants who sold them in Germanic lands and even in Constantinople. However, his masterpieces remained unique pieces. He did not like to repeat himself and was forever in search of something new, desirous to experiment and seek to conquer absolute perfection. Thus, since he had never pursued wealth, he had condemned himself to an uncertain and unsteady life.

"My oven burned down," he said in a hoarse voice and detached tone.

Tàtaro handed the junior assistant his blowing pipe, wiped off his sweat, and looked at him as if he were seeing him for the first time. "So?"

"I've come here to ask you to hire one out to me so that I can carry on working."

Tàtaro rubbed his hands on his apron and moved closer, with an expression of arrogance. Next to Segrado, he looked even more slender. "I have no oven for hire."

His eyes semi-closed and his breath heavy, as though about to fall asleep, Segrado waited with indifference for his destiny to be fulfilled.

"But I have a proposal for you. Come and work for me, I'll hire you as a craftsman outside the consortium—the pay is good."

The *garzoni* turned, curious to see the bald bear's reaction: he, who had years of experience and was considered one of the glassmaking geniuses, to be hired as an apprentice craftsman?

Segrado did not stir. His shiny skull suddenly glowed with sweat.

"I cannot work for you, Tàtaro," he said slowly but loudly enough for everyone to hear. "I'm not good enough . . . Not good enough at blowing pretentious, vulgar pieces. Not good enough at licking the asses of noblemen and counselors. I'm not good at thinking just about money when I blow in the pipe, and I'm also not good at taking away other people's ovens by any means necessary . . . "

His nerves tightened, like the strings of a bow, his veins swelled with black blood, and his metallic voice rose from his stomach as if from beyond the grave.

"What are you implying?" Tàtaro shouted. "Don't you dare insult me! Every oven I've taken, I've taken with my work, with a mouth burned by fire and lungs full of sand! I've built every other one with these hands and with my art." He came so close, he was almost touching him. "You, on the other hand, you've created nothing, you are nothing, you have nothing, and you'll end up like Balbo, with no eyes and no soul. And when they bury you, nobody will remember you or weep over you, because you'll have left nothing behind in which the people of Venetia can take pride. I feel sorry for you, Segrado."

In the hot, damp air, exhausted by the glare of the flames, the bodies of the *garzoni* grew tense, anticipating blood. Some said later that Segrado rose as if to strike Tàtaro, while the latter seized a pair of shears, ready to ram them into Segrado's belly. But that is not what happened. Nothing happened. The violence that might have exploded and blazed up continued to flash in their eyes until these were filled with tears of anger, yet it remained locked in their hearts. And so the air fed on hatred until it had created a self-enclosed vortex. Segrado did not utter a word. He was seen walking backwards toward the door without taking his eyes off Tàtaro, then vanished along the bank, amidst timber and sails.

VII.
LUPRIO*

Walking across the city, diving into the world, risking getting lost, facing dangers. Alone. Edgardo was trying to control the slight agitation quivering in his labored breathing. Ademaro had to stay in the abbey for the daily functions and could not have accompanied him without arousing suspicion. A cleric in search of manuscripts, however, is only praiseworthy.

Jacopo Zoto, the crystal-maker, lived in Luprio, an area made up of different small islands, near Campo di San Giacomo. Edgardo had followed Ademaro's directions to the letter. "Go along Calle delle Merzerie, past Karamago's shop, and you'll get straight to Rivoalto." And yet Edgardo had gotten lost. Perhaps "lost" was not the right word. Rather, he had fallen under a spell: a vortex of lights, blinding glares, land that appeared and disappeared, vapors that would suddenly wrap around you and drag you into the void, suspended between stretches of suffocating slime and gashes of turquoise sky. Paths that led nowhere but dissolved into water streams, reeds compact as walls concealing little houses that sprang, fragile, in a lagoon giving off odors that clouded your mind, triggering hallucinations and mirages. For a few minutes, Edgardo abandoned himself to this sort of dream, wondering if he would ever leave this labyrinth. Then, turning behind an imposing building made of wood and thatch, he suddenly found himself on the shore of Rivus Altus,* which cut Venetia exactly in half. In the blink of an eye, he was transported from his dream and immersed in a feverish and frantic wake. Large freight and transport boats loaded with timber, hay, baskets, sacks, and amphoras were sailing along the canal. Goods were being loaded onto and unloaded from other boats moored along the shore. Where the canal formed a wider bend, there were shops, boathouses, and warehouses, all clustered together, stealing space from the water, and a huge two-story building with a stone façade, one of the few, with an open gallery on the first floor, two turrets on the sides, and a portico on the ground floor, under which horses and travelers from faraway countries took shelter. Edgardo heard expressions he had never come across before, and saw faces, skin colors, and styles of clothing he had never seen drawn, even in the books of his library.

Ademaro had explained to him that he had to go beyond the canal that cut the agglomeration of smaller islands into two sections. He looked for a bridge or a passageway but could not find one. He did, however, see many *scaulas* that shuttled from one shore to another, transporting people, goods, and even horses and other animals. He paid a *quartarolo** and asked to be taken to the other side of the canal. Here too, there was a multitude of tradesmen crowding beneath the portico of a church. Edgardo made his way amidst the chaos of baskets overflowing with fruit and vegetables, cages with birds, cackling hens, rising pyramids of melons leaning against the pillars, amidst the shouts, disorder and swearing, to the edge of the *campo* where buildings were scarcer and the landscape was different.

The view was almost that of the countryside, with fields lush with grass, and privet bushes alternating with mudflats, mushy, treacherous land that emerged just below the water surface. Edgardo stepped gingerly amidst an intersection of streams and rivulets, sometimes crossing shallow waters or using barely visible wooden bridges or simple planks thrown between two banks. Escorted by a powerful stench of putrefying fish guts and rotting grass, he wondered if he would ever find this wretched crystal-maker known as Zoto.

When he began to despair of ever reaching his goal, he suddenly came out onto a large grassy *campo* shaded by elms and lime trees, where pigs, geese, and hens were quietly grazing. The far end of the *campo* was closed off by a church and surrounded by dwellings and warehouses. He approached a group of children who were amusing themselves by dismembering rats and feeding them to a sow in the shade of the bell tower, and asked the way. They confirmed that this was, indeed, the Church of San Giacomo di Luprio, and added, laughing, that Zoto was behind the *campo*, next to the saltworks.

The fact that he was on the right path was confirmed by the unbelievable crunching sound made by his every step. It was like walking on a blanket of broken bones. Then came the light. A blinding glow hit him in the eyes. A widespread flash, like an almost unnatural explosion of ice, forced him to shield his face with his hand. As he walked, the glare became more and more unbearable, to the point where he began to fear for his ailing eyes. The air was permeated with a sour, metallic smell that burned his lungs with every breath.

Before him there were wide swaths of swamp surrounded by banks of earth so as to form pools, while a system of minor canals drained the water coming in and out, making the salty liquid evaporate in the sun and leaving behind large patches of salt crystals.

At the edge of the saltworks there were buildings made of gray wood, pressed close together both for support and for protection against the saltpeter, as well as a huge windmill with large sails that cast a bit of shadow on that blinding clearing.

Edgardo plucked up his courage and shouted, "I'm looking for Zoto, the crystal-maker!" but his voice slid away, useless over the white surfaces.

"Karamago the merchant sent me!" he shouted again.

Only then did he hear a log rolling inside one of the huts, followed by a rhythmical grumbling like the sail of a watermill.

"The canker on you! Here I am—who's calling?"

A man appeared on the threshold of the hut, short and square like a die, with legs and arms half the normal length, long locks of hair on the nape of his neck that fluttered like a sail in the wind with every step. He walked slowly and with a limp. A severe limp. Karamago was right, thought Edgardo, the nickname Zoto suited him to perfection.

Together, Zoto and the Crooked One would have made a good team. All they needed was a dwarf, and they could have served as entertainment at the banquet of a prince.

Perhaps it was precisely Edgardo's crooked gait, and the hump on his chest protruding beneath his habit, that stopped the crystal-maker from chasing away the intruder.

"I am Edgardo d'Arduino," he said, giving him a level gaze, "a cleric from Bobbio."

"Jacopo, known as Zoto," the other man replied, rolling his bovine eyes. "Come inside."

They walked into a dark room, lit only by a gash in the thatched roof and an oil lamp hanging by the workbench, to which were attached a grip and an abrasive emery wheel for polishing and shaping the crystal. Zoto studied Edgardo in great detail, cautious and mistrustful.

"What do you want, monk?"

Once again, Edgardo felt that sense of frailty and uncertainty, as though the world around him were about to collapse on top of him. Trying not to give away too much, he told Zoto about the rumors he had heard concerning stones for the eyes, and that Karamago had pointed him in his direction.

To start with, the crystal-maker listened absentmindedly whilst tampering with his tools, but when he discovered that the cleric was a copyist from the Abbey of San Giorgio, his attitude immediately changed. He began showing off all his wares: buttons, handles, chalices, and candlesticks.

"I want to show you something that will make your eyes pop out," he said, opening a trunk he kept hidden under a rug in a dark corner. "Here's my masterpiece." From a crimson cloth he pulled a cross carved out of rock crystal. "Have you ever seen anything so wonderful? God himself guided my hand."

Edgardo was dazzled. An almost supernatural light glowed through this symbol of Our Lord's sacrifice.

"It was commissioned by a Germanic prince for his future bride. See the perfection of the cut, the light. I created it from a single block of crystal. It's worth a fortune."

Edgardo nodded. "And do you know anything about the stone for the eyes? Have you ever seen it?"

"Yes, of course, I've heard it produces miracles, but the first thing you need is crystal—rock crystal. The first element, nature's purest. The only one that possesses miraculous powers." He drew closer to Edgardo. "Unfortunately, crystal is extremely rare and so very expensive. If you want your eye stone, monk, we must obtain crystal."

Zoto seemed very sure of himself, but wasn't being very clear about how the stones had to be used. Edgardo became defensive.

"You need at least ten dinars for that kind of job," Zoto concluded.

"That's a huge sum."

"Rock crystal, good quality rock crystal, has its price, but in the end, you'll see, you'll be pleased with the job."

"As you can imagine, a monk doesn't have that kind of money . . . "

Zoto's attitude suddenly changed. His muscles stiffened, transforming his body into a block of stone, and his face turned purple. "You lazy monk!" he shouted. "Do you take me for a fool? You come here to beg for a miracle for your sick eyes and you expect me to work without a proper reward?"

"That's not what I said—" Edgardo tried to reply.

"You wasted my time and now you don't have any money on you?"

Zoto drew even closer, with an aggressive air, and Edgardo realized, with some surprise, that he himself was walking backwards toward the door, defenseless and incapable of reacting.

"You pig of a monk, you've got to pay me, you understand? You've just commissioned a job and now you're going back on it?"

"I've commissioned nothing . . . " Edgardo realized that no logical argument would prevail on this man who had fallen prey to senseless, brutal anger.

Zoto grabbed him with all his might and lifted him off the ground. "Are you going to pay, yes or no?"

Edgardo felt himself dissolve, overwhelmed by terror.

"Zoto, how dare you treat a servant of God like that?"

He would have liked these words to have been spoken from his own mouth, but that was not the case. Behind them, a kind of brown, hairless bear was watching them, motionless. Zoto's eyes grew wide as though he was hoping they would set fire to the apparition.

"Stay out of this, Segrado."

"Let go of the monk," the bear repeated.

There and then, Edgardo felt useless and ridiculous. An empty shell with no spirit, no strength, battered by the current. He felt a surge of pride, wriggled free, and stepped away from Zoto who, taken aback, did not react.

"That's right, go to hell, freak . . . only remember, if you want your eye crystal then you have to come back to Zoto. Nobody else can help you." He breathed out through his nostrils like an angry bull, and went back into his hut.

It had all happened so quickly that Edgardo was shaken and bewildered. He gave a nod of thanks.

"You'd better be careful with that animal. You mustn't trust him. He's a fine crystal-maker but he'd cut his own brother's throat if there was money in it."

"He wanted money for the rock crystal in advance . . . "

Segrado burst into a wild laugh. "And you would have waited quite a while for your crystal. Zoto is always up to his neck in debt. He would've used your money to save his own ass . . . " That said, he walked away toward a warehouse on the edge of the saltworks.

"Do you work with him?" Edgardo asked, following him.

"No, God help me. Zoto was the last card I had to play. I've lost everything in a fire and he was the only man left in Venetia who could hire me out an oven. He's a nasty piece of work and people don't want to do business with him, but I had no choice." He paused on the threshold and indicated the oven. "Look, it's in a really bad state but we'll get it to work again . . . "

Inside, limonium bushes had grown on the dirt floor, the wall beams had come apart and were rotting, and you could glimpse large gashes of cloudy sky through the roof made of reeds and thatch. Only the oven, in the middle of the room, had withstood the ice and the salt. Edgardo heard something rustle inside the furnace, like a rat rummaging among the twigs. From the loading hole a head, an arm, and finally, with an acrobatic move, a body appeared. A slim, lithe body covered in ash and coal. An indescribable being, a cross between an exotic snake and a segment of creeper vine bursting with bluebells, like those he had seen drawn in the miniatures of his beloved manuscripts. Only after it had shaken off the layers of soot did Edgardo realize that the being in question was female.

"Now empty it and clean it all out," Segrado ordered.

Kallis obeyed without even raising her head, almost as though, Edgardo thought, he was a mere ghost she had not seen.

"So how did a cleric like you end up in the clutches of someone like Zoto?" Segrado asked. "Forgive me, I don't even know your name."

"Edgardo. I am a copyist cleric at Bobbio."

"My name is Angelo Segrado, master glassmaker."

It felt natural for Edgardo to turn toward the girl, expecting to hear her name, but neither she nor the master seemed to consider that possibility, as though neither of them deemed her presence to be a reality.

"Forgive me if I speak out of turn, but what does a copyist need with crystal? Surely not to make jewelry or buttons . . . "

It was such a far-fetched story. If he told everything to a stranger, he would be taken for a madman. And yet the hairy bear had something good-natured and reassuring about him. Moreover, he had saved him from that brute. If nothing else, courtesy demanded that he respond.

He decided to let it out. "I'm losing my eyesight, and I've been told there is a stone for the eyes that can cure me." A strange silence, like an empty pause, lay spread before him, so much so that Edgardo felt he had to add, "Without writing, my life has no sense."

His words created an opening. Segrado's expression altered. A wave of understanding colored with melancholy seemed to break out of his animal body. Even Kallis looked up, surprised, and stared at him, trying to understand the reason for this transformation. That was when she saw Edgardo, perhaps for the first time.

Segrado tightened his lips, as though trying to keep the words in, then said: "What exactly do you know about this stone?"

"Nothing, just a story. Perhaps I'm clinging to a dream, perhaps God no longer wants my eyes to drink from the pages of a manuscript."

"God gave glassmakers the power of breath, and you the sharpness of the eyes, and to both of us He gave nimble fingers."

He turned the palms of his hands, as large as oars, toward the sky. "Our hands, though," he said, "are like waves against the cliffs of a stormy sea: coarse and violent, while yours are like a clear stream that laps, penetrates, and shapes. The eyes of a scribe are a gift from God that men must keep and safeguard."

"May Our Lord hear you." Edgardo thanked him, marveling at the glassmaker's profound words. He looked like a simple man of humble origins, and yet he showed uncommon sensitivity, wisdom, and eloquence.

Kallis had interrupted her work and gone to sit at his feet like a loyal dog, unwilling to move. She listened without taking her eyes off Edgardo. Maybe she had never seen such a poorly formed creature: crooked, hunchbacked, a shock of red hair exploding over a face as white as a baby's bottom, dusted with freckles, and eyes so transparent you could see through into his very thoughts.

"Maybe I could help you," Segrado suddenly said. His knobbly hand slid over the girl's head, slowly caressing it. "I've devoted my life to the search for the impossible," he said, a look of defiance in his eye, "and I like people who follow their dreams . . . "

The cleric was astounded and puzzled. "Thank you. I'm prepared to risk my life in order to recover my sight."

Segrado laughed heartily. "Don't worry, I won't ask you that much. If you like, meet me tomorrow at Terce at the foot of the tower, in front of the Basilica of San Marco, where there's a market. I'll be there, and I hope I'll be able to prove my good intentions."

Edgardo looked at the girl and thought he could see in her dark, narrow eyes a promise of hope, but also something he had never seen before: a gentle sweetness and a yearning that took his breath away.

"Very well, I'll be there."

VIII.
THE BASILICA

There were bodies strewn on the ground, dumped on top of one another, twisted, heads bowed, eyes full of suffering. The square in front of the basilica of San Marco was overrun by a multitude of slaves waiting to embark on a galley about to sail to Constantinople. As soon as he got out of the *scaula* at the dock, Edgardo felt as though he was on a battlefield following a fierce clash. He stepped over backs and heads, amid lamentations and insults, and managed, with difficulty, to reach the watchtower where he found Segrado waiting for him. The glassmaker was looking around as though searching for someone. Then he decisively walked up to a group of men engaged in a lively discussion near Rio Bataro. Among them, Edgardo immediately recognized the merchant Karamago. For a moment, they stared at each other in disbelief at meeting again, this time in the company of a man like Segrado. The merchant stepped away from the group.

"Are you already acquainted with this young cleric?" Segrado asked.

Karamago took a clumsy bow, impaired by his prominent belly. "I've had the honor of welcoming him to my shop."

"Good," Segrado cut him short, "so then you know what the problem is, since you sent him to Zoto."

Caught red-handed, Karamago grimaced and started toying with his long beard.

"A while back," the glassmaker said, "you mentioned a manuscript you'd bought from a Cairo merchant . . . a treatise describing experiments performed with glass globes, experiments with lights, recipes, and all kinds of witchcraft. You were hoping I'd know someone able to read it and who'd be interested in the subject. Well, I've found the right person." He looked at Edgardo. "The scribe would like to see that manuscript."

Karamago fidgeted, clearly embarrassed. "I'd be truly delighted to help you," he said.

"So where do you keep it, then?"

"Unfortunately," he said, gazing insistently at Edgardo, "it's no longer in my possession. I've sold it."

Segrado muttered an unintelligible curse. "And who did you sell it to?"

"Well, let's see, I don't know if I can, it's just that I promised not to say . . . The material has truly valuable value, and I was paid very well."

"Come on, speak," Segrado threatened him. "I want to know who you sold it to."

"I sold it to them." The merchant blurted, pointing innocently at Edgardo.

All the attention was suddenly focused on the cleric, who looked lost and almost offended. For a moment, they waited for an explanation that did not come, so Karamago continued: "I sold it to a monk from the library of San Giorgio. It was in Arabic and had to be translated. Nobody else wanted it."

"Do you know anything about this, scribe?" Segrado asked aggressively.

"No, nothing at all. I'm not a copyist at that scriptorium . . . and I've only just arrived here."

Segrado fell silent and Karamago took advantage of his uncertainty.

"I've told you nothing." He gave Edgardo a honeyed smile. "And now I must go. I'm expected elsewhere to close a deal. May God bless you." He rolled up his beard in an exaggerated bow and sneaked away. Segrado followed him with his eyes as he tried to blend in with the crowd that filled the piazza between the dock and the basilica.

In addition to the merchants and sailors, there were a large number of workers attached to the now ongoing building site established for the construction and embellishment of the basilica of San Marco. Under the guidance of Master Tàtaro, various mosaic-makers from Constantinople, together with young Venetian apprentices, were on the scaffoldings, working on the faces of apostles above the central door of the narthex.

Tàtaro had called Karamago to him. Segrado watched them talking conspiratorially, and very obviously discussing them. He could not stop himself from walking up to them.

"I'm here, Tàtaro. If there's anything you want to know, you can ask me to my face."

"Have you come here to steal the secrets of my mosaics?" Tàtaro smiled with contempt, then turned to Edgardo, who was following the pantomime uncomprehendingly. "Ever since we were apprentices, this honorable gentleman has been trying to copy my brilliant tesserae without ever succeeding." He took Edgardo by the arm and led him to the lunette in the entrance. "Just look at the flow of the drapery over Saint Peter, how the folds are broken up—they actually look as if they're moving . . . and look at the halo bursting with light . . . only a master who knows all the secrets of glass is able to produce such perfect mosaics as to transform images into living beings. Allow me to introduce myself. My name is Tàtaro and I am that master." He smiled, self-satisfied.

After listening to Tàtaro's ramblings without batting an eyelid, Segrado pulled Edgardo away, reclaiming his attention. "You're a copyist, you're not expected to know that what this arrogant sack of hot air isn't telling you, is that what's important in a mosaic tessera is transparency, and that transparency depends on the layer of glass you spread over the gold laminate. The purer and more transparent the glass, the more alive the mosaic. Right, Tàtaro? Why do you go around boasting you're the best glassmaker in Venetia when everybody knows that my glass is more limpid and more crystalline? No matter how hard you try, you'll never be able to find the correct formula to match the purity of my glass."

Tàtaro's body stiffened, tall and crisp like the mast of a ship, then he turned to Edgardo and resumed a self-confident, teasing expression. "Don't listen to this man's nonsense. Don't trust him, he's a braggart. All his life he's gone around saying he's going to make who knows what amazing discoveries, but he's discovered nothing, and created nothing except poverty and failure, so he harbors deep hatred toward all those more successful than him." Tàtaro cocked his head toward Segrado, like a crane. "Unless I am very much mistaken, the hapless Marco Balbo was your *garzone.*"

That was below the belt, and Segrado clenched his fists. "Just what are you implying, Tàtaro?"

"Nothing . . . I was just trying to remember . . . "

"You remember correctly, except that before that he used to work at your oven, but then he left because he wasn't learning anything . . . Isn't that true?" Segrado burst out laughing before Tàtaro had the time to retaliate, grabbed Edgardo, and dragged him bodily into the basilica.

From the floor of the atrium, you walked up a few steps to the floor of the church. This way, it felt as if you had to walk up to enter the church and so your attention was immediately drawn to the splendid, curved surfaces that demarcated the naves. Edgardo found himself immersed in an explosion of spaces, which the reflected lights rendered mysterious and misty. The complex crisscrossing of arches and domes, the decorative mosaics against a golden background, the Moorish-style marbles along the walls, the marble inlays of the flooring—everything contributed to creating a feeling of wonder and mystical vibration.

Segardo led him as far as the presbytery, which was raised a few steps from the floor of the basilica, then asked him to go down a narrow staircase leading to a wide space right beneath the altar: the crypt.

The middle of this space was dominated by an imposing stone sarcophagus, which in turn contained a casket of gilded wood.

"The body of Saint Mark, patron saint of Venetia, is preserved here," Segrado announced in an inspired voice. "It was two Venetians from the lagoon, Buono da Metamauco and Rustico da Torcellus, who found it. Many years ago, ten Venetian chelandions entered the Port of Alexandria. All contact with Oriental merchants was then forbidden to us Venetians, but the wind pushed the ships to that port against their will. Evidently, it was God's will. So the two merchants took advantage of the forced layover to go and worship the relics of Saint Mark, who had been martyred in that city. After many devout visits, they persuaded the Greek fathers to give them the saint's body, since the urn wasn't at all safe in that church, because it risked being turned into a mosque and profaned. Before Alexandria, Saint Mark had converted Aquileia and Venetia, so the lagoon has a legitimate claim to watch over his remains. After they won the argument, the Venetians carefully hid the relics under chunks of pork meat, and left Alexandria under the indifferent watch of Egyptian guards. The homebound journey was full of difficulties, but finally they were welcomed back with a triumphant ceremony by the Doge, who placed the remains in the basilica that now bears his name."

Edgardo listened attentively to the wonderful story, increasingly fascinated by Segrado's personality. For all his simplicity, he was turning out to be a learned man with a noble soul.

"But I haven't brought you here just to show you the remains of our Saint," Segrado said, approaching one of the niches carved out in the perimeter walls. "There are pieces from Saint Mark's treasure on display here. Look." He drew closer. "Here you see a beaker that belonged to the Caliph Al-Aziz Billah. It's carved from a single block of crystal and trimmed with animal friezes. Look at the purity, the transparency and the luminosity of it. Only rock crystal possesses such properties. There's nothing as limpid in all of nature . . . It's with this that Zoto promised to make your stones for the eyes, but he probably didn't even know how he'd do it."

Segrado took a deep breath, and his chest swelled so much that Edgardo thought he seemed even more imposing and gigantic.

"Man may aspire to reproduce the wonders offered us by nature, in fact, he must. All my life I've been chasing after a dream: to go beyond the limits of matter, to equal the transparency of light, and to transform the impure into the pure." He raised his eyes to the sky. "Only those who can read the signs of Our Lord can succeed in this enterprise. And God has put you on my path . . . "

Edgardo stared, confused and rather frightened.

Segrado continued: "Maybe there's information in the manuscript Karamago sold to your library—teachings or formulas that could open new roads for us. There are learned men in Arab lands with knowledge far superior to ours. I could never look through the pages of those books, and even if I could, well, I can't read. But you, you're a copyist. You have free access to the library. You could find out interesting information and recipes useful for your eyes." He came so close to Edgardo that even in the darkness of the crypt, the latter could see a flash of madness in his eyes.

"The abbey rules are very strict with regard to consulting manuscripts, and I don't even know if that book is actually there."

Segrado stared at him, confused, unable to understand his

reservations. "At times, Our Lord shows us a way but we don't want to see it. Do you think it's pure chance that we met? Think about it . . . "

The light seeping through the small windows had assumed a gray tint, and pale mist had spread through the crypt, erasing all contours. Edgardo suddenly felt lost, as though in a deep dark forest, completely alone with his conscience.

IX.
THE SCRIPTORIUM

The procession advanced slowly. Four monks were carrying the plank on which lay the body of their dying fellow brother. The *tramontana* wind lifted the cowls, swelling them like sails. The slender flames of the oil lamps wavered, projecting warm shadows on the refectory walls. The echo of the chanting that escorted the old, agonizing monk resounded beneath the portico vaults. They reached the field behind the church, where all the abbey brothers were buried. They laid the body on the bare earth and scattered holy ashes over it. In that humble position, a reminder of the transience of earthly life, the dying man would wait until his soul could free itself from his body.

Not a single moan came out of the old cellarer. After the abbot had administered the last rites, the procession broke up. In solitude, ashes to ashes, dust to dust, enveloped by the wind from the lagoon, soaked by the night dew, he waited for his heart to stop beating. Edgardo waited for the group of monks accompanying Abbott Carimanno to go to the dormitory before he approached Ademaro. During the day, the whole abbey had gathered around the dying man's bedside, so he had not found a private moment in which to confide in his friend.

"I need to speak with you," Edgardo whispered, leading him toward a forest of cypresses beyond the vegetable garden.

On that side of the island, which was not as well shielded by buildings, the *bora* wind was blowing even more strongly, knocking the tops of the trees together, as if in a fight.

"Do you have any news?" Ademaro asked.

Edgardo told him about Zoto, the crystal-maker, an untrustworthy, violent man, and about Segrado, who, on the contrary, seemed to be an honest man you could trust, even though it was not at all clear how he would be able to help his eyes . . . He spoke excitedly, skipping from one subject to another. Ademaro tried to calm him down. Above all, he tried to tell him to exercise prudence in every decision he made. Contrary to appearances, Venetia was a changeable, elusive place, where reality was constantly shape-shifting.

"Everything that appears definite and clear at a particular time of the day becomes obscure and unfathomable a few hours later. And the same is true of its inhabitants. They're difficult to pin down, mysterious men of a thousand faces who've learned to adapt to an ever-changing nature, to the sudden movements of the waters, and to the invasions of barbarians who want to conquer them. You must be prudent," Ademaro insisted. "You must be careful both in your speech and in your actions, like a knight riding through an unknown forest. In every ravine, and every thicket, an enemy could be lurking, ready to pounce."

Edgardo always listened to his friend's words with respect and consideration.

"Abbot Carimanno asked after you. I told him I'd given you the task of exploring Venetia's markets in search of manuscripts. He seemed content with that explanation. Still, don't lose heart. We have time. My work here at the abbey is going to be longer than anticipated. I have many codices to examine before I can decide which ones to take to Bobbio . . . "

"Now, on that subject. . . The merchant, Karamago, claims that a treatise in Arabic was sold to the San Giorgio library. Apparently, it actually deals with vision, and eyes, and perhaps with the manufacturing of glass and the transformation of crystal. Is he telling the truth? Have you ever seen that manuscript?"

Ademaro sank his head into his hood and hid his hands in his habit. Edgardo thought he looked like a man trying to stall, or elude the question. A gust of wind snapped a branch, which landed just a few feet away.

"Come, let's leave before the storm carries us away." Ademaro spoke firmly. "I don't know all the books in the library. Although there aren't as many as in Bobbio, there are still too many for me to have had a chance to look at them all during my visits."

Edgardo insisted. "So you don't know anything about any recently acquired Arabic manuscripts?"

"Venetia is a crossroads for a lot of commerce. Goods from the Northern Countries as well as the Orient arrive here, and there is a constant influx of new manuscripts."

"So you don't know anything about it?"

"I shall ask our fellow brothers in the scriptorium. I'm sure some of them know the library better than I do."

The sea must have risen also in the lagoon, because the gentle swish had turned into a deep roar.

Ademaro put an abrupt stop to the conversation. "Come, let's go in before they notice our absence."

They parted outside their cells without a single word. Edgardo had the sense that a shadow had fallen between them.

He threw himself on the bed and wrapped himself in the damp blanket, going over his conversation with his friend. He had found Ademaro's behavior odd, somewhat distant and reserved, avoiding direct answers to his questions, constantly shifting the conclusion of the discourse elsewhere. The final impression was that of a man trying to avoid the subject. But what possible reason could Ademaro have to keep quiet? After all, it was he who had insisted Edgardo embark on the search for the stone for his eyes. These questions tormented him, preventing him from sleeping. A keen wind that smelled of snow was whistling through the slit in the wall. Sharp pangs of pain, like being cut by red-hot blades, were stabbing him in the back. His thoughts were getting tangled up. He remembered that, soon after he had arrived, he had met a talented Arabic translator in the scriptorium. What was his name? That's right—Ermanno di Carinzia! It was Ademaro himself who had introduced him. So why had he not mentioned him just now? He could have answered his questions. Why had Ademaro refused to help him?

It was not so much his curiosity about the contents of that book that triggered Edgardo's reckless decision as the urge to appease the doubts that had formed over his friend's behavior.

He had never ventured into the abbey at night or without a light. The sky was overcast and there was not even any moonlight to guide him. He stepped lightly, wary of any creaking. At the end of the dormitory corridor, he stopped and listened to the sounds of the night. He thought he heard a litany dragged by the wind, knocked from one wall to another. The awareness of committing an act against the rules of the order made him anxious.

As he went down into the cloister, the litany became clearer. It was the lament of his fellow brother, abandoned to his solitude in the middle of the field, waiting for Sister Death to come. Edgardo's first impulse was to join him, to comfort him and keep him company in his final moments. He considered abandoning his foolish idea of going to rummage through the scriptorium and, instead, following the impulse of Christian charity that had reawakened in his heart. Something stopped him. A languor and a sense of unease. His legs refused to obey him, and he began to breathe heavily. He leaned against a pillar and took a deep breath, trying to gather his strength. The lament became fainter and more hesitant. Perhaps he was dying and his destiny had been fulfilled. There was nothing more he could do, so he pretended not to hear. He listened to the voice of the wind and retraced his steps toward the library. He felt something heavy weighing on his chest.

For the first time he thought of a word he had never used: coward. There was only one truth: that he was afraid of looking death in the face.

The scent of the library greeted him like a warm and welcoming bed: the acetate aroma of the inks, the acrid wilderness smell of the parchment, the perfume of dust and resin that had impregnated the wooden shelves . . . How he loved this place! It was his life, his breath, his refuge, his heaven, the very essence of his existence. When he was there his body would transform: the hunch would vanish, his hip straighten, his back lengthen and grow strong. And Edgardo the Crooked would turn into an intrepid knight illuminated by Divine Grace.

He groped his way to the staircase that led to the scriptorium. He took a tallow candle stub from the pocket of his habit and, after several attempts at striking the flintlock, managed to light it.

He remembered that Ermanno di Carinzia's work station was near the first window. He held up the light. The lectern was empty. Usually, after the day's work, the monks put the manuscripts away and then took them out again the following morning. Even if they followed the same rules here as in Bobbio, there had to be a bookshelf for all the books currently being worked on, whether copied or translated. He was right. He found the manuscripts arranged in order on the long wooden plank leaning against the south wall, which was drier than the others. With extreme care, he picked up the first volume. The pages had not been bound yet and were gathered between two pieces of parchment tied with ribbons. He untied them and brought the candle to the frontispiece, possessed by a kind of feverish excitement.

He shivered and felt a pang in his heart. His, weak, miserable, trembling eyes. He had forgotten the poor state they were in. Out of habit, he had acted like back in the days when, at first glance, and without any difficulty, letters would parade before him like a merry dance.

In a fit of anger, he wanted to throw everything up in the air, but managed to restrain himself. Very careful to avoid starting a fire, he brought the flame closer to the page and leaned forward so that he was almost touching the words with his nose.

The Ophtalmicus by Demosthenes Philaletes. He picked up another one: *Explanationes in Ciceronis Rhetoricam* by Victorinus. Nothing to do with the manuscript he was looking for. One more attempt. Unfamiliar signs, flourishes, and a huge, indecipherable drawing: it was Arabic—pages of an Arabic parchment. He had found the manuscript on which Ermanno di Carinzia was working. Still, he had no way of knowing if it was the one he was looking for, and certainly could not tell by these doodles. He shifted his nose onto the adjacent attached pages. These certainly sounded a different note . . . He recognized the writing, the strokes, the regular, round shapes. It was the familiar Carolingian minuscule, it was Latin.

He began to peruse the pages, trying to decipher their contents. On the first page of the colophon, he found the name of the translator: Ermanno di Carinzia, the date, MCVI, and the complete title of the book and its author: *De Aspectibus* by Alhazen Arabis.

Edgardo read on as quickly as he could, afraid that someone would discover him.

He had in his hands the translation of the Arabic manuscript Karamago had told him about. The translator had not finished his work yet, but evidently the treatise concerned optics. Perhaps he would find useful information about his eye stones among these pages. Segrado was right. He would have to read the entire manuscript, and that would take time.

He heard footsteps and subdued voices. Somebody was

crossing the cloister. Edgardo saw the reflection of lanterns flashing at the windows. He quickly replaced the papers in the order in which he had found them, put out the candle, and rushed to the staircase that led down from the library. The scriptorium did not have an external exit, as though they had wanted to isolate it from the rest of the abbey, leaving only one obligatory passage in and out, thereby monitoring all those who came and went. When he was beneath the portico, he leaned out toward the garden and saw a group of monks walking to the church. You could not hear the lament anymore. The cellarer must have given up the ghost.

Back in his cell, his thoughts took a logical turn, and were no longer influenced by emotions and feelings. Edgardo started to ask himself a list of questions. Did Ademaro really not know anything about the translation of the Arabic manuscript on optics? And if he knew, why had he kept quiet, especially with him, whose salvation might be found in that very book?

Slowly, like a slight temperature that rises during the night until it becomes a debilitating fever that makes your limbs shake, all these questions and the answers he could not find took over his mind and multiplied, dragging him into a state of prostration and anguish.

Was Ademaro, his only friend and point of reference, his support, and a role model of honesty and faith, no longer worthy of his trust? Could the people nearest and dearest to you also lie to you, betray you, fail in the duties dictated by honor?

His world was crumbling to pieces. The safe fortress he had built himself had collapsed in just one night. Edgardo felt like an empty shell at the mercy of ungovernable forces. Suddenly, the habit he wore lost all its significance and became a symbol of no worth.

Where was this place in the world where God had put him? Why had he never wanted to take his vows? Was the divinity he had so often named in his prayers his true light? Or had the monastery been only an escape from his deformed body? Had he immersed himself in study and writing because he had no other path? And now this path was also becoming less and less certain. He was not a monk, and he was not a copyist. He was nothing . . . Moreover, he was alone, because he could not even trust his dearest friend.

In this solitary night, his one glimmer of hope was Segrado. He would be able to advise him, guide him like a father—yes, he imagined him as a father figure, and the feeling surprised him.

He decided to meet with him as soon as possible the following day. He had to see him, to tell him about the manuscript.

But was it the glassmaker that he really wanted to meet? Was it not another thought, another desire, an insane restlessness he did not want to confess even to himself, that was slyly insinuating itself like a larva digging beneath bark?

Out! Out! Get your asses out of here!" Segrado shouted in a sudden fit of anger. Accustomed to the master's unpredictable outbursts, Niccolò and Kallis left the foundry without a sound. Whenever he reached a delicate stage of his work, or a new procedure that he wanted to keep secret, Segrado trusted no one. Every master glassmaker who developed, over years of work, a formula for the composition of various kinds of glass was very anxious not to have it discovered by outside observers ready to pass it on to his competitors.

Many formulas belonged to the public domain, such as the recipe for making glass salt or molten glass, or for manufacturing ordinary glass.

The others were the specialty of individual glassmakers, such as how to make marbled glass, or deep blue and delicate enamel, or gold and silver mosaic.

Many other craftsmen were working on the formula Segrado was in the process of testing, in Amurianum, Venetia and Torcellus, but nobody had yet achieved the much coveted result: crystalline glass—a substance so pure, transparent, and clear that it looked identical to rock crystal.

The latter was a hard and not very malleable stone, difficult to find, very expensive and almost impossible to shape. His ambition was to create glass that had all the qualities of crystal but was also thin, light, colorless, and without cracks. You could use it to craft objects that had been unthinkable up to then. The luminosity of the most important pieces, both in terms of finesse and value, was spoiled by an annoying blue-green or yellow-green tint nobody had ever managed to eliminate. Despite all their efforts, the ovens of Venetian master craftsmen had not been able to produce a substance as pure as rock crystal. Everyone knew that a discovery of this kind would bring wealth and fame. Crystalline glass was the dream of every glassmaker, and especially Segrado, who had been searching for it all his life.

His oven had been lit for hours, regulated by a light, smokeless flame. In the crucible, coarsely crushed pieces of crystal had been baking for twelve hours. Segrado had introduced great innovations in the preparation of these pieces of crystal, beginning with the raw materials at the basis of glass production.

Instead of white stone from a quarry, he had obtained several pounds of pebbles that came from the river Ticino, ground and sifted them, then mixed the resulting fine powder with the ashes, also known as *allume catina*, of certain plants that grew in Eastern Mediterranean countries. Then he had put the mixture into the lime kiln, a reverberation oven, until it was liquefied, in other words, until it became molten glass. Subsequently, he had put the resulting stew on the shelves, covered it with a cloth, and left it to cool so that the actual crystal pieces would be formed.

Segrado was very pleased with his work. He removed the crucible from the furnace. The molten glass was white, but not white enough. Greenish shadows were still soiling its purity. It occurred to him that the only way to cleanse it and purge it of old impurities would be to swish it in water until it was clear and transparent. He washed it obsessively, over and over again, so that the water would make it spit out the salt that made the glass cloudy.

He felt close to achieving the result. He had followed every step with care and the glass mixture seemed limpid and clear, as though it had been purified by a ray of divine light. A light that brings purity, peace, and the salvation of the soul. If Segrado succeeded in creating crystalline glass, he would offer his secret up to God. He was certain that God would accept it with a magnanimous gesture and, finally, would forgive him.

There was only one thing left to do—the fire test. He put the crucible into the oven. After the washing, the new fusion would produce the definitive result. To kill time while he was waiting, Segrado came out of the storehouse. The *bora* wind had swept away the fog and the blue reflection of the sky colored the stretches of salt, transforming them into an ocean of ice. Niccolò and Kallis were talking to the man who was operating the windmill. As soon as they saw him, Niccolò ran toward him, while Kallis remained apart.

"So, Maestro, have you figured out the secret of crystalline glass?"

"I don't know yet, but I hope so."

"It'll work out for sure with the river Ticino pebbles . . . "

Segrado's face clouded over. "How do you know about the Ticino pebbles?"

Niccolò hung his head, embarrassed, and tried to justify himself. "You told me when you brought them, don't you remember?"

Segrado could not remember. Maybe he had inadvertently let it slip. "You haven't told anyone else, have you?" he asked.

"Of course not, Master. You've ordered me never to tell anything to anyone about what we do at the oven."

"Not even to Tàtaro?"

"Tàtaro? That son of a bitch! He hates us and burned down our oven."

Segrado did not seem surprised. "What makes you say that?"

"Tàtaro is burning down the ovens of the glassmakers in Amurianum. He'll stop at nothing to be the only glassmaker in Venetia—even if he has to kill everybody."

Segrado frowned. Since Balbo's death, he, like all the other glassmakers, had felt unsafe. "Have you heard any rumors about the eye murderer?" he asked. "Have they found him?"

"Not yet. They're saying it's the devil . . . If it is, then we'll have to smoke him out of hell . . . "

Segrado glanced at the oven.

"How much longer do we have to wait, Maestro?"

"We have to wait for it to melt."

"And then we'll know?"

Segrado did not reply, but let his eyes wander over the expanse of salt. His lips barely moved, as though uttering a silent prayer.

Edgardo had left the abbey shortly after Terce, trying to avoid Ademaro. He was confused and tormented. The first light of day had scattered his darkest thoughts and the search for an explanation had emerged like a beam of hope. Maybe Ademaro knew nothing of Ermanno di Carinzia's translation work or, if he did, then he was not aware of the contents of the Arabic manuscript. Or perhaps he did not think that it would be useful in his search for the eye stone. The more reasons he found to justify his friend's behavior, the more relief he felt. Still, he preferred not to encounter him face to face, in case he was unable to conceal his thoughts from him.

The sharp air had a metallic smell. The cold light had tinted the water a dark blue, heavy with bad omens. It was like sailing through a hostile universe, about to be swallowed into nothingness. The gondola deposited him at Rivoalto, like the first time. There was even more of a bustle this morning. Where the banks of the canal were close together, something was being built. Standing on a row of barges, anchored side by side and tied together securely, workmen were leaning over the water, sticking logs into the bottom. Edgardo imagined they must be stilts on which an enormous platform would be erected—an imposing and difficult task. He stood there, fascinated, admiring these people's ability to build on water as skillfully as on solid ground.

He resumed his walk, allowing himself to be guided more by instinct than memory, and found the path that led to Segrado's workshop. The small *campo* in front of his storehouse was deserted and the foundry door was open. He looked in and was blinded by the glow of the flames. The room was permeated by a sour, vinegary smell. There were dark shadows moving around the oven: blazing trails, movements that cut through the air, canes that twirled as if dancing during a knightly tournament. After a while, his eyes grew accustomed to the darkness and he recognized Segrado, his upper body naked, about to slide a crucible out of the mouth of the oven. Niccolò was next to him, sweating, a mold in his hand, and behind them, in the semidarkness brightened by a blade of light, Kallis was pestling in a mortar.

Segrado approached the crucible and, with a slow and loving gesture, poured the molten glass into the mold Niccolò was holding with long pincers. In the unreal silence, it was possible to hear the voice of the glass sliding into the receptacle: a gentle melody, a liquid note that quivered through the air, infusing everything around it with profound peace.

Edgardo stared, stupefied, as though witnessing the birth of something primordial and absolutely miraculous: the very magma from which man was created.

They were all so engrossed that they took no notice of him. When the mold was filled, Niccolò brought it up to Segrado's face, and the latter motioned him to the exit. They fell into the full daylight, blinded and confused. Then the master bent over the mold to examine the result of his experiment: crystalline glass, transparent as rock crystal, pure as the eyes of God, who cleanses your soul of every sin.

Segrado studied the glass chalice he had crafted. He lifted

it to the light to check for imperfections. No, it was perfect. No bubbles, no froth or cracks, but the color and transparency . . . No, he still had a long way to go. A green, opaque shadow, like a sickly, pestilent complexion, had contaminated his glass. Neither the Ticino pebbles nor the repeated washes in the basins had been enough to achieve the real crystalline glass. Something else was missing . . . but what? Segrado hurled the chalice against a mound of salt. Shards scattered around. Kallis tried to approach, but Segrado pushed her away with a brutal gesture. Niccolò was bending over the fragments, staring at them as though refusing to accept that yet another attempt had failed.

Edgardo had watched the scene without understanding. Only then did the master seem to notice him.

"What do you want, scribe?" he asked.

Edgardo waited briefly before replying. "I've found the Arabic manuscript the merchant Karamago told us about."

Niccolò turned, attentive and inquisitive. Segrado, on the other hand, manifested no reaction, still lost in the nightmare of his failure.

"It's a treatise on optics by an Arab scholar. It's thick and complex."

"Is it about glass and crystal?" Segrado asked, as though waking from a nightmare.

"I don't know, maybe . . . I didn't have much time. Besides, the manuscript hasn't been translated in its entirety yet."

Kallis was listening to him with a feverish intensity, picturing the hidden meanings and miraculous powers books must possess.

"Can you find out more?" Segrado asked. "Can you read more?"

"Monks are forbidden to look at manuscripts without asking permission. Abbott Carimanno doesn't know the true reason for my trip."

"So you won't do it?"

"I'd be breaking the rules."

"Then you must do as your conscience dictates. I don't want to push you to commit a sin you might come to regret." All of a sudden, Segrado's voice had turned melancholy.

Kallis glared at the glassmaker darkly, with an air of defiance. Segrado went back into the storehouse without dignifying her with so much as a glance. Niccolò picked up the mold and followed him.

Edgardo remained alone with the girl. He felt uneasy but did not know the reason. He had a sense that her eyes were dismembering him, investigating him, digging deeply into his heart, his head, searching for something. Two slits, long and narrow, dark and deep, piercing through him like blades. Her slim, frail body managed to stay alive only because she stored the whole world's hatred in those eyes.

"You have to teach me to write," Kallis suddenly said. She had a harsh, vibrating voice, like a breath of wind in the reeds. "Can you do it?"

She had caught him unawares, as if in a trap. He felt himself blush.

"Can someone like me learn to write?" Kallis insisted.

Edgardo did not know how to respond. It had never occurred to him that someone outside a monastery should want to learn to write—and a woman at that! He had heard that there were nuns in some convent or other, but he had never seen them, so perhaps it was just fantasy.

"It's a long, arduous path, and you have to do a lot of studying," he stuttered.

"Look at me," she said, standing straight before him. "I'm strong as an ox, and I have the endurance and stubbornness of a mule." She raised her arms. "Look at my hands and tell me— are they suited to writing?"

Long, fine fingers worn away by water and work. Hesitantly,

Edgardo brushed them. It was the first time in his life he had touched a woman. He should not have, and he immediately pulled away.

"It's not about hands or strength but, yes . . . It's about endurance and constancy, willpower . . . and love." He was embarrassed to utter that word. "The love of knowledge."

"Then I am able," Kallis decreed.

Edgardo smiled, touched he knew not why, and thought he saw that Kallis too had to swallow some of the sorrow and hatred she kept jealously in her eyes.

"You must teach me," she repeated, "I want to learn."

He did not want to say yes, he tried to restrain himself, to stop his tongue, to tighten his lips, but all the while his mind kept repeating, yes, yes, yes! He did not even notice his head bend forward as a sign of agreement. Then he turned and walked away without saying anything else, inexplicably agitated. A sense of guilt mixed with turmoil of the soul, and a strange warmth. He did not look back. He left the *campo*, and walked around the saltworks toward San Giacomo di Luprio.

"Where are you running, monk? Wait."

He heard himself being called—a voice from beyond the grave, a voice of guilt. Where was it coming from?

"Stop . . . The stone for the eyes, I'm telling you."

Edgardo turned.

"Did a scorpion sting you?"

Zoto's square mug was proffering its best, friendliest smile. Sitting in his favorite spot, in front of a wine tavern, he had noticed Edgardo pass by and had run after him.

"I have good news for you. I've found the crystal. I've got it already, it's mine, it's very pure . . . Come and see it. It glitters and sparkles so much it looks alive. It's perfect to make the stones for your eyes. And you don't have to pay me in advance, only if you're satisfied. Your eyes are safe, it's better than any ointment. The magical power of rock crystal cures every disease. Come and see. Come."

Zoto was circling him, skipping around: with his stones for the eyes, crystal, ointments, magic . . . The words echoed in Edgardo's head like a witches' spell. It had become a kind of obsession. Everybody around him seemed to be competing to offer him a remedy for his eyes. He felt wrapped in a spider's web that was becoming thicker and tighter, until he could not breathe anymore. He managed to shake Zoto off by running toward Rivoalto. The hand that had touched Kallis's fingers was still burning.

"V*iderunt omnes fines terrae salutare Dei nostri: iubilate Deo omnis terra.*"

"*Notum fecit Dominus salutare suum: ante conspectum gentium revelavit iustitiam suam.*"

The faint early morning light was slowly penetrating the church windows, blending in with the voices of the monks who were gathered in a choir behind the altar, to sing praises to Our Lord.

The sharp cold bit at the knees and gnawed at the voice. Faces and hands were hidden under habits. Edgardo's thoughts were at odds with his words. No matter how hard he tried to keep harmony with the others, he kept losing his way, swerving, chasing after images: Kallis's long, tapered fingers, her hands outstretched toward him, and the impenetrable expression on her face, where a faint smile had emerged.

"Hallelujah," he repeated, and met the eyes of Ademaro, who was sitting right opposite him. He had an unfathomable expression that concealed a myriad of answers Edgardo preferred not to hear.

"*Laudamus igitur . . .* " Already, he was regretting his nod of agreement to Kallis's request that he teach her to write. Only a madman's mind could conceive of a cleric with a woman—a stranger working for a glassmaker— as a disciple.

For the first time he articulated to himself a question he had so far kept quiet: What was Kallis to Segrado? What did she mean to him? He had seen her take orders, blindly obey them, and work hard at the foundry. Segrado treated her with no regard and less attention than he used when addressing Niccolò, his *garzone*. Why did he always take her around with him? Was she living with him? Edgardo felt ashamed of these questions that set his mind alight.

"*Laudamus igitur . . .* " Sing praises, pray, lift one's purest thoughts up to an omnipotent God. The rest is dust, emptiness, the splinters of a fragile and transitory life. His eyes, writing, Kallis.

The morning prayers ended, and it was a relief, since the struggle with his mind was becoming unsustainable.

In the refectory, Ademaro came up to him and said, in a friendly tone, "I don't know anything about what you're doing anymore, my friend. I get the impression you're avoiding me."

Edgardo had a slight hesitation, and he wondered if Ademaro noticed. "Not at all, why would I? I would have spoken to you as soon as I had the opportunity."

They poured themselves a bowl of the wine the monks of San Giorgio produced from their vineyard, broke some oatmeal bread, added some goat cheese, and went to sit at the communal table.

"Have you made any progress in your search?" Ademaro asked.

Edgardo realized that he did not want to reveal too much, almost as though he no longer trusted his friend. "It's all very confusing, "he said. "Many people say they know about this stone for the eyes, but nobody has been able to show it to me yet or tell me how to use it, or even how it's made. They're all offering to help me and I get the feeling that there are interests involved that go beyond my simple search." Edgardo looked up from his plate and stared purposefully at his friend. "Do you know anything about this, Ademaro? Is there some secret behind the discovery of the stone that cures the eyes?"

Ademaro did not seem affected by the question, and carried

on eating thoughtfully. Chewing, he replied, "I have no idea . . . Maybe it's a very precious object and whoever manages to grab it or make it could earn a lot of money."

It was a satisfactory answer that seemed to dispel all doubts, but for Edgardo it was not enough. "I want to come to the scriptorium with you this morning. I miss the smell of ink."

Ademaro seemed a little surprised. "Of course, but bear in mind that you could bump into the abbot—he often comes into the library."

"I'll just have to risk an unpleasant encounter," Edgardo replied provocatively. Ademaro laughed, and Edgardo found that laugh very comforting.

He wanted to approach Ermanno di Carinzia to ask him questions about the Arabic manuscript and see Ademaro's reaction, as a kind of final test that would establish his innocence and clarify any misunderstanding.

It was a gray day and a faint light barely filtered through the waxed canvas, making the scribes' task even harder. They were bent over their lecterns, their numbed hands wrapped in bandages against the cold. Edgardo wondered if he was mad in his desperate need to return to writing and his struggle to search for a remedy for his eyes. Perhaps it would be better to be happily blind, working in the vegetable garden. The only man who did not seem to mind the adverse weather was Ermanno. His arms and head bare, his face red, he was working diligently on his manuscript, an ineffable smile on his face, and an expression of physical enjoyment. Ademaro had stopped to talk to the armarius, an old but still quite spry monk who looked after the library and kept a list of the monks who had borrowed books. Edgardo took advantage of this to approach Ermanno and ask him how his work was going.

"It's exhausting. This Arab scholar uses terms unknown to us and talks of truly daring experiments. But it's such a delight . . . Such stimulation for the mind!" He wiped his mouth as though he had just drunk a carafe of good wine. "His theories on light and vision are very interesting and very innovative. For example . . . "

However, he could not complete his sentence because Ademaro promptly—or so it seemed to Edgardo—came to interrupt them.

"Ermanno, the merchant Karamago has told me that new Arabic manuscripts from Constantinople have arrived in Venetia. He's waiting for us to go and see them."

"Spare me! This is more than enough . . . Give me Greek or even Spanish but no more Arabic. It's going to take me a long time and a lot of wine to finish this task." He burst into such uproarious laughter that the other monks turned, surprised. Edgardo peered into Ademaro's face, trying to work out if his interruption had been intentional or pure coincidence, and saw that it was open and smiling.

"I like it when the myth that a copyist's work is nothing but worries and tribulations is debunked." Abbot Carimanno was coming up the stairs with a steady step. "Our brother Ermanno should be an example to us all: a cheerful, playful spirit also nourishes writing . . . "

"It's not just that, Abbott," Ermanno added. "Good wine also nourishes writing . . . and protects from the cold." Thereupon, he gave another healthy laugh, joined this time by the other scribes.

The abbot demonstrated his approval with a wide, fatherly gesture. Ermanno was one of the very few Benedictine translators versed in Arabic as well as Greek, and so was held in high esteem and protected by any abbot who cared about his library.

"But look, today we have the honor of also having the young and talented scribe from Bobbio with us. Given how seldom you take part in the daily functions of the monastery, I must consider your presence as a special event."

Carimanno gave a foul smile and shook his head, scattering hair and lint from his nose and ears in the air.

Fearing Edgardo might respond in a slightly disrespectful tone, Ademaro intervened. "It's my fault, Illustrious Father. As I already mentioned, I charged him with the task of walking around Venetia in search of manuscripts and Edgardo is a very picky cleric. Even today he told me about some new arrivals . . . "

"Well done, but promise me you won't keep the best morsels for yourselves in Bobbio and leave your leftovers to us, your poor, minor fellow brothers."

"I promise you will be at the front of our minds." Ademaro's natural talent for diplomacy had managed to appease him, but there was still tension.

"In any case," Carimanno continued, "there's all the time in the world finally to give our young scribes a demonstration of your expertise. Don't you agree, Edgardo d'Arduino?"

It could no longer be put off. Ademaro tried to think of a suitable excuse to justify his friend.

"It will be an honor," said Edgardo, walking to the lectern.

The scribes left their stations and gathered around him, curious.

"As I was telling you last time, this young scribe, Rainardo, is anxious to learn all your secrets," Carimanno said.

The skinny young man handed him the goose quill with a wan smile.

"What are you copying?" Edgardo asked.

"As you yourself can see . . . The *Topics*," he replied knowingly. "Translated from Greek into Latin by Cicero, and explained in commentary in six volumes by Boethius."

"Good." Edgardo came closer to the parchment: a meaningless blur of out-of-focus symbols. "I see you've done an excellent job."

"But you can do better, I'm sure," the young man replied. "We're all anxious to see you at work."

A deep silence descended on those present. Ademaro's face had turned pale and his features were tense. Edgardo dipped the tip of the quill in the horn filled with ink and, trying to follow it with his body as though assuming a position more adept to writing, drew his face close to the Cicero manuscript. Even with a huge effort, he could barely make out the words, while the letters blended into one another and the lines flickered in a kind of nauseating dance. He would have liked to come even closer, until his nose touched the page, in order to see clearly.

Ademaro realized that he would never manage it. He was about to intervene and help his friend, but Edgardo anticipated him. He straightened up, gave all those present a long look, and stood right in front of Carimanno.

"I want to confess a secret I have never revealed to anyone, Your Worship. The first rule that has guided me in my search for perfection when copying was given to me by an old master at Bobbio."

Ademaro looked at him, incredulous. What on earth was he making up?

"In the beginning, he always said, copy under dictation. Don't worry about committing the pericope to memory. Concentrate exclusively on the shape of the words, the neatness of the signs, and enjoy shaping the characters. Young scribe, would you like to dictate to me a couple of lines from Cicero's original manuscript?"

Carimanno nodded, satisfied, and the young man prepared to dictate.

What Edgardo had to do now was follow his instinct and his memory. He could see a little and, with luck, he would manage it. His hand was steady and he could still follow the lines. The young man began to read slowly, pausing every so often to allow Edgardo to transcribe.

The nib ran freely and the characters took shape on the parchment as if by magic until they made up words. He found the pauses, the blackletters, the hairlines, and the flourishes. He felt joyous and transported as though it were his first time. As though his hand were dancing on the sheet. And he was overwhelmed by a kind of languor, a physical pleasure he had never experienced before.

Carimanno was following the hand with an entranced expression, emitting little gurgling sounds of delight. Ademaro breathed a sigh of relief and looked around. Nobody suspected anything. Edgardo was safe.

Later, Ademaro said, "I confess, I thought I knew you very well, but I was wrong."

"What do you mean?"

"You managed to astonish me. I never thought you'd find a way out with the abbot."

Edgardo laughed. "Neither did I. The idea came to me out of the blue, like a flash of enlightenment."

"You filled us all with wonder. Carimanno won't persecute you for a while."

Ademaro was serene and his tone complicit. It seemed to Edgardo that his doubts were unfounded, and that he had found his friend again.

Karamago the merchant was waiting in his shop to show them the manuscripts that had just arrived from Constantinople. As usual, they took a gondola as far as the dock, where a galley was anchored. It was a tall, wide ship with sails, a rounded bow, raised forecastles at the bow and the stern, and two rows of oars.

"I've never seen a horse fly!" Edgardo said, astounded.

Ademaro stopped with his nose in the air. At that very moment they were loading onto the ship the horses that were to be kept in the hold, and because it was impossible to lead them across the gangplank and the narrow bridges, a system had been devised to lower them from the top. Tied with leather straps that went under their bellies, they were then lifted up by means of a capstan and carried over to the main deck where the trap door was open. It was a complex operation, with which the animals did not happily cooperate. Some were neighing and kicking, and every so often one slipped out of its harness and crashed to the ground.

A multitude of people gathered outside the Orseolo Hospice, near the watchtower, waiting to embark. Well-dressed men with an aristocratic demeanor mixed with simpler folk, such as craftsmen and tradesmen, and, rather unusually, there were also many noble-looking women escorted by their maids or by poor peasant women. There were carefree children running after one another, weaving between the legs of the adults. Edgardo noticed that all these people were calm, and that their faces were luminous, almost inspired. They were patiently waiting their turn as though under a spellbinding influence.

"They're pilgrims waiting to embark for Jerusalem," Ademaro explained. "They're going on a pilgrimage to the Holy Sepulcher. There are more and more of them coming from every country. Shortly after the year one thousand, Doge Orseolo had this hospice built especially to welcome and offer shelter to pilgrims, women, and the sick."

Edgardo felt a kind of envy toward these people who were about to embark on a long and perilous journey just so they could go and pray at the tomb of Our Lord.

"What makes them so . . . so luminous?" he asked.

"This holy voyage is a preparation for death and the promise of salvation. The pilgrim leaves his home, severs relations with his family, relinquishes any protection, and disengages himself from any emotional ties, in the certainty that with this journey he will secure life eternal. That's what makes them so trusting. They abandon themselves to the hands of God."

"They have a deep faith."

"It's the same faith that guided our choice to shut ourselves in a monastery."

Edgardo hung his head and fell silent.

To avoid the crowds in the Calle delle Merzerie, they took a narrow and smelly side street, covered in rubbish and excrement, with low, mold-infested houses, corroded by salt. With every step they took, they sank into sticky, smelly mire that lapped at their habits.

Karamago received them with the usual bowing and scraping. Teodora's bed was empty and the room was saturated with an acrid smell of incense that overwhelmed the odors of all the other spices.

"I have the complete works of Aristotle, Hippocrates's *Aphorisms*, Galen's *Ars Medica* and, besides, little morsels by Horatio and Juvenal that are impossible to find . . . So, what do you think?" He gave the monks a complicit look. "I'll give them to you for little, and if you buy them all I'll give you a good price. Wait, I'll go and get them."

He tottered, took a step and then, as though he had changed his mind, turned to Edgardo. "Will you be so kind as to help me carry them? They're in the attic. It's the safest and driest place now that the waters are high."

Karamago went to a ladder that was leaning against an open trapdoor in the ceiling. Edgardo followed him.

"Mind your holy skull."

They climbed through the hole into a low attic where they had to move on all fours. They began crawling on the floor covered in dried bird excrement. The smell of feces made it hard to breathe. Karamago stopped in front of a trunk.

"I wanted to speak to you in private," he whispered. "It's better if this remains between you and me."

"What is it?"

"I found your eye stone."

Edgardo stared at him in disbelief.

"I've already spoken to him and he's willing to meet you."

"Who?"

"Master Tàtaro. You saw him outside the basilica. He's the most important glassmaker in the whole of Venetia. He wants to see you. He's expecting you at his foundry in Amurianum."

Edgardo was hesitant. Another offer of the stone, and maybe another disappointment.

"I'm warning you, be discreet and silently silent with everyone, especially Segrado."

"But why all this secrecy? What's behind this stone?" Edgardo asked.

Karamago rolled onto his side, trying to find a more comfortable position. In such conditions, the conversation had something both absurd and funny about it.

"Something big is happening in the world of glassmakers. They're all looking for the same thing and want to be the first to get there . . . So when I mention your eye stone, everyone gets very agitated."

"Yes, I've noticed."

"The very word throws even the most peaceful souls into turmoil. And let's not forget that a glassmaker has just been killed in that barbaric manner. Also, let me tell you that many ovens are catching fire in ways I'd say are, to say the least, mysteriously mysterious. In my humble opinion, there is a fight currently being fought. It's hard to say who the eye murderer could be. Maybe that glassmaker had found a new formula, or had stolen it so somebody decided to punish him. We don't know. In any case, Tàtaro is a trustworthy person, so don't be afraid . . . " The merchant gave him a long look. "Still, you must always exercise prudent prudence." And, twisting his behind in a semicircle, he reached the trunk, opened it, and pulled out the manuscripts.

"Here they are," he said, blowing on the frontispieces. "Nice and fresh. Firsthand Greek stuff, not a copy of the translation of a translation."

Edgardo took them delicately in his arms, like newborns just out of their mother's womb. They crawled backwards to the trapdoor. As they were about to go down, Karamago stopped.

"By the way . . . that Arabic manuscript, the one I sold to your fellow brothers, did you ever find it? Is it still in the library at San Giorgio?"

Edgardo was about to answer "yes" without thinking. After all, why should he lie? But then he froze and took a deep breath.

"I don't know, I haven't seen it in the library," he lied.

A stain, a sin: lying. What kind of path was he embarking on? Where would this road bordered with temptation and flattery lead him? Ever since he had left Bobbio to search for the stone for the eyes, Edgardo had done nothing but slide down a dangerous and treacherous slope. He had broken the rules of the order by secretly spying on Ermanno's manuscript. He had gotten close to a woman, even touched her and also, this was an even graver fault, he had experienced an indescribable feeling of turmoil. And now, finally, this lie. Why had he not told Karamago the truth? Out of fear? Or because he did not trust him? Or was it to protect himself against some harm?

He showed Ademaro the manuscripts.

"You could take them to Bobbio," Karamago butted in. "It would be quite a coup for your abbey."

"I serve the interests of knowledge," Ademaro interrupted. "For me every library is equally important. What counts is collecting books and passing them on."

"Yes, yes, of course," Karamago sniggered, "but let's just say that every abbot hopes to have the most prestigious books . . . and that sometimes this results in such bitter competition that the rules of good manners are forgotten."

Ademaro started looking through the pages. Suddenly, a whiff of Arabic incense invaded the room, announcing Teodora's entrance.

She was struggling up the stairs, huffing and puffing and complaining. When she appeared on the doorstep, she was bright red and dripping with sweat. Her flabby, ivory flesh was bursting at every seam of the long velvet dress she had fruitlessly tried to tighten at the waist, under her breasts, and at the armpits. Her body rebelled at being constricted. It wobbled with every movement, trying to free itself from its bonds and giving off a whiff of perfume in every direction. When she saw the monks, she burst into a kind of tearful lament.

"God, I thank you! It's a miracle! A miracle! I knew Our Lord wouldn't abandon me, and your being here is proof of that. I prayed for a sign and you appeared, sent by Divine Providence."

She went up to Ademaro and tried to kiss his hand, but he pulled it away. Then she threw herself on Edgardo, tugging at his cowl.

"My young and saintly monk, you must hear me out. I want to open my heart to you, please enlighten me."

Rather embarrassed, Edgardo glanced at his friend, who, unperturbed, had gone back to looking through the manuscripts.

"I had a dream, a terrible dream . . . and you must tell me what it means."

"I don't interpret dreams," Edgardo replied.

"Listen and you'll understand. The other night, before Lauds, I suddenly woke up. I thought I heard noises. This animal here," she said, indicating her husband, "was fast asleep, so I lifted myself up and looked around . . . and there, in the semidarkness, at the foot of the bed, what do you think I saw?

It was a kind of horrible dwarf. From what I could make out, he was short, with very black eyes, the beard of a goat, pointy, hairy ears, disheveled, bristly hair, teeth like a dog, a pointy skull, a swollen chest, a hump on his back, quivering buttocks, and strange clothes; he was leaning forward with his entire body. He was looking at me without saying a word."

"It was the devil," Edgardo said casually and with a touch of sadism.

"That's exactly what I thought! It was him, the devil, but why was he staring at me that way? What was he trying to tell me?"

While she was recounting her story, Teodora had become so heated that her body was quivering like ibex broth jelly.

"That maybe you shouldn't try to sell false relics," Ademaro commented casually.

At this point, Teodora unleashed an endless litany of complaints. "It's true. I have sinned, but in good faith. I didn't know, I acted foolishly, but I'm ready to repent and make amends. I've just come back from the basilica where I spent the morning praying to Saint Mark. I've renounced idleness and perfumes . . . Every morning, I sprinkle myself with ashes and incense . . . "

Poor Karamago nodded with a disgusted grimace.

"And I'm ready to renounce all worldly goods, free myself of all the relics . . . Isn't that true, Karamago?"

"You did promise," said the merchant.

"All of them without exception: Saint John the Baptist's foreskin, Saint Paul's tibia, the humerus of Saint Callixtus, Saint Sebastian's fingernail, a splinter from the cross of Our Lord, a piece from the stone pillar at which he was whipped, a thorn from his crown, a milk tooth of the Virgin Mary, the eyes of Saint Cosmas and Saint Damian, and of a baby from Herod's massacre, and even a lock of Mary Magdalene's hair that I was very much attached to. Out, all of them out of this unworthy house."

Edgardo nodded, satisfied.

"There, if you want you can take everything away with you, I don't want anything, just a small offering, I'm relying on your kind heart, just a little charity for this sinner who looked the devil in the eyes. I leave it up to you!"

After pleading her cause, Teodora dropped, exhausted, on her bed, making the floor shake.

As though nothing had happened, Ademaro returned the manuscripts to Karamago. "I'll talk to Abbot Carimanno, and see what he says. It also depends on how much you want."

The merchant bowed. "I'm sure we will reach an agreement."

"Let's sort out a price to include the relics," said Teodora.

Edgardo approached the woman and, with a cavernous voice like thunder, which seemed to come from beyond the grave, said, "Quiet, woman. Those relics are cursed now, the devil has tainted them. Get rid of them, throw them into the lagoon, burn them, but whatever you do, get them out of this house as soon as possible if you don't want the devil to pay you another visit. Get them out!"

Repeating the anathema together, the monks left Teodora prostrate and terrified.

XII.
CA' TATARO*

He felt close to achieving his goal. This time, the stone for the eyes could definitely become reality. Edgardo could not account for his feeling. When the boat left him at the tower of Amurianum, he was certain that the meeting with Master Tàtaro would be conclusive. He immediately found the foundry at the start of the *rio* of glassmakers, and asked a *garzone* where the master was.

"He's at the palace," he replied. "Follow the *rio* and it's on the same bank as the basilica of Santa Maria. You can't miss it. It's the only real palace in Amurianum."

The *garzone* was right. Crossing the island, Edgardo went past low warehouses, wooden huts, boathouses, and an arc-shaped bridge made of beams that were fitted and nailed together, supported by logs fixed in the canal. He went past two more churches and, finally, on the shore of a larger canal, saw the only building that might look like a palace . . . or rather like the idea of a palace, since construction was still in full swing. Still, what could already be seen was a princely building of Istrian stone and marble, something seldom glimpsed in the whole of Venetia, let alone on the island of Amurianum.

He saw the skeleton of the two-story building, which, despite its size, gave the impression of extreme lightness, of weightlessness. That was because the first floor was made of a tunnel with large central lancet arches wedged between two filled lateral screens, and a portico with two small towers on the sides. Another porch opened onto the ground floor, which led straight to the bank, giving the impression that the building leaned over into the void, creating a play of light and shadow. To make way for the construction, the canal had been dammed and drained, so that Edgardo could see how they had made the foundations to support the weight of such a large building.

In order to firm up the earth and increase its density, thus ensuring that the foundations were more stable, eight or nine very long wooden poles had been planted. The tops had been leveled and two wide beech platforms had been nailed to them, from which issued the foundation walls. The wood, immersed in damp mud and shielded from any contact with air, was preserved in excellent condition, guaranteeing that the deepest part of the foundational structure would remain functional.

One side of the façade was already plastered in marble and, under the portico, *pateras** and ornamental tiles depicting floral patterns and mythical animals were set. Builders were still at work inside and on the banks, but the palace already looked magnificent.

Master Tàtaro, standing on a freight boat loaded with timber, like the captain of a ship, gave orders as he admired his creation. As soon as he saw Edgardo, he abandoned his command post and went to meet him with an affable manner.

"I'm glad you came. You're the first cleric to cross the threshold of my new home. What do you think?"

"Magnificent," Edgardo agreed.

"I still have other embellishments and clever solutions in mind. I heard from a glassmaker who visited the abbey of Monte Cassino that there they closed the windows with glass circles of different colors, tied together by a string of lead; it keeps the ice and rain out and the light projects colored reflections on the floor and the walls, creating a fairy-tale atmosphere. Glass on the windows . . . Master Tàtaro will be the first and only one in Venetia—as usual."

"It's a wonderful idea, I've never seen anything like it. It would be very convenient for us too, in the scriptorium," Edgardo said.

Master Tàtaro assessed him with a look. "Still, you haven't come here in order to admire my home, right?" Edgardo nodded. "Then come, there's something I must show you."

They entered the palace. The rooms were empty and their footsteps created a sinister echo on the terrazzo flooring.

Inside, a courtyard surrounded by a portico opened up. In the middle, two workmen were building a well. After digging out a large square reservoir underground, which had then been lined with clay and sand to stop salt water from seeping in, they were erecting a flue of curved bricks in the center of the tank, leaving a gap between each so that rainwater—by means of *pilelle* (perforated slabs of stone attached to the four corners of the floor around the cistern)—could gather in the flue and, by passing through it, be purified until it became more natural than springwater. The city subsoil had no freshwater, and it had always been difficult for Venetians to quench their thirst.

At the back of the house, Tàtaro had set up a kind of museum where he kept his most valuable pieces on display, in permanent memory of his genius. He pulled out a parchment from a shelf and, with a theatrical gesture, unrolled it before Edgardo.

"This is what your eyes long for."

It was a drawing, the strokes vague and faded; a sketch with writing.

"*Lapides ad legendum*," Tàtaro said in a loud voice, emphasizing his understanding of the writing.

All Edgardo's hopes and delusions vanished in a flash. A simple drawing? Is that all it was? Edgardo had expected to see this stone for the eyes, touch it, try it! Instead, he had to content himself with imagining it, and even that with great difficulty. The object represented had an oblong shape, flat on the bottom and curved on the top, like a tortoise shell, but it was impossible to tell how big it was or from what kind of material it was made.

"It's certainly rock crystal," Tàtaro added. "A huge piece of crystal that's been cut and smoothed."

"And how does it work?" Edgardo asked, trying hard to imagine the relationship between the eyes and that heavy stone.

"We don't know exactly. The scholar who asked me to reproduce it thinks that the stone must be placed on the page of a parchment and that, if you draw the eye close to the part that's curved, you can see the letters reflected there, magnified, a remedy for eyes like yours that can no longer make out very small things."

Edgardo tried to imagine the effort it would take to push the stone across the page to be transcribed, one word at a time . . . a huge task that would make copying take much longer. Still, it would be better than a world that was uncertain and out of focus.

"Have you managed to reproduce one of these stones?" he asked.

"Well . . . I've tried with the help of a crystal-maker I trust. We're working on it but it's not easy to find the right curvature. If the proportion between the base and the curve isn't exact, the letters get deformed, melt, and break up, and everything blends into a nightmarish mixture."

Edgardo stared at the drawing, not knowing what to think.

"So that's why I wanted to meet you." Tàtaro took his time to roll up the parchment and put it back on the shelf. "You're a talented cleric and you have access to the library of San Giorgio . . . "

Edgardo was beginning to understand.

"I know that Abbot Carimanno keeps precious manuscripts that come from the Orient, and apparently there is among them a volume that deals precisely with vision, eye function, and experiments performed with crystal and glass. With this information I think I could make considerable progress in reproducing *lapides ad legendum.*" His face grew pointy as he peered beyond the tip of his nose. "I imagine it wouldn't be impossible for you to take a peek. With your knowledge and my genius we will certainly succeed in solving the problem. You'll have your eyesight and I'll have the secrets of Arab scholars."

Obviously, news of the existence of Alhazen's book was spreading fast, reawakening the interests of many. Karamago had started it, but what had really stirred the waters was the arrival of Edgardo, who could read, had access to the library, and in addition, in order to save his eyes, had a vested interest in divulging the contents of the book. A poor monk, easy to blackmail.

"What do you think? It seems like a fair exchange," Tàtaro concluded.

His immediate reaction was one of disgust. The very word "exchange" made his blood boil. The prospect of doing something against the rules, of having recourse to subterfuge, and bartering his learning with a pompous craftsman for his personal gain made him feel like a despicable being. It was an action unworthy of him, of the habit he wore, and of his heritage, to strike a deal with a plebeian! His noble origins reemerged with arrogance. Edgardo d'Arduino, known as the Crooked, was about to respond with outrage that he would never . . . but then he stopped, lost and confused. What dignity, what family name was he thinking of? Had he not already broken the rules by going to the scriptorium in secret and reading the Arabic book? Was he not lying, resorting to subterfuge, and betraying a friend? Who did he think he was fooling? He was hardly that pure and noble cleric he deluded himself that he was, but just a common mortal desperately trying to find a way to save his eyesight and give his life purpose. And perhaps he would stop at nothing to reach that goal. Therefore, he did not respond with his instinctive outrage but, instead, took his time and prevaricated diplomatically.

"I don't know anything about that book." Another lie. "It could be there, I won't deny it. If I have the opportunity to—if by chance I happen to find it . . . I'll bear it in mind . . . I'll try to see . . . "

Accustomed to haggling and bargaining over the price of his glass, Tàtaro understood that the door was not shut, and that the negotiations could continue.

"It's important," the glassmaker continued, "that a particular kind of knowledge should fall into the right hands. Venetia is full of braggarts and adventurers who boast about discoveries, magic arts, and secret formulas—especially among glassmakers. Don't let them cheat you, they only want to take advantage of you. And don't let yourself be impressed if they announce that they've made an extraordinary discovery or new experiments. Glass is glass, and crystal is crystal—nobody can substitute the one for the other. Only that madman Segrado goes around announcing he has revolutionary formulas that will change the course of history." Tàtaro laughed, enjoying the sound coming out of his mouth. "That braggart will end up begging outside San Marco together with his foolish slave. You'll see . . . You'll see . . . " As he said this, he had a sniggering fit.

His slave . . . So Kallis was his slave. Edgardo felt somewhat confused. It was logical and he should have known it immediately. It was exactly the behavior of a master toward his slave, so it was not in the least surprising . . . But then why did he feel that uncontrollable anger rise in his chest? Tàtaro was laughing and laughing . . . Edgardo was tempted to punch him in the face, ram his teeth down his throat, and put a stop to that stupid, inappropriate laughter. He turned abruptly and, without so much as a goodbye, walked out of the palace.

XIII.
ARSENAL

He left Amurianum on a *scaula* loaded with cloths, which would take him back to Venetia. He was ever more confused and tormented. Edgardo felt caught up in a vortex that was dragging him down, with no hope of returning to the surface. He began wondering if he should give up. He was paying too high a price for the recovery of his sight. But was that what was really happening? Was the search for the stone for the eyes not an excuse, a cover he had created himself? Giving up would mean returning to confinement and solitude. He did not want to admit to himself that the freedom he was savoring filled him with excitement and curiosity. It was the first time he had plunged into life, and he was discovering its ugliness, its tricks, its unforeseen events, its torments and fears. However, together with that, he had savored moments of immense joy: the celestial vision-like enchantment of the impalpable lagoon landscape, his spirit quivering while visiting the basilica of San Marco, and the feverish emotion he felt in Kallis's presence. His soul was all mixed up, and the reality about him appeared deformed in both good and evil ways. In the end, his ailing eyes were showing him reality as it was: a confused and sublime alternation of unfathomable events.

The boatman left him at the castle of Olivolo, in a quarter he had never been to. Edgardo had reached the stage where he was convinced that he had somehow mastered the city layout and that, in any case, he would be able to find his way to the basilica, his reference point for returning to San Giorgio.

The island of Olivolo, in the far eastern extremity of Venetia, was home to the Church of San Pietro, one of the oldest bishoprics of the *gens venetica*, an orderly who was distributing food to the poor in the *campo* outside the cathedral explained. In the old days, the island was enclosed within fortress walls, designed to protect it against Narentine pirates, who ruled in Istria and Dalmatia, as well as across the mouth of San Niccolò del Lido, and had even pushed deep into the heart of the lagoon. Hence its name: castle.

Edgardo walked across the wooded *campo* outside the bishopric and, crossing a rickety wooden bridge, reached a stretch of land that emerged from the waters. He crossed uncultivated fields that gave the impression of being in the open countryside except for the pools and ponds that suddenly opened up beside the paths. He went past two monasteries, Sant'Anna and San Domenico, walked around a large lake on the bank of which was the church of San Daniele, and reached an area where he began to notice large houses, huts, and warehouses along the canals. This reassured him because it meant that he had chosen his route wisely and was approaching the more populated center.

As he walked, with a sense of satisfaction, he was surprised to notice above the roofs of the huts, as if out of nowhere, the swaying mast of a ship with shreds of loose sails. This watery city seemed to spontaneously create ships and sails out of bare earth. He slipped between two little houses and found himself before an extraordinary sight: a large basin of water surrounded by a crenellated wall several workmen were still building. In the middle, proud and imposing, a galley was anchored, its sails lowered and its oars at rest. Around the pool there were open sheds and naval building sites where boats and ships of every shape and size took shelter. A chelandion had been pulled aground and various shipbuilders were busy working around the keel, where you could see an enormous gash. Heaps of rigging, hemp, timber, and towropes, as well as barrels of pitch, were piled up behind the warehouses.

He had come across an arsenal. Edgardo had read about them in manuscripts about Constantinople and Alexandria, but never imagined that Venetia might have one.

He was still admiring the display of timber and sails when a deep rumbling sound swept over him like a gust of wind, a vibration that originated from the depths of the earth.

Edgardo looked around but could not work out where it was coming from, but then he heard from afar, like a forgotten echo, shouts, voices, and crashing. A moment later, they had increased and he felt surrounded by an impending din that suddenly materialized.

A multitude of men of different ages, brandishing pitchforks, poles, swords, and torches, were running, enraged, after two defenseless young boys. The crowd was moving toward him and, to avoid being knocked down, he hid under the arch of a warehouse. The shouts were deafening. A vague shrieking, like the cries of a demented flock of seagulls.

One of the fugitives managed to find refuge inside a nearby monastery, but the other was reached by the angry crowd, held down, and tied to a pole.

Edgardo could not understand what was going on. The voices were confused and everything happened very quickly. A well-dressed man brought a flaming torch to the boy's face and threatened to set fire to him. The prisoner struggled, crying out in pain. His hair caught fire and a blaze caressed his face. The crowd was laughing and spurring the torturer on. The torch moved closer to his eyes, closer and closer . . . Edgardo heard a sharp, final cry, thin as a whistle, blend with a soft crackling and the bubbling of roasted marrow. It was a terrifying scene. The boy fainted. Suddenly, there was silence, like a void in the air before a storm. Then he heard other distant voices and footsteps. From the opposite side of the *campo*, another gang of young men appeared, armed and wearing red coats.

As soon as they saw them, the first crowd dropped the pole to which the boy was tied. The fire had already spread to his clothes. The two groups stood studying each other, then a man threw himself on the burning body to extinguish the flames. It was the signal that triggered the clash. It was a senseless and chaotic unleashing of bodies: blows, cuts, crunching bones, blood, screams, and moans.

Someone had set fire to the timber gathered for the ships. Edgardo was overwhelmed by a feeling of impotence, annihilated by this senseless violence. Afraid, he took refuge inside the warehouse, among the remains of abandoned boats, but after a while he realized that he was not safe there either. The fire was all around him. Taking advantage of a pause during which the brawl moved inside the arsenal, he rolled out and began running at breakneck speed toward the lagoon, stepping over bodies, avoiding flaming beams, thinking only of saving himself. He ran and ran for what felt like an eternity, with that poor crippled body that could not keep up with the mounting terror in his heart.

When he reached the bank, he felt a deep sense of relief at finding himself before the open lagoon, navigated by ships and boats. He stopped to catch his breath, unsure of which way to go, when he heard someone calling him.

"Scribe! Scribe! Where are you running?"

It sounded to him like a voice from heaven, and he looked around, panting.

"Here we are, man of God!" There was a laugh.

A *scaula* was approaching the bank. Segrado was rowing, and Kallis sat in the bow, wrapped in a turquoise cloak.

"Quick, get in."

Without even thinking, Edgardo leapt into the boat. With

four well-delivered strokes of the oar, Segrado took them out to sea. A light, cold wind was blowing over the surface of the water, which was lead-gray and waved, thick and soft, as they moved. Edgardo breathed deeply the cold air that chilled his habit, still drenched in sweat. A deep sense of shame prevented him from speaking, or even looking up. Kallis was watching the horizon, looking blank and absent.

"What happened? Did they try to disembowel you?"

Segrado's voice came from behind, like a stab in the back.

"Venetia has become a bubbling cauldron of madness. Everything is still and quiet, and then suddenly there's trouble. You found yourself right in the middle of the usual brawl between hotheads. You should be careful. They can be a bit rough . . . even with monks."

Edgardo listened with his head down, glad not to have to speak.

"It's an old story that goes back to the beginning, when people from the mainland escaped from barbarian invaders and took refuge on the islands. Ever since there have been two factions made up of those that came from different lands. The Castellanis, who live in the far eastern part, and the Nicolottis or Cannaruolis, who live in the far western part. The castle of Olivolo and San Niccolò are the oldest settlements in this treacherous city, and their inhabitants hate one another and use any excuse to beat each other up. For people like me or you," he laughed again, "who don't want anything to do with them, it's hard to stay out of it. Look over there," he indicated the bank. "They've set fire to the arsenal while it's still being built. They burn things and cut throats and our Doge Falier does nothing. And you know why? I'll tell you. Because it's convenient for him, and because he doesn't want to upset any of the powerful Venetian families who use those poor wretches to their advantage. The Nicolottis are backed by the Candiani family, who have large holdings on the mainland and business interests they need to preserve with the Franks and the Germanics. The Castellanis, on the other hand, are manipulated by the Orseolos, who have close blood ties with Slavic and Hungarian kings, and want Venetia to be tied to the court of Byzantium. So you see, it's all a war between lords who use deadbeats like beasts for slaughter. Doge Ordelaffo is a great knight, of course, and a truly brave fighter. When we intervened in Schiavonia* because they wanted to take the cities along the coast away from us, he gave them a really good beating. However, with all the mainland wars and those he fights in the Orient to keep on the right side of the Pope, he doesn't take much care of his city, where it's the rich families who rule, and they have no time for the poor . . . "

The wind had increased in the bow of the boat as it struggled to cut through the waves. Kallis was sitting huddled up at the bottom of the keel, right in front of Edgardo.

"In any case, thank God for saving your life today," Segrado said in conclusion.

Edgardo lifted his head. Kallis was observing him. In fact, she was probing his soul. He felt himself searched in his mind, his body, and beneath his habit. The eyes of that invasive and brazen woman were stripping him of his dignity. Through the eyes of a woman, his crippled body was being exposed in all its nakedness.

He felt himself being born a second time and became even more painfully aware of his deformity. Thanks to Kallis's gaze, which had generated a new monster, Edgardo discovered the power of a woman's eyes and felt ashamed.

"Where are we going?" he finally found the strength to ask.

"Home," said Segrado. "I can't take you back now. It's almost time for Vespers, and it'll be dark soon. You can stay with us. We live on an island in the middle of the lagoon, in the north. It's called Metamauco."

Distanced from the familiar world, in an unknown hemisphere, the city skyline had slowly disappeared behind them. Before them and all around there was nothing but water, water and sky, which blended into each other in a unique lead-gray reflection. A thin layer of mist blurred the substance of the shoals that were peeping out just below the water's surface. They were navigating through the void, without a point of reference, in dense and heavy silence. A voyage into the beyond.

Edgardo felt as though his body was crumbling into an infinite number of particles that were being ravished by the humid veil of sunset. Only his spirit remained, dragged along on that unstable boat, carried into a new dimension. So he gave himself up to the unknown. He put himself trustingly into the hands of Segrado, his boatman, before the eyes of his guide, Kallis, and was surprised to find that he was no longer afflicted by the weight of life, by torments, by physical pain. With carefree hopes for the future, he wished that this journey would never end, so that he could stay forever in this state of unfathomable bliss.

The current pushed the boat north and the strokes of the oars became more intense and decisive. The fog dissipated, the sky resumed its position, separating itself from the surface of the water, and in the distance a white stripe appeared, sucked in by the fading light. A long, deep beach of white and very fine sand surrounded the entire island and dense vegetation came as far as the dunes that waved uncertainly at the horizon. Segrado turned east and followed the coast for a long stretch until he reached a landing.

The island of Metamauco had a well-equipped harbor where a variety of galleys, warships, and freight boats were anchored. Not far from the mainland, between the mouths of Medoacus Maior and Minor, it served as an outpost for goods from Padua bound for the city of Venetia.

Segrado pulled alongside the bank. Kallis leapt on the *junctorio* and moored the boat to a pole. The district was bustling. Sailors, merchants, and fishermen were busying themselves around the boats. It was surprising to see so many people and such impressive buildings on an island in the middle of the lagoon. In the main *campo*, next to the church of perforated bricks, there was a white two-story stone building with a wide loggia, and coats of arms and sculptures on the façade. It had once been the Doge's residence and was now the see of the bishopric. All around the *campo* and in the adjacent streets were rows of simple, well-kept houses of painted timber, with vegetable patches, orchards, and gardens at the back. Much of the island was occupied by vineyards. The white beach, lush forests, and the farming reminded Edgardo of the descriptions of earthly paradise he had read in sacred books.

Segrado left the *campo* and walked toward the building Edgardo immediately recognized as a monastery. Then they followed a path that snaked through marshes and minor canals until they reached a small, shabby bridge made of beams, which led to a bare and muddy little island surrounded by rushes, in the middle of which, on top of a raised, solid mound, stood a little house. The walls were made of planks coated with tar, the roof out of woven reeds and covered in stubble. At the back there was a tiny vegetable garden and a fig tree to which a goat was tied. Segrado took off the chain latch, flung the door open, and walked in.

"Tonight you'll do penance," he said defiantly. "You monks are used to comfort."

"Perhaps you should take a closer look at me," Edgardo replied touching the hump on his chest. "I do penance every day . . . "

Kallis let loose a gurgling sound, like a repressed laugh, then rushed to the hearth, which was dug out of a brick shelf; there was a hole in the roof overhead to let the smoke out. With a torch, she set about starting a fire. Segrado indicated a corner of the hut.

"All I have is a bit of straw and a bench for the night."

"That will be fine, thank you for your hospitality," Edgardo replied.

The dwelling consisted of a single large room. In a corner, hidden behind hemp canvas hanging from a rope, were two high beds made of rough wood. A table and four stools stood by the fireplace, with a chest and a trunk making up the rest of the furniture in that basic abode.

The fire grew, the room lit up, and Edgardo looked around, stunned. The floor seemed to glow with its own light and the walls glistened with colored dots in blue, green, yellow and ruby, as though a swarm of multicolored fireflies had suddenly flown into the room. In a second, the modest home had turned into a magical place. Seeing the amazement on the cleric's face, Segrado burst out laughing.

"It's an invention of mine. What do you think of it?"

"I'm speechless. It's like a starry sky. It's magic."

Kallis smiled.

"There's nothing magic about it," said Segrado. "When I made the lime cast for the *terrazzo* flooring, I mixed in colored stones, fragments of glass, leftover enamel, and cast-off mosaic tiles. This way I can walk on a carpet of precious stones and sleep beneath a starry sky."

"It's very clever," Edgardo concurred.

A blanket of darkness had now stifled what was left of the light on the horizon. Even the seagulls had stopped crying, and the hut was wrapped in a stagnant silence. They sat around the table. Kallis brought a large pan blackened by the fire, full of oatmeal. Then she took three salted sardines out of a jar and put them on the plates. A mixture of oats and fish: this would be dinner. They ate without talking and Kallis did not raise her head from her plate. Segrado kept stealing glances at the cleric, the hint of a sly smile on his face, watching his reaction to the poor meal. Edgardo ate without paying any attention, contentedly, in fact. He did not know why, but he felt calm and at peace. It was the feeling of being welcome and of belonging: to a roof, two people, and a table. A state of mind he had never experienced while sitting with his fellow brothers at Bobbio Abbey, let alone in his father's house.

"We'll even attack the emergency supplies in your honor," Segrado said, giving Kallis a nod. From a shelf hanging on the wall, she fetched two bunches of dried black grapes and laid them delicately on the table, so as not to lose a single one.

"Help yourself," Segrado said.

Edgardo pulled off one grape, as did Segardo and, finally, Kallis. He felt he was taking part in a pagan ritual.

"So, what have you decided to do?" Segrado asked, sucking hungrily at the sweet pulp.

Edgardo did not understand to what he was referring. "About what?"

"About the Arabic manuscript."

Edgardo studied the face of the man opposite him. He tried to read his eyes, to see if there was the trace of any stain there; he searched the lines of his face, his shovel-like hands, trying to decide if he could put his trust in him and speak to him as honestly and openly as he wished.

"Everybody wants to know what's in that book, but we don't know if it contains information useful to you or me."

Segrado spat out a skin. "That's why I'm asking you to investigate further. Who else knows about the book besides the merchant?"

Edgardo hesitated for a moment and turned to the woman, almost as if he were waiting for her approval. Kallis plucked a grape, lifted it slowly to her mouth and, with her lips slightly parted, sucked in the pulp in one quick slurp. Edgardo lowered his eyes.

"Master Tàtaro wanted to meet me. He has a drawing of the stone for the eyes: *lapides ad legendum.* He's promised to make the stone with rock crystal in exchange for information about the Arabic book."

"He's lying!" Segrado railed. "Tàtaro doesn't know the first thing about working with crystal. He wants to swindle you. All he wants is to discover a new formula for glass."

"I'm telling you, I don't know if there's anything about that in the optics treatise."

"All the glassmakers would be ready to cheat in order to discover the pure glass that transmits the purifying light of Our Lord." Segrado wiped his toothless mouth with his sleeve. "Tàtaro cares nothing about your eyes or your failing sight. Tàtaro cares for nothing but himself."

Edgardo leaned toward him. "And you? What do you care about?"

Kallis placed her hands on the table like a little girl and waited.

"I don't know you, scribe, but I know why God decided to put you on my path. For you, losing your eyesight is like losing my breath for me: I couldn't live without it. There is creation in my breath, and in your eyes there is knowledge. It's the meaning of our earthly lives. I believe that uniting our skills could sprout a plant that would give both you and me new lifeblood."

Segrado stood up and went to the corner where the beds

were arranged. Kallis picked up the dishes and wiped them down with a cloth. Then she turned to Edgardo.

"The well is behind the house, and the latrines by the canal." She opened the trunk and took out a blanket. "Take this," she said. "At night, the chill rises from the ground and seeps into your bones."

"Thank you."

They were standing very close. Edgardo felt her heat, a strange wave of warmth smelling of myrrh, like a *scirocco* wind that enveloped and dazed him.

Then Kallis stepped out of his aura and went to her bed behind the hemp canvas.

It was the first time in his life that Edgardo had slept under the same roof as a woman. Although their beds were not close, he thought he could hear her breath and heartbeat. Even when the mind is not willing, and the body is not willing either, desire awakens and sin takes over your soul. He tossed and turned under the blanket, unable to sleep. The night silence had turned into a racket. The swish of the waves along the shore had become a waterfall, and the cry of an owl had become a call of death. The faint flame of the oil lamp squashed the shadows onto the floor, awakening glistening eyes and fragments of stars.

Edgardo started to pray as he had been taught to by monks when he could not sleep for love or money. However, Kallis's breath and heartbeat seemed to grow louder and dance around him. He continued to repeat his litany to chase away thoughts and images.

A creaking sound made him jump. Somebody was moving behind the hemp canvas. It was a vague rustling. Perhaps a blanket being lifted or clothes slipping off? Then there was a faint, slightly hoarse gasp. A body melting in an embrace? Was he dreaming? Was it a child's nightmare? Or a demon's temptation? Edgardo curled up against the wall, hiding his head under the blanket so that he would not hear, or see, or even imagine. Kallis the slave had turned into Kallis the concubine. It was no use praying, except to curse his own body, hide from nightmares and stifle dangerous dreams, the sound of her increasingly deep breathing, and the flame of the lamp that wavered, about to go out. It was not the breathing of the lagoon, nor the beating wings of a kite that had landed on the thatched roof, but the soul of Kallis the concubine arrogantly coming out to flaunt her insane pleasure to the world. Her skin, sweating salt and milk. Her numbed fingers digging into the bear's back.

Pray, Edgardo the Crooked, pray—not that it helps, except to hide your hump. Pray to that God who has punished you from birth and who continues to proclaim His omnipotence in your failing eyesight and in the shadow falling deeper and deeper over your poor eyes with every passing day.

He fell asleep once his prayers had worn out his limbs and intoxicated his mind. It was a brief, restless sleep, light enough to allow an apparition so clear it looked real. The naked body of a woman was leaning over him, stroking his head and tucking him in like a child. It was the body of an old woman, all wrinkled and white as milk. The body of the servant who would rock him, as a child, when he could not get to sleep because of the pain in his crooked bones, and who would leave the scent of burned acorns in his hair.

He was awoken by the desperate bleating of the goat. Strips of light filtered through the reeds on the ceiling. The hut was empty. Edgardo got up, with excruciating pain in his joints. He suddenly remembered the night before, with all its torments. A naked woman had leaned over him . . . Who was she? He was unable to reconstruct a clear picture. He stepped out of the door. The sky was so clear and bright, it seemed to vibrate. He rubbed his eyes. They were watering, and a sharp sting made it so that he could not keep them open. He went to a small canal, to rinse his face and soothe the burning sensation. Against a blurred horizon, he recognized Segrado and Kallis, standing in water up to their waists, working by the bank outside the house. He approached with an unsteady step. Segrado was planting sharpened sticks into the muddy bottom, to which Kallis was attaching a wicker trellis that she then covered with slime and clay, building a kind of barrier.

"The water has been rising for months." Segrado did not lift his head and spoke without interrupting his work. "I don't know what's happening to the muddy sea. We keep having to reinforce and raise the banks in order not to be submerged, and have our houses flooded, our fields destroyed, and our vineyards burned by salt water. Old people talk of times gone by when you could walk from Altinus to Torcellus and when the islands of Aymanas and Costanciacum were part of the same land. There were herds grazing free where right now there are marshes and reeds. When I took over this little island, it was a submerged shoal. I broke my back digging canals, carrying soil, reinforcing the banks—I stole this land from the water and managed to build a home on it."

He stopped and looked up as though to check that what he was saying was true. Kallis had collected some stones on a board tied with two ropes and was about to pull them to the shore. The load was heavy, and despite all her efforts she was struggling to move it. Edgardo picked up a rope and started pulling with her. Kallis gave him a grateful look. Segrado was putting mud on the dam and paid no attention to them.

The stones had to be put behind the stilts. Kallis started moving them on to the bank, one by one, with Edgardo helping her. They worked together in perfect harmony, their movements almost blending together. They were glistening with sweat. Edgardo felt his muscles tighten and his body obey, relaxed, agile, as though his crookedness had miraculously disap-peared. At the abbey, because of his disability, they had always exempted him from heavy work. And now, maybe for the first time, he was discovering muscles and strength in his arms. His hands were not just made to hold a goose quill. Kallis lifted the last load, bigger than the others, and reached out to Segrado. Perhaps she put a foot wrong in the mud, or perhaps it was too heavy for her, but the stone slipped and fell into the water, grazing Segrado's leg.

"Bitch like your mother!" he cried. "Do you want me to be crippled? Stupid woman!"

He struck her violently across the face. A bear's paw on a slender reed. Kallis bent double, swayed, but did not fall. Edgardo felt the impulse to pounce on the man and punish him for his cowardly action. Yet he did not move. An unnatu-ral silence had suddenly fallen over them, interrupted only by Kallis's panting, full of rage.

Segrado resumed his work, still swearing. She remained there for a few seconds, straight and motionless, like one of those poles stuck in the mud; then, without saying a word, walked toward the hut. Segrado did not stop her. Edgardo wanted to catch up with her and comfort her: an action that would not have been appropriate to his role. A master has full power over his slave. He can beat her and also enjoy her favors. A monk must not get involved.

Edgardo had contrasting feelings toward the man. On the one hand he admired and trusted him, recognizing his honesty, his purity of spirit, and a certain degree of knowledge. On the other hand, he felt in him a shadow of ambiguity, depths of vio-lence that frightened him.

"Don't worry, scribe, you'll be safely back in your abbey by Terce. Go home and wait for me there. I'm going to pick up some materials from the harbor, and then I'll come and get you."

Edgardo obeyed. Kallis was feeding the goat.

"Where is he?" she asked.

"He's gone to get some stuff, then he's coming back."

Kallis looked at him with surprise. "He went alone?"

Edgardo nodded.

She shook her head thoughtfully. "Are you hungry? There's some oatmeal left."

"Thank you."

They went into the house. Edgardo sat at the table while Kallis gave him a bowl and a glass of water. They were alone. Segrado was far away. Edgardo was forcing himself not to look at her, but a magnetic force emanated from her soft, graceful movements and her amber skin. All of a sudden, Kallis came and sat down opposite him, and he could not help admiring her.

"Have you thought that perhaps your eyes won't last much longer?" Her tone was hard and severe.

"I think about it every day. "

"Then you must act quickly. Maybe there's a recipe in that book that can cure them . . . If you wait too long you'll never know. You must read it and copy it, while you still can. It could be your salvation."

Edgardo stared at her, astonished by her determination. "You have no idea how long it takes to copy a manuscript . . . It takes months, years."

"Then copy only what you need for your eyes." Her voice was like a low and monotonous chant, yet full of deep energy.

Kallis reached out with her hand. Edgardo watched her fingers draw so close, they turned into a blurry shadow. He was overwhelmed by her spice-scented breath. A light touch brushed his eyelids and a blinding light exploded in his head, accompanied by a wave of heat. Edgardo opened his eyes again, frightened. Kallis was sitting there, opposite him.

"You're a witch!" he said.

Kallis started to laugh, to laugh without stopping. He had

never seen a woman laugh in such an unseemly, unrestrained manner.

"Me, a witch?" She was laughing and laughing.

Edgardo leapt to his feet, offended, and grabbed her by the wrist. "That's enough. I will not allow you to make fun of me."

"Make fun of you? What are you saying?" A note of surprise had crept into her laugh. "It's me I'm laughing at . . . If only I was a witch! People are afraid of witches and keep away from them. While I am nothing, nothing . . . You can beat me if you want, you can throw me out or forget me. You can even kill me—nobody would notice, nobody would cry over me."

Edgardo let go of her. He had behaved like a petty man, merely following his pride. After all, he too, had treated her like a slave.

Kallis left the room but Edgardo went after her. "Wait!" he shouted.

At that moment, the *scaula* was turning into the stream outside the house. Segrado shouted to get their attention. Kallis quickly picked up her things, closed the door with the chain, and went to the bank. It all happened very quickly, and Edgardo did not have the time to speak to her. They got in from the bow. With a stroke of the oar, Segrado pushed the boat toward the open lagoon.

Kallis noticed a small, dark sack on the bench. It seemed full. She was about to put it at the bottom of the boat before sitting down.

"Don't touch it!" Segrado's brusque tone stopped her. "Give it here!" He put the little sack at his feet, as though protecting a treasure of inestimable value. By now they were far away, with Metamauco behind them, going toward the island of Popilia.*

XV.
DE ASPECTIBUS

He waited late into the night. The abbey was plunged into an unnatural silence. Not a breath of wind or a swish in the waves. Only a gurgling sound that came from underground, as though the lagoon was simmering beneath the island. For hours he had mulled over the right thing to do. Kallis's words were still echoing in his head. "Have you thought that perhaps your eyes won't last much longer?" She was right. He did not know if, only a few days hence, he would be able to read, even with difficulty, the page of a manuscript. He had noticed that the illness was progressing very fast. In old people, he had seen it advance very slowly and over many years. In his case, though, it was different. It was not just his near sight that had deteriorated. Even in the distance, contours looked out of focus and wobbly. Perhaps an evil disease was taking him toward blindness in a short space of time. In that case, not even these magical stones for the eyes would be able to save him. However, he still had one hope, so why give up? He could not consider living deprived of the supreme joy of being able to see. Not just seeing words but the entire world that surrounded him. A shadow, a dark veil would fall over the sky, nature, and men. Kallis's face appeared before him, clear and luminous. That too would be obliterated by the darkness of blind eyes.

Edgardo left his cell. He had made his decision. The candle he had kept lit barely illuminated his steps. He did not encounter any difficulties on his way to the library; he was accompanied only by that underground rumbling which grew louder in the cloisters. When he had reached the scriptorium, he looked for the shelf where he had previously found the manuscript. It was still in the same place, together with the yet incomplete translation. He took it and placed it on the lectern. The pages had not yet been bound. It was a thick manuscript. Finding in so little time—that is, if there was anything to find—the passages that could bring him knowledge about eyesight and optics seemed like an impossible enterprise. Alhazen's *De Aspectibus* was divided into seven books, and he began to look through the index: The Mechanics of Vision, The Nature and Propagation of Light, The Nature of Colors. Physiology of the Eye, Optical Cone, The Light Required by Vision, Reflection and Refraction.

With difficulty, he started reading. Alhazen claimed that if vision was possible, as those who sustained visual rays said, thanks to the eye's emission of rays similar to sticks able to examine the external world and provide the psyche with elements to discern shapes and colors, then looking at the sun should not be painful, because the eye would not emit rays if emitting them hurt. On the contrary, reality demands that there should be an external agent operating in the eye, so that when this agent is too strong it causes pain to the sensitive organ.

Edgardo found the argument very logical and sensible. Once again, he drew close to the manuscript and continued to read.

Alhazen's theory was that the beam of light emanated from objects and not from the eye. "Tiny slivers of peel"—a kind of shadow that envelops bodies—get detached from the bodies themselves and reach the eye. Once they penetrate the pupil, these slivers of peel are able to reconstruct inside the eye an ordered object like the one that has emitted them. Alhazen called this external agent capable of acting so as to trigger vision, "Lumen."

Edgardo had never asked himself how his eyes or vision in general worked. He just looked at the world and was pleased with what he saw. Now, discovering that there were such complex mechanisms that explained such an immediate act filled him with amazement and curiosity. However, he could not yet understand how these notions could be related to his illness, the stones, or the crystalline glass Segrado had mentioned. He continued perusing the pages. He did not have much time left. Soon the bells would be ringing Lauds and the abbey would be awake.

Book VII: Refraction. Through a series of experiments which involved making the sun's rays pass through glass receptacles full of water, Alhazen had discovered that when they traveled through air, glass, or water, beams of light changed their angle of impact according to precise formulas: this means that when it goes through a body, the speed of light changes and does not remain constant, as had been claimed by Ptolemy.

Edgardo felt he was close to a concept, an explanation that he was not yet able to grasp clearly. He was trying to find his way through thick fog, sensing the existence of a gash that did not seem to open.

He persevered. There were many pages: the theory of spherical lenses, experiments on the behavior of flat, convex and concave mirrors of different shapes, experiments on the magnifying properties of glass spheres and semispheres.

Edgardo stopped. Had he read correctly or were his eyes playing a trick? The words "magnifying" and "glass semispheres" startled him.

He remembered the drawing of the *lapides ad legendum* Tàtaro had shown him. It was a semisphere of rock crystal that, when placed on a page, magnified the written characters beneath. Perhaps he had really found something. He had to study this attentively, copy it, and show it to Segrado.

The sound of bells tolling for Lauds made him jump. He had lost track of time. He quickly put the manuscript back on the shelf and left the scriptorium. He needed more time and would have to come back.

Niccolò ran across Campo San Giacomo di Luprio. He was in a rush. His master was waiting and he was late already. The boat from Amurianum had taken longer than usual because the lagoon was rough and there was an adverse wind. He heard someone call him. The *campo* was deserted at that time. There were only penitents praying under the church porch, beggars, cripples, and lepers. He turned and saw Zoto walking toward him. Niccolò carried on walking briskly but the crystal-maker caught up with him.

"Where are you running, you peasant, wait a moment!"

"Maestro Segrado is waiting for me."

"What's the rush? The oven isn't going to run away. What do you have to do that's so important?"

"Earn my living." Niccolò did not like the crystal-maker.

Zoto tried to keep up with him in spite of his limp. "And you think I don't? We all have to work for a living, that's why we should help each other out. Glass and crystal makers have always had a good working relationship, helping and supporting one another—"

"What do you want from me, Zoto?"

"I don't want anything. Only remind your master he should be grateful to Zoto if he's still working. I rented him a foundry. Otherwise, you'd all be stuck in the mud with them," he indicated the beggars outside the church.

"He pays you what he owes you, doesn't he?"

"Yes, I know, I'm not saying anything—just that if we need to help each other out . . . "

Niccolò stopped and stared at him inquisitively.

"That cleric . . . " Zoto started again, "I heard they've seen you together. He was looking for rock crystal . . . And I've got some that's pure and perfect . . . If you see him again, tell him Zoto is a talented and honest crystal-maker who can make anything, even if I've never actually seen these stones for the eyes in my life." He burst out laughing and coughed. "Zoto can even make the impossible. Just give him a piece of crystal and he'll make anything you like out of it, even a beautiful woman's ass." Once again, he laughed so hard he nearly choked.

They had almost reached the shop near the foundry. Kallis saw them walking together, with Zoto laughing without restraint.

"All right, if I see the cleric, I'll tell him you already have the crystal."

Niccolò was about to walk away but Zoto pulled him toward him as though trying to confide a secret. "If you ever wanted to make a little extra . . . I can't imagine the master pays you all that much . . . If you ever wanted to make something out of green or ruby glass suitable for imitating gemstones, then I'd know just how to cut them perfectly and set them so well they'd look like real precious stones . . . "

"Let go of me, Zoto." Niccolò broke away from him, annoyed.

"You don't think I can? I dare anyone to discover the truth. You just give me the right color glass and you'll see what Zoto's capable of."

But Niccolò was now walking away.

"So?" Zoto shouted after him. "Who do you think you glassmakers are? Craftsmen, my ass!"

Niccolò stopped, ready to come to blows. He could not bear to be insulted, but then decided it was not worth soiling his hands with someone like Zoto and pressed ahead.

Outside the foundry, he found Kallis sifting ground pebbles through silk sieves to obtain powder as fine as flour.

"He doesn't want anyone," she said, with an eloquent hand gesture. Niccolò crouched down by the door and waited.

Old glassmakers in Venetia used to say that in the olden days there was a powder that could cleanse the glass mixture. Segrado wanted to try adding this substance to the molten glass. It was tartar salt, also known as wine dregs because it was obtained from that thick, dark brown scale you find at the bottom of the barrels.

He took from the trunk, where he had hidden it, the little sack he had picked up at the harbor in Matamauco. He did not want anyone to know about his gut feeling, yet he needed the help of an assistant. He came out and motioned to Niccolò. He did not have to explain anything to him. All the boy had to do was follow orders.

He approached the oven, and a wave of heat made his skin glow red-hot. Even though winter was upon them, and with it ice and rain, the heat around the furnace was unbearable, so they worked with the upper part of their bodies naked, bathed in sweat. Niccolò took the crucible out of the fire. Segrado mixed the molten glass with a blowing pipe. It still had that green tint that marred its purity. He took a pinch of tartar from the bag. Niccolò watched him attentively, not understanding.

At that moment, Kallis appeared at the door, carrying the powdered pebbles. Segrado frowned. "What do you want?"

Kallis looked at him, surprised. "The pebbles," she said, indicating the bag.

"By the blood of the canker!" Segrado shouted, suddenly angry. "Out! Go to hell! Get out of here!"

Kallis put down the bag, gave Niccolò, who lowered his head, a puzzled look, and walked out without saying a word.

Segrado panted to cast out all his anger and, once he was calm again, poured the tartar into the glass. He did not know how much he should add, since nobody had passed on a rule.

He watched the glass paste as a change took place: the green grew pale, turning almost ocher, then the color faded to the point where it almost disappeared. Segrado thought for a moment that he had before his eyes a light, pure and limpid paste. He felt a sense of freedom, as though the bolus was his soul and suddenly, thanks to divine intervention, it had been purified of all sin and feelings of guilt, all the terrors that tormented his nights.

He remained there, spellbound, staring at the miraculous substance, and thought for a moment that he had achieved the perfection of crystalline glass. Then, inexplicably, the incandescent mass changed color, as though dragged toward impurity by a devilish force. Segrado saw a stain creeping into the original purity, a purple shadow that quickly took possession of the whole substance, destroying his illusion of achieved transparency.

Once again, he had failed. Still, he had picked up a sign: for a moment, the glass had become pure. He had to work out what had triggered that phase, and why.

The following night, Edgardo did not wait too long. He had a lot of work to do and he needed as much time as possible. After the monks had gone to bed, he listened until the noises in the abbey had died out. Then he went to the library and the scriptorium. Everything seemed calm and quiet. He looked for Book VII among the translated sheets on the shelf. He had decided to copy that one because it contained the description of experiments with glass spheres and the magnifying process. It was too dangerous to work in the scriptorium. The only solution was to take Book VII to his cell, spend all night copying whatever was possible, then take it back before Lauds.

He took a few blank sheets of parchment, a goose quill, and a horn full of ink. He smelled it. They used a slightly different blend in Bobbio: cabbage juice, copper sulphate, gall cooked over fire with arabica and beer. The color was not as red as this one in San Giorgio. Then he looked for pumice for erasing, and a few pins to fix the parchment to the table.

Loaded with all the equipment, he returned to his cell without difficulties. Time was flying, so he had to start copying right away. He did not have a pulpit, but only a small table and a stool. He organized himself as well as he could, but the position was uncomfortable and painful. His hump pressed against the wooden edge of the table and his back was bent in an unnatural pose. He brought the tallow candle as close as possible to the pages to be copied, and dipped the goose quill in ink.

He was both scared and excited, as always when he was about to start copying a manuscript. In that moment, he felt exactly like the sage who had written the original. Copying was as important and emotional as the initial writing. It was as though the concepts, the words, the very structure of the sentence belonged to him and were pouring out of his mind. In other words, he would identify with the work he had before him, and be transfigured within it.

The light was pale and wavering as he tried to memorize the first line. He had not forgotten about his eyes but he thought that perhaps God, in his mercy, would envelop him in His miraculous light. An illusion. The delirium of a madman. The letters, the words, the lines of the sentences were ever more vague and blurred. He had to get even closer to the sheet to understand the meaning, and his body was bent like a bow is, as tautly as possible, just before the arrow is shot. In the end, he began to copy slowly, hesitantly, in fits and starts, like a novice with his first assignment. Where had his former mastery gone? And what about his enjoyment, and his boldness? He had to content himself with memorizing just one word at a time before transcribing it. He did not even follow the sense of what he was reading. He was just copying it, mechanically.

The cell was so cold that he had lost the feeling in his fingers and the goose quill seemed guided by somebody else's hand. Nevertheless, Edgardo the Crooked kept going. He managed to copy a few pages in spite of excruciating pain. There was absolute silence and the world around him seemed to have stopped in order to allow him to bring his enterprise to term.

Then, suddenly, it was there before him. The killjoy, the pedant, the copyist's most feared visitor: Titivillus, the demon who sneaks into the mind of the poor copyist and who, with tricks, jests and impure thoughts, tries at all costs to distract him and trip him up.

Edgardo noticed Titivillus's arrival immediately because on

the same line he omitted two letters, added a syllable, and repeated a word. He had to do some precision work with the pumice to mend the disaster.

When Titivillus chose to disturb a copyist, it was very difficult to get rid of him. He remained for as long as he had not filled his sack with omitted letters to take down to hell. The only way to chase him away was to stop your work. However, Edgardo could not do that, as the night was drawing to a close.

"Leave me alone, go away!" he muttered. "You've come at the wrong time. I have to finish this work before Lauds. My back is aching, I can't feel my fingers anymore, my stomach is in turmoil, I'm a poor, crippled cleric. Take pity on me."

Titivillus laughed, leapt onto the sheet and tugged at the quill. "Donkey! Here's another missed letter for my sack." Then he slipped between his fingers, confusing them. "Donkey! You've just repeated a word." Finally, he roused lascivious thoughts of naked women with their legs spread open, their asses in the air, dancing on the edge of the parchment.

"That's enough! Stop it! Go away!" Edgardo did not know anymore what to say in order to chase Titivillus out of his cell. "I warn you. If you don't let me finish, you'll end up losing a client—I will be through with you forever."

Titivillus paused, suspended, one paw on the tip of the goose quill.

"That's right, you heard me. If you don't let me finish copying these pages I'll never be able to copy anything else again, because my eyes are forsaking me and these pages contain formulas that are my last chance. So, what do you say?"

Titivillus began nibbling thoughtfully at the point of the quill: the situation seemed serious.

He looked into his sack and saw that he had already collected a fair number of letters and words. They might be enough. It's never in a little demon's interest to lose a client. He leapt off the quill, causing it to slip into one last doodle, and spat a tiny ink spot on the parchment. Then, with a fart, he went back to where he had come from, through a secret tunnel between the beams of the floor, which no copyist had ever been able to discover.

Edgardo breathed a sigh of relief and rushed to copy the final pages. It must soon be Lauds. When he heard the bell start to toll, he picked up the manuscript and the equipment, hid the copied pages under his mattress, and rushed out of his cell.

It was still pitch dark. He covered his head with his hood and went along the corridor of the dormitory. Going past his fellow brothers' cells, he heard signs of awakening. A creak, a cough, a chair leg scraping against the floor. He rushed to the staircase. He had to go down to the ground floor, cross the cloisters, go into the library and up to the scriptorium. Fortunately, the church was on the other side of the abbey. Under the portico, he kept as close to the wall as he could. He tried to make as little noise as possible. The celebrant monk was probably already getting ready for the ceremony.

Once in the library, he felt safe. There was never anybody there at that hour. He went up to the scriptorium and put away the manuscript and the equipment. He was smiling, satisfied, when he suddenly stopped. Had he sunk this low? Like a thief proud of his crimes, happy to have gotten away with breaking the rules? If anybody had come into the library at that moment, he would have been lost. Trapped like a rat.

He rushed to the winding staircase and walked down carefully. Not a light, nor a sound. The library was dark and empty. By now he knew the way by heart, and he kept to the middle in order not to trip over the heavy lecterns lined up along the walls. As soon as he was out, he would consider himself safe. In any case, he could find an excuse for being there.

As he approached the door, there was a rustle, an eddy. A chair was moved. Something was pulling at his habit, holding onto him. Perhaps the habit had caught on something. There was breathing and a pungent smell. A hand grasping the hem of his habit, tugging hard. He was trapped. His blood drained away and his face turned to ice. He yanked at his tunic and managed to free himself. He heard a bustle in the dark. Perhaps somebody had lost his balance. He threw the door open, was out in a flash, and started to run like a frightened child who has lost his mind, throwing all caution to the wind.

He reached the end of the cloisters and climbed the stairs. Not a sound behind him. Before tackling the corridor of the dormitory, he stopped to catch his breath. He was in a sorry state, terrified and shaking. He could still feel the grip of the hand trying to hold onto him. A knobbly, predatory hand, like that of a demon. When sin enters your soul, raging demons are unleashed against you. And his soul was now tainted with too many stains.

He forced himself to keep a calm and regular step, and went toward his cell. He had almost arrived when, out of nowhere, a hand landed heavily on his shoulder. His heartbeat pounded in his head, and his vision began to fail. He turned abruptly.

"I see you're ready. Shall we go down together?" By the light of the lantern, he recognized Ademaro, who was looking at him sleepily. Edgardo took a step back. He did not want his friend to notice his pallor.

"Very well," he whispered.

"I slept badly," Ademaro said, walking toward the exit. "I was tormented by a terrible nightmare all night. A thief had entered the library, to steal the most precious manuscript. It's absurd . . . "

Edgardo hid his face under his hood. Ademaro had dreamed correctly.

"Karamago! Karamago!"
The powerful cry rose and somehow made its way through

the bustle by the dock. The merchant turned so abruptly that his belly dragged him and he almost lost his balance and fell into the water. The *scaula* rocked dangerously but the oarsman managed to hold onto the helm. Who was shouting his name so rudely and unrestrainedly? Karamago looked around. Outside the basilica, carried on the back of a tall, strong servant who did not seem bothered by the backwash of putrid water that came up to his waist, he saw Maestro Tàtaro, waving his arms about like a bird of prey.

"Here, here," he kept squawking.

Karamago gave a polite smile and ordered the oarsman to get close to San Marco. It was the height of chaos. During the night, the water level had risen enormously and very suddenly. Pushed by a *bora* wind, it had totally submerged the Brolo, the ground floor of the Doge's palace, and the Orseolo Hospice, and had even penetrated the narthex, threatening to flood the entire basilica and endangering the patron saint's relics in the crypt.

For centuries, Venetia had been used to high water incursions that would break through the barriers, invade and destroy the embankments, seep in through the stones and the timber, gnawing and crumbling, pleased to watch as the city that had dared stand up to the power of the marsh died.

Venetians had always fought against the muddy sea and the floods caused by the impetuous rivers Sile, Piave and Medoacus, which discharged rubbish and detritus into the lagoon—and won. In recent years, however, the power of the water had become ungovernable. The level had constantly risen, grabbing tidal shallows, shoals, and entire islands. Many monks from monasteries scattered on the islands had had to abandon their residences and move to safer places closer to the city. And now the tide was becoming more and more violent and unpredictable, making people's lives even more difficult and uncertain.

Karamago's *scaula* made its way among the other boats and

managed to reach Porta di Sant'Alipio. Tàtaro slid off his servant's back and dropped into the boat.

"We're about to lose the sacks with gold mosaics! The water has flooded the atrium and the workmen are stuck on top of the scaffolding." Tàtaro was highly agitated. "You must take me to Amurianum. I have no boat and I have to get other workmen."

"Actually, Maestro, I was about to pick up a shipment of fabric that's just arrived, so I'm expected."

"Never mind, you can do that later. My mosaics are more important than your fabrics. These are the mosaics of San Marco, the mosaics of Venetia. In any case, you'll never be able to load anything in this chaos. Trust me."

Karamago agreed willy-nilly and motioned to the boatman.

It was true that the dock was completely blocked: *scaulas*, gondolas, and freight boats dragged by the current were drifting toward the Brolo. There was abundant screaming, swearing, and insulting by everyone and against everyone. A long procession of wheelbarrows was carrying the sick and dying from the hospice to the Doge's castle in search of shelter on the first floor. All kind of filth was floating on the water: leftover food, dead cats, pieces of furniture, clothes, wooden utensils, and naturally, since the tide had penetrated the inner streets, there was a substantial amount of excrement in all shapes and sizes.

"If nothing's done about this as soon as possible, this city's going to sink," Tàtaro muttered.

"It's always been like this and always will be," Karamago said philosophically. "You just need to adapt . . . I've taken all my goods to the first floor, so the high water doesn't scare me."

"And what are you going to do when the water reaches your first floor?" Tàtaro asked, stung.

Karamago laughed. "I'll swim!"

"Don't be foolish. Something has to be done. The embankments need to be raised and the river mouths diverted. Our illustrious Doge won't listen to wise advice. The Brolo in front of San Marco should be lengthened so that it buries Rio Batario and the dock should also be covered because it's too close to the church. That way, we would have a barrier against the water in front of the basilica. It's very simple, but our beloved Doge says there isn't enough money in the city coffers. No wonder, since they spend it all on those useless crusades to please the Pope. Why don't we sort out our city before sending money and ships to Rome to fight the infidels?"

Karamago pursed his lips. This idea of widening the Brolo and eliminating the dock sounded odd to him. Where would they moor the ships and how would they unload the goods? Still, he said nothing, not wishing to antagonize a man as powerful as Maestro Tàtaro.

The *scaula* glided lightly toward Amurianum. The wind had dropped and the surface of the lagoon looked like a slab of burnished iron. From the bow, Tàtaro was looking at the mountains on the horizon.

"The water is glowing like a topaz," Karamago said, fancying himself a poet.

"Don't talk nonsense," Tàtaro scolded him. "What do you know about gemstones and colors? I'm the glassmaker, so let me be the judge."

"Certainly, Maestro . . . " Karamago coughed and spat into the water. A mullet peeped out of the water and quickly swallowed a shred of dog intestine floating nearby.

"I've heard Maestro Segrado is messing about with new recipes. Do you know anything about this?" Tàtaro asked.

"No, Maestro. Segrado does not do me the honor of confiding in me. I'm sure you're better informed."

"You don't suppose that cleric found the Arabic manuscript and then took it to Segrado?"

"The monk hasn't been back to my shop," Karamago answered on cue.

"In that case, find a way of meeting him. I want to know . . . "

They were approaching Amurianum. Tàtaro stood up, ready to disembark. "Also, if you managed to lay your hands on that manuscript, you'd be amply rewarded."

Karamago believed that a merchant should always try to satisfy his clients' every whim, no matter how.

"Don't worry, Maestro, I'll see what I can do."

Tàtaro leapt onto the steps. The water kept rising.

XVII.
THE EYE MURDERER

It was like lying on a bed of fire. An inexplicable heat seemed to come from the depths of the earth, wrap around him, and burn him up. Drenched in sweat, Edgardo rose and slipped out from under the mattress the manuscript he had copied the night before.

"Is this stopping me from sleeping?" he wondered. "Is this generating the fire that's burning inside me? Is it guilt that's tearing my soul apart?"

Yes, he had acted selfishly and allowed himself to be carried away by an evil impulse. He had listened to Kallis, and a woman's advice had pushed him on the road to sin. Still, perhaps those pages were concealing the remedy for his eyes.

What was God's will? A blind copyist or a scribe who devoted his life to transcribing sacred texts? He could not find a solution for his torment. Only Segrado could help him find a way out. If, in the manuscript, he was able to glimpse the possibility of creating the stone for the eyes, then it would mean that God was showing him the right path.

He rolled up the pages of *De Aspectibus* in coarse parchment and slipped them under his scapular. Prime had not rung yet. Taking advantage of the faint light of the winter twilight, Edgardo left the abbey. He woke the boatman asleep in his gondola and asked to be taken to Rivoalto. The high waters had decreased, leaving behind breakage and ruin. The embankments of many canals had collapsed and the waters had invaded squares and streets, creating large pools and stretches of mud.

The Rivoalto shops were overflowing with slime and mud, and a large number of goods had been ruined. Along the paths lay the abandoned leftovers of the tide: tree trunks, leaves, straw, canes, strange red algae. The residents were already working on clearing the passages and cleaning the warehouses and boat sheds. Progress had been made on the jetty. The walkway was already nearly halfway across the Rivus Altus.

With some difficulty, Edgardo managed to reach Campo San Giacomo. The tide had erased the paths and many stretches of grass had been turned into impassable bogs. With every step, he sank into sticky and treacherous slime that seemed to want to swallow him up. The icy air had the ferrous smell of flooding mountain streams. The winter had come down from the north in full strength and invaded valleys and plains all the way to the sea. The *campo* was deserted. The fishermen's huts were shut, the nets had been gathered, there were no children playing at the foot of the belfry, and even the beggars had taken refuge under the church portico. A heavy silence weighed over everything. Even the saltworks had lost their shine. The mud had got mixed with the crystals, creating a wide, gray sea, a creaking, frozen expanse that stank of rancid wine. Segardo's foundry was boarded up and even Zoto's workshop next door gave no sign of life. Maybe it was too early and the high water had made the trip from Metamauco difficult. He tried calling out.

"Maestro Segrado? Maestro?"

His voice slid over the surface of diseased salt and scattered among the tidal shallows. Edgardo decided to wait. Maybe the mill watchman would offer him hospitality while he waited.

He went to the thatched cottage where the mill watchman lived, which marked the beginning of the saltworks with pools demarcated by dams.

A dark spot, right in the middle of the brine, caught his attention. It looked like a dirty sail torn by the wind and dragged by the tide. The crystals moaned and cracked under his feet with every step. As he drew closer, his eyes managed to compose a clearer image. The abandoned rag had two legs, a head, and an arm folded under the chest. It was the back of a man. Edgardo rushed forward and bent over him. The face was immersed in sandy slush. He tried to turn the body over, but the salt mixed with the mud had formed a crystal sarcophagus.

Perhaps he was still alive, and had just fainted. He took him by the arm and started pulling. He was not thinking or reasoning but using his strength like a peasant trying to pull out a root. Finally, the mass came out of the salt. He kneeled and tried to turn him over. The head turned first as though independent of the rest of the body. Edgardo pulled away, raised his hands, and held his breath. His thoughts became entangled, at odds with his soul. Merciful God. It was Niccolò. Niccolò. Segrado's *garzone*. There was no doubt about it. It was him. Then came the horror that almost made him swoon. The eyes. The eyes were now two black, bleeding holes. Two dark wells that vibrated with an infernal light. Instead of the eyeballs, there were two white glass spheres with, in the middle, fiery, ruby-red irises. His mind was suddenly swallowed by the void. He wanted to scream and call for help but he felt a lump of glass in his throat that prevented him from breathing. He got unsteadily to his feet. Niccolò, poor Niccolò . . . He wanted to kneel, say a prayer, give a blessing, but he could not. Something inside his head snapped and he lost all restraint. He took a step backwards and began to run haphazardly. He slipped, fell, and got up again. There was a voice calling in the distance but he did not stop. All he wanted to do was run away, as far away as possible from that horror, from that mutilated body, as though a demon were after him, a demon who wanted to inflict the same torment on him.

Just before Terce, when Segrado and Kallis arrived at the foundry, they saw a few salt workers gathered in the middle of the basin and the mill watchman talking to the district constable. A boy stepped away from the group and ran toward Segrado.

"Maestro, Maestro! It's the devil! The devil. Come and see."

Segrado followed him. The workmen stood aside, revealing Niccolò's body lying in a sea of salt.

"Look at his eyes . . . Just like Balbo. They killed him exactly the same way."

He looked like an ancient Greek mask. The mouth was wide open, and the hollows of the eyes were glowing.

Segrado staggered. As though pierced with a lance, the bald bear gave a hopeless roar, then dropped to his knees. For the first time, people saw tears running down his face. He leaned over, kissed the glass eyes, and slid the palm of his hand over the pale face, closing the eyelids and the lips.

"May God have pity on him and may whoever has soiled himself with this crime burn in eternal hell." He crossed himself. Behind him, Kallis, her face like an olivewood carving, had followed his every movement without betraying the slightest emotion, cold and detached as though suspicious of his expression of pain.

"Are you Angelo Segrado, master glassmaker?" the constable asked.

"Yes."

"The mill watchman says this young man was your *garzone*."

"That's true."

"When was the last time you saw him?"

"Last night. I left him at the foundry when I went home."

"Did you leave him alone?"

"Yes."

"Do you have any idea of who could have wanted to kill the boy? Did he have any enemies, or rivals?"

"There's someone intent on killing off glassmakers," Segrado replied. "Perhaps there are too many of us in Venetia."

"And what's the meaning of the glass eyes? What do you think, since you're in the trade?"

Everybody turned to look at Segrado, hoping for a logical explanation for an act that had something diabolical about it.

Segrado shook his head. "I don't know. It's an atrocious torture . . . Maybe the murderer wants to convey a message."

"What kind of message?"

Segrado said nothing.

"The mill watchman says he saw a monk lurking around here at dawn," the constable said.

"A monk?"

"A cripple with fiery red hair."

Kallis stiffened and gave Segrado an imploring look. He said nothing.

"We're going to look for this monk," the constable concluded. "We'll see what he has to say. And now, pull out this boy and take him back to his family. I insist, don't tell anyone about the glass eyes. It's the second time . . . The people get agitated and want us to find someone to hang immediately, and if we can't find him, they do it all themselves and often pick the first stranger who happens to walk by."

The workmen lifted Niccolò's body and made their way to the mill. Segrado approached Kallis, who looked tense and upset.

"We must track down that cleric immediately. Otherwise, we'll find him hanging upside down in the courtyard of the Doge's palace before sunset."

Without wasting precious time, Segrado and Kallis began searching for the cleric. They went toward Rivoalto in their *scaula*, checking the internal streams. Segrado rowed with hard, decisive strokes. The boat moved fast, gliding along the water. In the market, shopkeepers were busy repairing the damage done by the high water and there were still few residents about. Kallis looked between the houses, under the porches and in the under-porticos, but with no luck.

"Maybe the scribe got scared and went to seek refuge in San Giorgio."

"Is he safe there?" Kallis asked.

"I wouldn't bet on it. He's just a cleric. If there's any trouble, the abbot won't want any conflicts with the Doge's authorities."

They traveled a few fathoms up the Rivus Altus, in the hope of seeing him crossing on a barge, but could not find him. So Segrado decided to venture through the minor streams of the area known as Dorsoduro, so called because of its dense, hard soil rising higher than its surroundings, like someone's *dorso*, or back. Here there were few inhabited islands, so the probability of noticing a monk's habit fluttering in the wind was very high.

Their persistence paid off. Kallis saw him emerge from behind a bed of reeds, following a path that ended in a canal, his head held low. He was brooding, agitated, talking to himself.

"Why did I run away? I should've stopped, looked for

help . . . You run away only if you're guilty but I'm not guilty of anything, so why . . . ?" He kept asking himself the same question over and over again and could not find the courage to admit the one and only answer.

"Edgardo!" Kallis shouted.

His name, called in a woman's voice. It was a strange, unreal feeling. He could not even remember his mother's voice ever calling him by name. Kept away from his parents' room, raised by servants, he had only seen her a few times. Even a mother does not enjoy holding a crippled baby in her arms.

"Edgardo!" Kallis called again. "We're here!"

He turned and saw her not far away. He felt a sense of liberation and lightness and jumped into the *scaula* without a single word or question, finally feeling safe, like the time he had fled from the arsenal. He thought Kallis appearing was like a savior angel sent by God.

Segrado put pressure on the rowlock and, with four strokes of the oar, navigated the boat out of the narrow stream toward the Vigano canal.

For a while they did not speak. Edgardo kept stealing glances at Kallis, as though he felt he needed to be forgiven for a sin. Then Segrado's deep voice resounded behind him.

"It was you at the mill at dawn this morning, wasn't it?"

Edgardo hesitated for a moment, but all he wanted was to free himself of that load. "I came to look for you," he confessed.

"And you found poor Niccolò's body!"

Edgardo nodded.

"You stupid scribe! Why did you run away? They saw you and now they're looking for you. You acted like a murderer, you of all people, why?"

Edgardo did not have the courage to confess the truth right in front of Kallis, and to utter the word *fear*. He lowered his head guiltily.

"You risk being hanged. It's the second glassmaker who's been murdered in this terrible manner, and here they tend not to stand on ceremony with murderers."

Kallis looked at him. It did not seem like contempt, but rather something akin to compassion.

"He didn't deserve to die that way . . . He was a good *garzone*, loyal and capable and like a son to me." Segrado hit the oar flat on the water with an angry gesture. "By the way, it wasn't you, was it, who did that chisel job?"

"Of course not!" Edgardo flared up. "How could you possibly think—"

"Why did you come looking for me at the foundry?"

Edgardo slipped his hand into his cowl and pulled out the rolled-up parchment. "I managed to copy one chapter from the Arabic scholar's book, *De Aspectibus*, like you asked." He searched out Kallis's eyes, but the girl had lowered her head again. "I was bringing it to show you."

Not a word. Just a more powerful and longer stroke of the oar that propelled the *scaula* faster, almost making it fly.

It was only then that Edgardo realized they had distanced themselves considerably from the shore.

"Where are we going?" he asked.

The girl looked up at him reassuringly. "To Metamauco. They won't look for you there."

The journey seemed to him quicker than it had the first time. The island appeared in the middle of the lagoon like a miniature drawing, with its white sand, its forests of willows and oaks, the sails spread out in the wind, coming down from Medoacus Maior and seeking shelter in the harbor before continuing their long journey to the sea through the Orfano canal.

The roof of Segrado's house and the surrounding fields, covered in brine, were oozing shiny drops that beaded the air with an unreal light.

Kallis immediately lit the fire and brought in spelt bread and cider.

"You've gotten yourself into a real mess," Segrado said. "If they get to question Zoto, who has seen you with Niccolò many times, they'll trace this back to Karamago and then they'll come looking for you at the abbey." He broke the bread and gave a piece to Edgardo. "You must be very careful."

"Who killed Niccolò in such a barbaric way?" Edgardo asked.

Segrado threw his knife on the table. Kallis winced and a log rolled out of the fireplace.

"I don't know but they'll find him. In Venetia, sooner or later, filth rises to the surface. They killed him to get at me. They're taking everything away from me. First, they burn down my oven, and now Niccolò. These are warnings. They want me to stop. I could be next."

"But who could possibly want you dead, Maestro?" the cleric asked naively.

Segrado was chewing with his eyes half open, mulling over his obsession.

"Tàtaro!" Kallis burst out, her voice like an out-of-tune song.

"You be quiet. Who asked you to open your mouth? What do you know about it?"

"Does Maestro Tàtaro want to eliminate you?" Edgardo asked. "Why?"

With a theatrical gesture, Segrado pushed away the stool, got up, and went to warm his hands by the fire.

"Those who seek out the new are frowned upon. The powerful want everything to carry on according to the old rules. If there's a novelty, if you make a discovery that upsets their way of working, they risk being left out and losing power and money. They know nothing of the force of nature, so want others to share their ignorance. They don't want people to look too deeply into things. They want us to believe what peasants believe. But we say it's necessary to seek the reason behind everything. And so when they find out that someone's trying to study these things, they cry heretic and wage war on him."

"So that's why they want to stop you from carrying on," was Edgardo's conclusion.

"Maybe somebody said something . . . They know I'm close to making a discovery and they want to stop me before I get there. If new doors are opened, then the entire glassmaking industry could be turned upside down. . . "

Edgardo admired him: his strength, his tenacity, his courage, and his knowledge. He wished he were like him, a solitary knight trying to reach his goal while fighting against the world. He sought Kallis's eyes and thought he saw in them an expression of great pride.

"Did you say you managed to copy the Arabic manuscript?" Segrado asked.

"Just a few pages. The ones that seemed the most interesting. I know next to nothing about optics." Then he added, apologetically, "I had just one night and I risked being discovered."

He took the rolled-up parchment, opened it, and laid the sheets on the table, securing them with logs.

Kallis stepped away from the fire and stood close to him, so close that Edgardo could feel her breath and smell her amber scent.

"Alhazen's manuscript is divided into seven books. It's very thick and it would take months to copy it all. I've read parts of it. It's difficult to understand and only a scholar could decipher it. There are complex calculations and drawings—"

"Have you found glass recipes or anything like that?" Segrado interrupted.

"No, I don't think so. However, there are some interesting new notions, like this one, look." Edgardo put his finger on the manuscript and let it slide down the words, almost caressing them.

Kallis was listening, entranced, panting slightly, as though she was in the presence of an inestimable treasure.

"This Arabic scholar claims that rays of light don't come out of the eye to penetrate objects in order to understand images, as Galen says, but, on the contrary, it's bodies themselves that produce the rays that reach the eye and transmit the images. Also, he adds that the rays that reach the eyes vary in strength and in angle when they meet and travel through other substances."

Segrado stopped him. "It sounds like a muddle. Do you mean that if I place a substance between my eyes and what I want to see, the image can change?"

"That's how I understand it," said Edgardo.

Segrado scratched his bald head as though trying to rekindle the memory of the thick hair he once had. Kallis was leaning over the pages and brushing the words with the tip of her finger, slowly, with concentration, as she had seen Edgardo do.

"Do you read with your fingers?" she suddenly asked.

Edgardo smiled. "No, unfortunately I don't. It would be useful, though, now that my eyes are letting me down."

"Maybe one could feel the shape of the letters, and absorb them that way," Kallis added as she continued to stroke the page, word after word, entranced.

"And what's this?" Segrado asked, pointing to a drawing Edgardo had reproduced imprecisely.

"It should be a glass sphere. Alhazen conducted some experiments where he filled glass spheres with water and made beams of light go through them. He observed that when they went through the liquid, these beams changed direction."

"So does water alter the light?" Segrado asked, intrigued.

"So it would seem."

"And what kind of glass were these spheres made of?"

"The treatise doesn't say. But it also talks about spheres through which you can see distorted and magnified reality."

"So if one can see through it, it means it's either very pure rock crystal, or else . . . " Segrado paused, excited and out of breath. "Or else it's glass similar to crystal."

"I think you're right," Edgardo said.

Segrado bent over the manuscript, attempting to make sense of those symbols he could not decipher, as though trying to feed his hunger with food he could not taste. Then, irked by being unable to make any sense of those words, he uttered a curse and left. He needed to walk.

He was very close, though he did not yet know exactly to what. Close to achieving his aim. Glass, crystal, stones for the eyes, spheres—everything was an unstoppable whirl.

Inside the hut, Kallis was still admiring the manuscripts: looking at the sheets, and touching them as though wanting to absorb them.

"I can't imagine that you are actually the one who created this work," she said softly.

"I only copied it," Edgardo replied shyly.

"That's what I find most extraordinary. That you should devote your life to the words of others. Not to studying, like the scholars, but to the art of drawing words. You see, since I can't read, for me this page is like a magnificent ornament, a jewel, a damask cloth, a painting . . . and it has much more value than the original work."

Nobody had ever praised his work quite so highly. Kallis had seen something even he had not been able to grasp.

"So you really want me to teach you?"

Kallis's eyes became two slits so narrow, they almost disappeared behind a smile wide enough it practically swallowed her face. "Would you really do it?"

"Of course, if you like."

"Will your abbot allow one of his monks to teach writing to a foreign woman?"

"I am not really a monk. I've never taken the vows."

Kallis looked at him with surprise. "If you're not a monk, why do you wear a habit? You've lied to me."

It was not easy to explain. "I'm a cleric. Some noble families send their sons, while they're still boys, to live in monasteries so they can learn to read and write. These boys share the lives of the monks in every way, but many of them don't take vows, so they can't administer sacraments, even though they live just as their fellow brothers do."

Kallis did not look very convinced.

"Now you tell me—will Segrado allow you to devote some of your time to taking up this art?"

She thought about this. "Now that Niccolò isn't here anymore, my work load will be even heavier. The Maestro has no one but me . . . However, there are quiet days when the molten glass needs to rest, or when the Maestro goes to buy pebbles in Ticino or timber on the mainland." Her face grew stern and her expression sharp. "Besides, the Maestro doesn't have to know everything I do."

At that moment, Segrado returned. Edgardo suddenly felt lost, as though caught red-handed. Segrado's face had lit up, and his movements were decisive and full of energy.

"Let's to go back to the foundry. I want to work," he told Kallis. "Take back your manuscripts. If they find them here, they'll accuse me of stealing them and they'll tear off my hands."

"I was really thinking that you should keep them. I don't know . . . "

Kallis looked at Segrado with eyes full of hope, like a child about to be deprived of her toy.

"The canker on me! Take them away. I don't want anything to do with them . . . "

Edgardo picked up the sheets and rolled them up delicately.

"It's better if you're not seen gallivanting all over the city," Segrado added. "I'll leave you at the abbey. At least there you should be safe for a while. In any case, listen to me, confide in the abbot. Tell him the trouble you've gotten yourself into, so that he can protect you if necessary."

Edgardo said nothing. He knew perfectly well that Abbot Carimanno would not spare a single word in his defense. The only person he could count on was his friend Ademaro.

He made up his mind to tell him everything. He simply had to free himself of that burden. He found Ademaro in the novices' cloister, meditating. When he saw Edgardo, Ademaro seemed irked.

"What happened to you? You disappeared. You didn't even attend the services."

"Forgive me. Something serious happened."

Ademaro looked annoyed. "A few nights ago you didn't sleep in your cell—tell me the truth." Edgardo bowed his head. "Our Order is built on precise rules that help us lead a life that's as close as possible to Our Lord's commandments. You, Edgardo, are no different than the rest."

"I got caught up in turmoil . . . and the darkness took me far away."

"I don't want to know where you spent the night or with whom. That's between you and your conscience, but your behavior is unacceptable to the Order."

Even though he knew his friend was right, Edgardo felt a sense of irritation, a slight desire to rebel, to react. After a struggle, he regained his self-control and told him all that had happened the day before—finding Niccolò's body, running away, meeting Segrado. However, he said nothing about the copy of Alhazen's manuscript. He had the impression that there was something rather unclear concerning that book and that subject, something in which his friend was also involved. In any case, Ademaro would never accept the idea of a monk secretly copying a book and then taking it outside.

Ademaro looked very worried. To be implicated in a murder, and such a horrific one at that, was an event of unheard-of gravity that could cast shame on the entire monastery.

"You allowed yourself to become too involved," he said, reproachfully. "I told you to be cautious."

"I found myself there by pure chance. It's not my fault."

"Your search for the eye stone has led you to have dealings with treacherous and disreputable people. You should have stayed away from them."

"It was you yourself who brought me to Venetia," Edgardo replied, astonished. "It was you who prompted me to start searching."

"An enlightened person knows when it's time to stop. You went too far. You crossed the boundary."

Ademaro was embittered, as though he had discovered that his friend had somehow betrayed his trust. Did he harbor suspicions about him with regard to the manuscript?

"If anyone saw you, they'll come looking for you here."

"There are many monasteries in Venetia."

"Yes, but there aren't many monks who look like you."

Edgardo was overwhelmed by a deep sadness. "You mean there are no crippled monks like me in the whole of Venetia?"

Ademaro said nothing, not wishing to offend him.

"Of course, you're right," Edgardo continued. "There aren't many like me, crippled, with a hump on the front, hair red as a ripe orange, and a face full of freckles."

"Listen, my friend," now Ademaro had a softer tone laced with affection, "perhaps it would be better if you went back to Bobbio. You're not safe here."

This took Edgardo by surprise. It was a possibility he had never considered. To go back to his previous life, to shut himself up in a monastery again. To do what? Now he could not even copy his beloved books anymore. He had come to Venetia to find a remedy for his eyes. Maybe it was just an illusion, a dream, but he had tasted freedom, and a rich, eventful life, so now the prospect of sinking into the shadows, into the darkness of a cell, made it difficult for him to breathe. Was that all? If he probed deeper into his soul, would he find an even stronger reason not to leave Venetia?

"I'll think about it," he said in order not to disappoint his friend.

Ademaro hugged him. "I trust in your wisdom," he said.

"Wise? Me?" Edgardo thought. Perhaps timid, fearful and scared by the world. But he decided to keep these thoughts to himself.

As soon as he approached, he realized something had happened. There were strange noises coming from the foundry: a disorderly rustling and small, repeated taps. The door chain was still in its place, attached with the padlock. Kallis leaned against the door and also heard the same confused scuffling sounds.

"There's someone inside," Segrado whispered.

He picked up a strong, gnarled branch of oak from the ground, carefully unfastened the chain, and threw the door open with a decisive kick. At the noise, all hell broke loose. In a cloud of dust, a group of panic-stricken seagulls sought to escape, beating their wings violently, colliding with the walls and ceiling, and dropping stunned to the ground.

Segrado and Kallis stood aside and finally the birds found a way out, leaving behind a whole host of feathers.

"Bloody canker on them!" Segrado swore. "How did these smelly creatures get in?"

Kallis pointed at the roof. The hole in the ceiling that acted as a smoke vent was now a large gash. The canes had been torn apart and the straw was hanging down on the inside. It could not have been the seagulls that had caused the wreckage, nor the wind. This was a man's handiwork.

Only then did they notice that the foundry was a total mess. There were benches knocked over, shelves on the floor, the fire was out, and the most recent pieces of blown glass were completely destroyed: bottles, glasses, beakers, beads, and rosaries lay in fragments on the floor, forming a luminous carpet that seemed to move in the light, to undulate like a drifting slab of ice. The trunk where they kept their tools had been turned upside down. Nothing had been left intact.

After a moment of shock, Segrado began to scream and rail against heaven and men. It was an inhuman scream, a kind of deep roar that came from his belly and exploded like thunder, making all the scattered fragments vibrate.

"This damned life! I was conceived while Satan was combing his tail! Bloody canker!"

Kallis crouched in a corner, afraid that the roar would turn, as had happened before, into an explosion of uncontrollable, devastating violence.

"Are you trying to kill me a little at a time? Why don't you just cut my throat now, once and for all? Come on, strike me, here!" He hit himself on his chest. "Right here! The canker on you all!" He walked out still screaming like a madman.

Kallis looked at the hole in the ceiling and then at the mess: they had destroyed everything but stolen nothing. If they had wanted to stop him from working, they would have taken away his tools and demolished the furnace. There was something strange about this incursion. She went out to join Segrado.

"They came looking for something," she said in a soft, fearful voice.

Segrado shot her an irritated glance. "Don't talk nonsense."

"If they'd wanted to stop you, they would've destroyed the furnace . . . and the tools are still there. But they turned the trunk upside down . . . "

Segrado was chewing saliva in his toothless mouth. It was a sign that he had to think things over. "All right then, what do you think they were looking for?"

"I don't know," Kallis replied, drawing closer. "Maybe someone found out about your experiments and wanted to find proof of the existence of crystalline glass."

"Quiet!" he warned her, pressing the palm of his hand over her mouth. "You must never ever utter that word, you stupid fool! Pure glass does not exist, and nobody will ever find it, is that clear?"

Kallis bowed her head.

What had happened to the righteous path he had followed, head high, proud of his destiny? For many years, Edgardo had lived in the certainty that his fate had been sealed and that God had chosen a path for him. And now, everything was crumbling and all his certainties and convictions seemed to be crashing against a wall of doubts and unexpected events. Ademaro was right, it would be more prudent to return to Bobbio and give up searching for the eye stone.

To go away and leave Venetia. Yes, this was the only possible choice. If he still had a fraction of reason left, he would listen to his friend.

Except that the very idea filled him with a deep sense of yearning he could not explain. Perhaps it was the life of freedom he was experiencing, or perhaps it was the place: this dimension suspended between the sea and the sky, these oily, ever-changing colors that blended into one another, stirred by the wind, so as to create a hue that he had never seen anywhere else. And then there was this brazen, elusive light whose reverberations would dissolve into a sudden chiaroscuro, into night shadows, doubled and amplified by the reflection of the water, that self-propelled expanse of liquid that surrounded everything. Never before had he felt such intense emotions, such ups and downs of the heart, such movements of joy and deep turmoil, as he had in the land of the Venetians, so much so that you could say that this all-encompassing light was a sign of God's eyes in the world.

However, his decision had been made.

An image flashed clearly before his eyes, a ghost he could

not banish: Kallis. He could not just leave like this, he had promised to teach her to write . . . He had to see her one last time, to explain, to say goodbye. He thought it would be kind to leave her a souvenir, a symbol of the art she so wanted to learn. He prepared a rough sheet of parchment and a goose quill to take with him. Then he looked for a hiding place for the manuscript. It was not safe under the mattress. He noticed a loose plank of wood under the bed, lifted it slightly, and slid the sheets into the gap. It was more prudent to leave the abbey before morning prayers, while it was still dark.

There was not a single star or even a sliver of moon in the sky, which formed one thick black expanse with the lagoon. There was no line on the horizon to mark where the earth ended and the celestial vault began. Venetia was sunk in absolute, hopeless darkness. He was guided only by sounds and noises amplified by the silence of the night, like signals originating from the world beyond the earth. Edgardo listened to the undertow of the oar as it cut through the water: it was like the rattle of a dying man spitting out the last chunk of his life. Every stroke was an omen of death. He was suddenly seized by inexplicable anxiety. That total darkness seemed to presage all that awaited him if his eyes were to fail completely.

A crack, like a broken branch, echoed from afar, followed by a squeaking noise on the water. The boatman kept rowing. Above them, a soft, gentle sound of flapping wings. He thought it was an angel come to get him, but the healing presence dissolved immediately, chased away by a long scream, the voice of a little girl, which then turned into desperate weeping, not far from the boat. Edgardo thought that perhaps they had reached Rivoalto. The boat advanced into the void and the weeping floated away like the memory of childhood pain.

In his own family home, weeping had not been allowed. His father would reward tears with the whip, so Edgardo and his brother had learned to swallow them before they could reach their eyes. Complaints, pain and fears were punished with dreadful physical torments. And so the body had become like air and the heart like a stone.

As they penetrated deeper into the Rivus Altus, the sounds became more familiar: a dog barking, a drunk vomiting, footsteps sucked up by mud, screaming, calling, the sound of a name. The boatman left him on the usual bank. On the one hand, he was comforted by the pitch black because it meant nobody would see him, but on the other hand, he was afraid of getting lost amid paths and streets, and of falling into a stream.

Edgardo groped his way uncertainly, unable to see where he was stepping. Soft, unstable ground, and then the creaking and echoing on the wooden planks of the bridges, and a gust of nauseating miasma, rotting meat chased away by the acid smell of tar. He knew he had reached the *campo* because he smelt the sharp stench of heaps of abandoned grapes still fermenting despite the cold.

As he walked past the church of San Giacomo he thought he heard a rustle behind him, a hem brushing against the grass. Edgardo stopped, alert. The noise seemed to be moving around him.

The air carried a familiar scent of wilderness but he could not remember where or when he had smelled it before. Perhaps it was an animal. He took another step and thought the sound turned into a bustle, into small, short steps that were coming closer.

"Hey! Is someone there?" he shouted.

His voice echoed in the distance. There was no reply. Edgardo was suddenly assailed by a sense of powerlessness and disorientation. All at once, he felt lost, like a child abandoned deep in the forest. He quickened his pace and the bustle turned into a series of sharp taps, like someone running. He did not know where to look or which direction to take. Somebody was following him, perhaps about to attack him.

He took a narrow *calle* between huts of rotting timber and felt as though he were surrounded by the footsteps without ever being reached by them, like those dreams where you are falling forever into the void.

Breathing the terror of that endless fall, he finally reached the saltworks, and felt the crystals crunching under his feet. He had to find a hiding place, a shelter where he could wait for the dawn. He remembered that next to the mill, behind Segrado's foundry, there was a hut where they stored salt, hay, and wood. He groped around in the dark until he found it, then crouched amid the heaps of salt.

He was panting with terror and tried to control his breathing. The crunching footsteps continued in different directions for a while. He heard them approach, then walk away, until they finally vanished in the distance. Whatever, whoever, it was, had gone. There was a stench of trough in the air and he wondered if he had been pursued by a sow, but no, it had been a man, of that he was certain. He could not have been so frightened by a pig. He felt ashamed, closed his eyes, and remained crouching in the hut, waiting for it to get light.

He was awakened by the squeaking sound of the mill sails turning in a strong wind. The white glare of the salt hurt his already painful eyes. He had fallen asleep without noticing. The sun was high. He crawled out of his shelter and looked around. The salt workers were gathered in a basin, raking up the crystals left by the evaporation. Other workmen were finishing the framework of a dam with strips of reed and clay. Nobody had noticed him. He walked determinedly to Segrado's foundry and entered without knocking.

He was somewhat startled to see Kallis in front of the furnace, wearing an apron, about to take some molten glass from the crucible with a blowing pipe. Her movements were confident and harmonious as though she had always blown glass.

Edgardo had seen her perform humble tasks and never imagined she could be familiar with the art of masters. In spite of his presence, Kallis did not interrupt her work but grabbed the pipe and started blowing the small ball of incandescent glass, which immediately turned into a hollow body. Every so often, she turned the soft mass on the marble slab to stop it from losing its shape. When she noticed that, in between one breath and another, the mass was hardening, she would stick it back into the furnace to soften it. In just a few moments, she had forged a pale yellow glass. Using a jack, she detached the crafted object from the cane with a sharp gesture and placed it on a plank to cool. Then she looked at Edgardo, satisfied.

"You're as good as Maestro Segrado," he said.

Kallis shook her head, but kept her proud smile. "The maestro isn't here," she said. "He's gone to pick up materials on the mainland." She indicated the glass debris piled up in a corner. "They broke in and smashed everything. They were looking for something."

Edgardo looked around, embarrassed, as though feeling responsible.

"You mustn't be seen here. It's not safe after what happened to Niccolò. Zoto could see you and report you to the constable."

"I've come to take my leave . . . to say goodbye. I've decided to go back to my monastery in Bobbio. I'm sorry the maestro isn't here."

The muscles of Kallis's face tensed with shock. She put down the tools and approached. "You promised you'd teach me to write." Her voice was hard and resolute, like someone who has been betrayed.

"You're right." Edgardo pulled out the parchment and goose quill from under his habit. "I want to leave you these as a gift . . . so that they might bring you luck. You'll find some-one else to teach you."

Her body, graceful as a thread of wool, now seemed trans-formed into the blade of a sword.

"Are you making fun of me? Do you think it's easy to find a scribe who'll teach a slave?"

"I know but . . . " Edgardo tried to find a reason to justify his decision, "my presence here can put the Abbot of San Giorgio in an embarrassing situation."

"Do you fear for your life?" Kallis asked, provoking him.

Edgardo did not have the courage to be completely honest. "It's not my life that is at risk . . . at least I don't think so . . . "

"I can take you to a secret place where you'll be safe. Nobody would find you there."

"You're very kind, but I can't hide forever. And I *don't want to* hide."

"Only in case it's necessary, in case you must run away, there's a hiding place nobody knows about. Come with me."

Edgardo tried to resist, but Kallis took his hand and squeezed it. At that moment, he lost all willpower, the reasoning of a wise mind got mixed up with the babblings of a madman and the warmth of his hand being squeezed flooded him with happiness. It was as though he had been bound with a chain of fire and there was nothing he could do except follow her.

The *scaula* was moored in the stream behind the foundry. Kallis slid the oar out from the bottom, leaned it on the rowlock, and, standing in the bow, started rowing. Edgardo watched her in awe. She moved with assurance, using strong, precise strokes, and in a few minutes they were out of the labyrinth of streams and canals and going toward the Vigano canal. Just as had happened before the furnace, Kallis looked completely transformed to Edgardo: she was not just a strong woman—of that he already had proof—but independent and determined: characteristics that were generally attributed to men.

With Segrado not there, she seemed finally able to express herself and set her true spirit free. Her slim body that seemed so fragile had taken on unexpected authority and dignity, and he allowed himself to be led without putting up any resistance, as if under a spell, stunned by her beauty and regal demeanor.

He did not want to know where they were going. He asked no questions and abandoned himself to a soft and languid pleasure, as though the moment had finally come to give up fighting for survival and trust the path that had been preordained.

They left the island of Spinalunga in the south, passed San Giorgio, and cut across the canal at Olivolo to reach the north of the lagoon.

It was a cold January morning and the air was so pure and insubstantial that you could almost touch the peaks of the mountains on the horizon. Edgardo saw Amurianum and, for a moment, thought that Kallis was taking him to the *rio* of the glassmakers, but then noticed that the bow was facing east, past the island of glass manufacturing, toward the interior of the marshes.

Kallis was rowing calmly, with a slow, constant rhythm, almost absentmindedly, lost in her own world, a world Edgardo would have so much liked to discover and share with her. She had a relaxed expression, and for the first time her eyes lit up her face with a serenity that bordered on joy. Edgardo felt the same: it was just the two of them, alone, lost in the meanderings of the lagoon, far from all turmoils and fears, on a journey he wanted never to end.

The landscape was different now. Wide expanses of tidal shallows alternated with shoals that surfaced just above the water. Here and there, on more substantial protruding islands, forests of elms, willows, poplars, oaks, Mediterranean pines, and brooms stood out. Wide expanses of marsh reeds and rushes bordered streams and canals. Past a large area of reed beds, they reached a *piscaria,* a big, shallow stretch of water closed off with artificial borders made of poles and netting that prevented young fish from leaving the basin once they had grown. The surrounding lands were cultivated with vines and vegetables. Edgardo would never have expected to find such luxuriant crops in an area that seemed dominated by insalubrious marshes and stagnant waters. He felt as though he had arrived in a kind of promised land.

He was even more surprised when he saw the silhouettes of towers and many belfries rise on the horizon. As they advanced, all around on the land above water, surrounded by fishermen's huts, sprouted churches and vast monasteries. He had never seen such a large number of holy places in such a small area. It was as though all the priests, monks, and hermits had gotten together and agreed to build places of worship on that stretch of muddy sea.

By now they had reached a large, densely-populated island crisscrossed by streams and canals. Kallis pushed the boat along a man-made canal that ran horizontal to the natural streams and crossed the whole of the inhabited area. The surrounding lands were cultivated and there were small herds of cows grazing in the fields. Outside the huts, along the bank, barges were moored loaded with hay, and nets were drying everywhere, hanging from poles. In the distance, large expanses of salt glistened.

They passed palaces, two monasteries, and a church, following the canal until they reached the district's main *campo.* Edgardo noticed that it had nothing to envy the wealthiest Venetian *campi.*

Surrounded by two-story patrician houses and buildings made of stone and marble, the center was dominated by an imposing cathedral, a circular baptistry, decorated with a tub fed by jets of water that flowed from the mouths of symbolic animals, and a small church laid out like a Greek cross and surrounded on all five sides by a portico. The religious complex, in its harmony, conveyed a sense of spirituality and profound peace.

Edgardo could never have imagined that there were islands besides Venetia—considered the main religious and political center of the lagoon—so densely inhabited, so wealthy and important for trade, business and farming, that you wondered if the civilization of the *gens venetica* had been born and developed precisely in this periphery.

"What's the name of this island?" Edgardo asked in awe.

"It's called Torcellus," Kallis replied, continuing to row.

"It's a place where you can hear the voice of Our Lord."

Kallis turned her face to the sky as though searching for that voice. "Sometimes Our Lord is silent and distant, or perhaps he simply doesn't condescend to talk to slaves."

Edgardo had never heard her speak with such bitterness.

They left Torcellus and other churches and monasteries behind, and went deeper into an area of shallow, slimy waters, grass-covered shoals that sank or emerged depending on the tide, giving the impression that perhaps once upon a time these islands had all been connected to dry land.

"We're nearly there!" Kallis exclaimed. "Those islands you see are Costancianum and Aymanas. Many years ago they were all the same land but now the rising waters have separated them."

On a small stretch of land, on separate islands along the main canals, Edgardo counted two churches and ten monasteries. The boat went toward one of these, which stood on a tiny island.

When the *scaula* finally touched shore, Edgardo realized that the abbey was totally abandoned. Kallis tied the boat to a willow.

"This is the convent of San Lorenzo. The nuns who used to

live here have gone. The lagoon grew so much that they were completely isolated and every time the waters rose, they were completely submerged." She set off for the convent. "It belongs to me now," she said, walking in the tall grass, "me and my fellow snakes." She laughed, satisfied.

Privet, beds of reeds, and rushes had invaded everything. The paths had been erased, submerged by mud.

Kallis skipped from one protruding stone to another with animal agility. With his clumsy, crooked demeanor, impaired by his habit, Edgardo tried to keep up with her.

Inside, the church was completely devastated. There were only a few slabs left of the marble floor. The altar, broken in two, was lying on the ground, caked with salt and shells from the sea, a sign that the water had reached that far. On the walls were a few frescoes that crumbled with every gust of wind and torn pieces of mosaic, as well as bas-reliefs and tiles with barely recognizable patterns. A Jesus Christ carved from a log watched from the apse, powerless, as his house went to ruin.

"They've taken everything away," Kallis said with contempt. "They come from Venetia and take stones, marble, and even the pillars, so they can build rich people's houses."

They crossed the central nave and came out into an inner cloister at the back. There were only a few poplars left in the garden, the other trees having been cut down for timber, and medicinal herbs had invaded every corner. The roof of the refectory and the chapter had collapsed, leaving a heap of logs, reeds, and bricks inside.

"Be careful, it's full of snakes," Kallis said, almost flying across the vegetable garden now corroded by sand and brambles. They reached the foot of the tower behind the church. "Wait here, I'll be back soon."

Edgardo watched her disappear behind the church, toward a small, fenced-off *campo* strewn with uprooted slabs of stone. The tower was the only building left that was still in good

shape. Built from solid Istrian stone, it had withstood the devastating tides that had eaten away at the rest of the convent.
Shortly afterwards, Kallis reappeared. She looked sad and her
eyes glistened as though she had been crying.

"Come, let's go up."

The inside staircase was steep and narrow, and stank of saltpeter and mold. They reached the top and entered a circular
room connected to the belfry by a trapdoor. Two slits let in the
light. The walls were bare, with heaps of straw on the floor, and
only a table and stool against the wall.

"This is my hiding place," Kallis announced proudly, looking
around as though showing a guest the hall of a palace. "Nobody
knows this place exists." Her voice cracked. "Not even Segrado.
You're the only one who knows. Everything is abandoned here.
The peasants stay away because they're afraid of the snakes. I'm
the mistress of this island—a slave mistress . . . "

She burst into a fierce, almost unnatural laugh, which
chilled Edgardo's blood. She approached the slit. "Look, from
here you can see the whole lagoon, the mountains, the river
mouths, the sea, Venetia, and all the islands and dry lands. You
can see the whole world from here."

Edgardo's eyes wandered as far as the horizon. A luminous
strip quivered above the waters, transforming the landscape
into a vision of unreality, like a painting discolored by rain.

"When I'm here I feel as free as a bird. I have no master and
no remorse. My soul can fly through the air."

Her voice was now warm and sweet as a songbird's.
Edgardo could have listened to her forever.

"Come," she said, sitting at the table. "You promised to
teach me to write. I'm ready."

It was he who was not ready now. He had not expected this.
A little awkwardly, he sat next to her, unrolled the parchment and
picked up the goose quill. He bent over the sheet, but stopped.

"We have no ink . . . "

For a moment, Kallis looked at him, puzzled, then stood up decisively and took from under the straw a small box of coarse wood that was all cracked. She opened it, took out a cloth wrapping and a glass jar, and put them on the table. The box was full of colored beads and she poured them out. "They were my mother's," she said, gesturing toward the beads and the wrapping. "It's all I have left of her." She remained with her hand in the air, transfixed, staring at the little beads rolling around freely.

"Is she dead?" Edgardo asked.

Kallis's eyes narrowed. Two black slits, like cuts, as though she had been stabbed in the chest. She nodded.

"Where do you come from?" Edgardo continued.

"From the Orient. My mother was abducted by Saracen pirates and was supposed to be sold in Alexandria. During a clash with the Venetian fleet, the pirates were all killed and my mother was brought to Venetia, as a slave."

Edgardo did not dare ask anything else. Kallis unfolded the wrapping, a piece of linen dyed with indigo. Inside, she had a knife with a thin, long blade. With a sharp gesture, she ran the tip across the crook of her arm. Blood began gushing out. Kallis placed the jar under her arm, to collect it. When the jar was full, she pushed it toward Edgardo.

"Here. Now we have ink."

Then she tied the piece of cloth securely to stanch the wound. It had all happened too fast for him to stop her. Besides, it would have been futile. Edgardo had read in her gestures a determination nobody could have stopped. It frightened and overwhelmed him. He said nothing and, with a sense he was performing a primitive rite of initiation, he dipped the quill in the dark liquid.

"The Latin alphabet is made up of twenty-six letters, five vowels and twenty-one consonants. We'll begin with the vowels. Watch carefully."

With difficulty, he drew close to the sheet to make a start, and began drawing the letter *a* on the parchment.

"Now it's your turn. You must copy the whole alphabet, and then learn it by heart."

He handed Kallis the quill. At first, she was almost afraid to touch it. The long, tapered fingers remained suspended in midair, spread out and quivering, then she plucked up the courage and gripped the quill. She dipped the tip into her own blood and rested it on the sheet. She looked into Edgardo's eyes, waiting for his approval. He smiled at her.

"Go on."

The quill creaked, moved forward a little, but then everything precipitated, and the hand slipped down and lost its balance.

"Not like that. Lightly. It must be a light touch."

Without thinking, Edgardo put his hand on Kallis's, in order to guide it.

"Let's try again. This is an *a*."

Kallis's arm became soft and tender and her hand turned into a tangle of warm, welcoming wool. Trusting in his ever more uncertain eyes, he led her to draw a vague, unsteady vowel.

"You've chosen a terrible teacher who can't see anymore."

"Again." Kallis's voice was thin and childlike.

"Now let's try an *e*. Repeat after me: *e*."

The pupil repeated, and once again the teacher took her by the hand and guided her on the sheet and as he did so felt her hand melt, open, and change shape and consistency . . . That blood letter assumed body and heat. The writing became alive and slid under his skin like a shock. Everything blended into an unstoppable vortex. Kallis's languid eyes led him to the land of madmen and, in an instant, the hand became a mouth and the mouth became a body. Edgardo felt limbs merge and blur. His mind turned to liquid and slipped out of his head, distancing itself from his will.

Swept along by an unstoppable wave, his body melted with Kallis's. He lost his arms, his legs, his stomach, his head. Everything was topsy-turvy, broken, sinking into a salty, aqueous humor.

For the first time, Edgardo discovered the wonder of flesh, skin as soft and smooth as silk, eyes full of desire caressing his naked belly, breathed in the moist, pungent scent of a deep well, and heard words in a foreign tongue pouring out of Kallis's throat.

Then the hands flew away, they entered and exited their interlaced bodies, held each other tight and were sucked again into a void where only chaos reigned.

Finally, Kallis's lips pressed against his. A veil of sweat and the taste of almonds. A light kiss that grew deeper and more intense. Kallis sucked in his breath with long, deep breaths. Edgardo felt his lungs and entrails empty and his life force slip out of his mouth and penetrate her body. As though she had stolen his soul with a spell. Then Kallis saw Edgardo's body light up and fly away, and Edgardo saw Kallis's narrow eyes suddenly open and burst in a confused, overwhelmed expression that enraptured him.

When he came to, he had no idea where he was, who he was, or to which life he belonged, the earthly or the spiritual. It took him some time to put back together the pieces of his body that lay scattered about the room. With difficulty, he found his stunned mind and pulled it back into him, sticking it back into the shell that had housed it for all of his brief existence.

He looked at Kallis's body lying naked beside him. He wanted to caress it but was afraid of losing his mind forever. A thread of amber wool, slim and perfect, which possessed a harmony that had nothing human about it.

Kallis was staring at him with a bewildered expression.

"What happened?" Edgardo asked, still in shock. "I felt I was being dragged into a vortex, then emptied of all energy."

Kallis smiled, satisfied. "I've stolen your soul, so now there's a part of you inside me." She spoke with a certainty that frightened him.

"Did you cast a spell on me?"

She burst into a full, sincere laugh that put his mind at ease. "No, no spell. I've just taken a tiny bit of your knowledge without asking your permission."

Edgardo was confused. He suddenly remembered his naked body and felt ashamed of it. He looked at his odd, crooked limbs and wondered how such a beautiful woman could willingly join herself to a rough, twisted branch.

Kallis seemed to read his mind, because she reached out to him and lightly touched the hump on his chest, like a tortoise's back.

"God hasn't been generous with me," Edgardo said. "He chose to mark me from birth with this repulsive shell."

"My mother always used to say that it's the light that outlines shapes. In the dark, everything is without substance. And the light within you illuminates you and transforms all your features. It erases all deformities."

"You're generous, but my soul is not illuminated at all, on the contrary . . . " And he stopped as though only now becoming aware of the catastrophe. He had coupled with a woman. He had committed a mortal sin. But that was not the only thing that frightened him. He felt that this act had capsized his life, making him tumble into an unknown and primitive world.

"I'm lost," Edgardo could not help saying in a whisper.

Kallis suddenly hugged him, with all the strength of her slim arms. "You were born crippled and I was born a slave. We've always been lost and yet here we still are, alive and strong."

Where did this woman come from? From which lands? Which oceans had she crossed? Where had she learned this princely dignity? Edgardo looked at her in awe. Kallis kissed his eyelids.

"Don't go. You still have to find the stone for the eyes."

Edgardo smiled. "My eyes . . . They suddenly seem like a distant memory of no importance."

"Your eyes are important. You must teach me to write."

At that moment, Edgardo knew he was lost forever.

XX.
THE WONDER

The rumor spread instantly and the whole of Venetia rushed to see the monstrous wonder with its own eyes. Since early morning, there had been an unusually large crowd in front of the Orseolo Hospice, so much so that Doge Ordelafo Falier had called in the guards to keep the peace. And so all the curious folk formed a line and waited impatiently for their turn.

Those who came out, after ascertaining that the tale on the street corresponded to the truth, would stop and comment with astounded expressions and excited gestures and leave saying that this prodigious event had to be an ill omen. Disorder was spreading and nature was rebelling against man. The Lord's wrath was at its peak and a disaster would befall the whole of humanity.

At the Hospice, in a secluded room, a young beggar girl from the Bergamo region who had been admitted with a nine-month belly, bloated like a goatskin and lumpy like a pumpkin, had given birth to a little monster.

Nobody had ever seen anything like it, not even when Barbarians had come down from the lands of ice and mated with sows. There was no restraining the curiosity of the people, or even of the nobility. They were all lining up as though it were a relic, their hats in their hands, in religious silence, to pay homage to that trick of nature.

Lying on a straw mattress, the mother smiled, grateful for so much attention, lovingly holding in her arms the grotesque being she had just birthed.

A huge, oblong head with a disproportionately large skull splattered with stains like black sausage, from which sprouted two spindly legs that ended in two soft, dangling feet. It had no torso, no shoulders, no arms, and no back. A pink ass began at the neck and the genitals dangled right under the chin. It was nothing but a head and a pair of legs. Nothing else. You could not tell where the heart, lungs and stomach were.

Some quacks were certain that life resided in the abnormally large skull. Wherever that life might have resided, the newborn did not seem in the least concerned with it, as long as he could hungrily suck at his mother's breast, almost as though the absence of a proper body meant he required extra energy to keep himself alive.

What added to the horror of the picture was the baby's face. In that macrocephalic skull there was somehow a little, delicate mouth, a small, almost feminine nose, two well-defined eyebrows, but no eyes. Instead, there were two deep black holes covered with purple skin, as though a trickster demon had scooped them out with a spoon before he had seen the light of day.

More than the incomplete and deformed body, it was the absence of eyeballs that captured the imagination of the procession that went to pay homage to the freak. Too many signs, too many coincidences had been piling up, and it was impossible not to connect them. Two dead men, murdered by a joker who had gouged out their eyes. And now this big-headed monster born without eyes, as though come to tell people what awaited all Venetian newborns if the perpetrator of those killings was not found and punished as soon as possible. People were blathering away, gathered on the Brolo outside the Hospice, and the crowd grew more numerous as the day went on.

On the way back from Costancianum, Kallis left Edgardo in a deserted area near the Arsenal, on the bank of an internal stream, so that no one would see them together. Edgardo headed toward the dock at San Marco to find the gondola to take him back to the abbey of San Giorgio. He walked with his head down, without looking around, shaken by a riot of thoughts and emotions that made him swing from a state of feverish excitement to one of heavy torment, fueled by the guilt of having so wretchedly given in to one of the most reproachable sins: the sin of the flesh.

Yet he could not help missing the moments of extreme joy and heavenly confusion, the sublime pleasure he had felt while lying with Kallis, and he wondered how, after experiencing such sensations, a man could consider giving up that life forever.

Even though he realized that he was now a sinner who deserved nothing but to burn in the fires of hell, he had to admit that he had never before felt so strong, so full of energy, so hungry for life. Even more surprising was the feeling that his body was a harmonious and balanced whole, a feeling that made him forget his hump and his crippled bones.

He reached the Brolo without even realizing it, saw the crowd outside the hospice, and, forgetting all prudence, approached with curiosity.

"Most illustrious cleric . . . Master copyist . . . "

Were they calling him? Nobody had ever called him "master." Edgardo looked around and, among a group of citizens gathered to discuss the event, he saw Karamago's belly protrude.

"Are you also here to gaze at the wondrous wonder?" the merchant asked, approaching.

"No, I don't know anything about it. What happened?"

"A beggar from Bergamo has given birth to a head with no eyes, two legs and a pendant under the chin. It's an extraordinary sight. All Venetia is rushing to see it. Everyone's saying that there are too many evil signs multiplying over our heads. Something terrible is about to happen."

An image flashed in Edgardo's memory: that of the cow with a head instead of an udder, which they'd found in the lagoon the day he arrived.

"Our meeting is timely," Karamago continued. "I wanted to talk to you about a delicate question that concerns your stones for the eyes . . . You haven't found them yet, have you?"

"No, unfortunately, not yet," Edgardo answered, hesitating.

"Good, well, don't despair. Maestro Tàtaro has taken your tearful situation very much to heart. He has great respect and esteem for copyist monks and would like to help you."

"Yes, I know. He told me."

"Exactly. Maestro Tàtaro is convinced that the Arabic manuscript contains information that could be very useful for creating these miracle stones . . . So Maestro Tàtaro has a theory that since you have access to the library where this manuscript is kept, perhaps you've been able to take a peek inside it . . . And if you felt so inclined, the maestro would be delighted to hear about it and, if so, would of course not fail to show his gratitude, perhaps even by applying his expert expertise to make you the stones you need."

Edgardo tensed. "As I've already said, the library rules do not allow me access to a manuscript entrusted to another skilled monk."

"Yes, of course, I understand." Karamago pushed his belly forward as though to find an opening in the conversation. "But I'm sure that, even taking into account your commendable cautious cautiousness, not wishing to offend anyone, you could find a way to take a quick look."

Edgardo's face darkened. He was about to reply firmly when a loud voice rose from the crowd.

"There's that monk!"

A confused buzz spread like a swarm of bees after their hive has been destroyed. Edgardo realized that all eyes were upon him.

"He was at the mill when they gouged out poor Niccolò's eyes!" the voice shouted again.

Edgardo searched among the gathered crowd and recognized Zoto, the crystal-maker, pointing at him.

"He's the eye-gouger!" another voice cried.

"He's the murderer!"

"Call the gastald!"

Other voices followed, one on top of the other, the crowd swayed, and Edgardo felt the ground shake beneath his feet. A wave of heat poured out of the multitude: breath, humors, and sweat throbbing in the air and getting closer.

With a jerk, Karamago tugged at his habit. "Quick, come away, or these people will tear you to pieces."

Edgardo stepped back, trying to distance himself from the crowd, which was still agitated and confused, not having yet found an order or a direction. Trying hard to find the logic behind what was happening, the scribe moved slowly, sleepily, as though his body did not belong to him and what was happening did not concern him.

"Don't let him get away!" someone else shouted, and the words echoed in his head as if in a dream.

"Quick! Run! Come with me," Karamago prompted.

A stick flew through the air and a sharp blow burned his shoulder. Only then did Edgardo become fully aware of the danger he was facing and begin to run, following Karamago who, although dragged down by his belly, had acquired speed.

For a moment, the multitude remained still, as though to consolidate the communal feeling and work out a plan of action, then it began running after him.

Like two foxes with hungry hounds at their heels. Legs, arms, breath. Splattering mud, your heart in your throat and a sharp pain in your chest. Behind you, the shouting of the pack at your back, and the stench of wildness. The two fugitives slid into a narrow, twisted *calle* at the far end of the Brolo. The crowd could not have followed them there. They ran through a labyrinth of paths, corners, under-porticos, banks, and rickety bridges. They could hear the deep murmur of the pursuers all around. They were surrounded, encircled.

Edgardo was following Karamago mechanically, his crooked bones creaking and causing him excruciating pain. Suddenly, the barking of the dogs grew closer and he felt lost. Karamago gave him a shove with his shoulder, and pushed him through a low, vaulted door. They crossed an inner courtyard covered in rubbish and excrement, climbed a few worn-out steps, and reached a walkway that acted as a bridge between two houses. Karamago brutally flung open a door.

"Get inside."

As if by a miracle, they found themselves on the upper floor of the merchant's shop, before an unmade bed and heaps of merchandise stacked against the walls.

Teodora surfaced from under a stack of fur blankets. "Heavens, what's this Sodom and Gomorrah?"

Karamago did not pay the slightest attention to her.

"Quick! Go upstairs!" he commanded Edgardo and opened the trapdoor that led to the attic. "Hide there and don't move. In a little while they'll calm down. It's always like this. After a while, they calm down and give up."

Edgardo stared at the face of this man he barely knew, trying to read signs of pity and charity in his features. He really knew nothing of the human soul! The merchant was saving his life without any hope of profit or ulterior motive. He could have left him to be savaged by those dogs and yet he had generously given him shelter in his home. How wrongly and superficially he had judged him at first.

On an impulse, he hugged him. "Thank you. May God reward you for this."

"Go, go, don't waste time," Karamago said, pushing him up the ladder.

"Is anybody going to tell me what's going on?" Teodora grumbled. "What's the cleric doing in our house?"

"Don't worry. Go back to sleep."

"I was praying, you idiot!" With a theatrical turn, Teodora hid her flabby white flesh beneath several layers of furs and scented wool.

The racket and shouts under the windows subsided for a while and it seemed as if the danger had been averted, and Karamago was about to tell Edgardo that he could leave his hiding place.

The sound of knocking at the door stopped him. He leaned out of the window overlooking the *calle* and saw a group of hotheads led by Zoto.

"What do you want?"

"We're looking for the monk who ran away with you."

"There's no monk here."

"Open up or we'll kick the door down."

Reluctantly, he had to let them in.

"You've got the wrong place, I told you," Karamago insisted.

"Then you won't mind us having a look."

Zoto pushed the merchant aside and, followed by the others, climbed the stairs.

There was nobody in the room and they began rummaging around. A petulant grumble coming from a strange swelling in the bed attracted their attention. A skinny, pockmarked youth pointed at it. Zoto approached it silently and, with a sharp motion, turned over the covers. Before the eyes of the hotheads appeared an oversized white ass, bursting out of a pair of night drawers. Teodora screamed and hid her head under the pillow. Karamago burst in with an oath that triggered general laughter, then ran to cover up his wife's behind. Still, the tension had been dissipated and the merchant sighed with relief.

"I told you—there's nobody here."

"You call an ass that size a nobody?" Zoto replied.

A boisterous laugh echoed as far as the loft. Karamago too

laughed to keep them happy. They were already going down the stairs when a small boy with the face of a hound began screaming like a lunatic.

"Here! Come quickly! Come and see what I found."

Zoto immediately backtracked. Karamago grew pale. The little hound was kneeling on the floor, his head stuck in a chest. The merchant heaved a sigh of relief.

"Help me, it's heavy," said the boy.

Zoto bent over and they started to rummage. The merchant watched on tiptoe, he too curious to find out what they had discovered in that chest that he had not opened for months. With some difficulty, they lifted out a large green glass bottle, closed at the neck with a cork as big as a pan. Inside, a thick, cloudy liquid with a yellow sheen was swishing about; there were strange white shapes floating in it.

"Go on, open it," Zoto ordered the boy.

With a sharp knock, the cork flew up in the air. At that moment, Karamago remembered what was inside the bottle, and felt his blood slide down to his sphincter.

A stench of rotting alcohol was released into the room. Zoto took a leap back. The boy, however, accustomed to the most evil smells, since he frequented the most secluded *calli*, leaned over the cesspit. White spheres were quietly floating in the liquid, streaked with light blue lines, wrapped in a kind of transparent, flabby film, like jellyfish.

"What's this stinking slop?" the boy asked.

Zoto came closer. "Good God . . . They're eyes."

Karamago wished he could have pulled his head into his belly and rolled down the stairs. Everybody approached the bottle. "It's true, they're human eyes," they said in chorus.

As a matter of fact, there were splendid, perfectly preserved eyeball specimens casually floating in the nauseating liquid.

The men turned to the merchant with threatening expressions.

"Where did these eyes come from, merchant?" Zoto asked.

"Just a moment, I can explain . . . They're relics, it's my wife's obsession, holy relics from the Orient. Tell them, Teodora."

The woman's chubby face emerged from under the covers in a flash.

"Yes, yes, I swear it, they're holy relics I got from a merchant in Constantinople. They're the eyes of Saint Lucy, Saint Lazarus, Saint Ermagora and Saint Pancras, and many others."

Zoto looked at the woman, then at Karamago. "And you expect us to believe this nonsense?"

"I swear it on Saint Mark's body," Teodora sniveled.

After a brief silence, the oldest man, who seemed to represent the group's voice of reason, stepped forward.

"Tell me, merchant, and be honest: if you were looking for a murderer who tears men's eyes out and, by chance, while pursuing a monk who was seen near where they found the last gouged man, you found yourself in the house of the man who helped him escape, and if, by chance, you found there a lovely bottle full of floating eyes . . . now what would you think?"

The logic was twisted but it seemed to have a certain effect on the group.

"I would think it's a coincidence . . . Just pure chance," Karamago replied, shaking.

"Well, I would think that the two of them are accomplices. The monk and the other man . . . That one of them tears out the eyes and the other one preserves them to perform who knows what kind of witchcraft."

"They sell them to alchemists and Jews for their experiments—I know it's true!" cried the boy.

"You're wrong. That's not it at all," Karamago insisted.

"They're relics of saints," Teodora repeated.

"Monstrous wretches are being born without eyes," the old

man declared. "For as long as the eye murderer isn't hanged, this curse will continue to befall our city."

"I beg you . . . "

"The Council will decide. Let's take him to the Doge, to the castle."

"No, no, my husband hasn't done anything," Teodora was crying.

"Take him," Zoto commanded.

There was some commotion but Karamago did not put up any resistance. They lifted him bodily and dragged him down the stairs. Teodora leapt out of bed and, wrapped in the furs, followed her husband, constantly proclaiming his innocence.

Edgardo had heard everything from the loft. Zoto's accusations against him and the merchant, Karamago's defense, and Teodora's lamentations. From the noises that came from downstairs, he had imagined the movements of the hotheads as they were taking him away. He had lived every moment of it . . . And yet he had not moved or spoken out. He had remained hidden behind the trunk, huddled like a frightened animal, holding his breath.

He would have liked to come forth, to stand up for the merchant, to tell the truth about why he had been at the mill when they had found Niccolò. He could have shown courage and shared Karamago's fate by facing the tribunal of the Council.

That is how a knight would have acted.

But he had done nothing, nailed down by fear and cowardice, mulling over a thousand reasons: such as that he could be more use to Karamago as a free man, that he would go to testify about Teodora's trade in relics . . . But only one thing was true: that man had saved his life, sacrificed himself without denouncing him, and he had done nothing to prevent this injustice.

To ease his sense of guilt, he started thinking about the possibility that Karamago might really be guilty of the killings, but the more he thought about it, the more ashamed he was of this theory. It just did not add up. Gouging people's eyes out was not very profitable. It made more sense to make a deal with the undertakers and take the eyes from corpses. Besides, all the victims were connected to the world of glassmakers and their eyeballs had been replaced by beautiful, well-crafted and polished spheres of glass. Karamago was a merchant and knew nothing about the art of glassmaking. After listening to the witnesses, the Doge's judges would reach the same conclusion and release him. He had to stay calm. Karamago was in no danger.

Freed from that worry, Edgardo regained some of his courage. There was no noise coming from downstairs. The room sounded empty. He remained hidden a little longer, waiting for the pale evening light to trail off completely, then left the attic.

He pulled the hood over his face and walked down deserted streets submerged in the darkness of a moonless night. He kept close to the walls like a thief, listening out for any creaking or sucking sounds, his mind obscured by a muddle of contrasting thoughts and feelings. He reached the Brolo. The shadow of the basilica suddenly appeared before him, like a huge whale emerging from the water, barring his way. He walked swiftly toward the dock, in search of a gondola to ferry him to San Giorgio.

When he neared the Doge's castle, he noticed near the tower a dark shape swaying in midair. He approached hesitantly.

Suspended from a long pole with a rope around his neck, a man's body was swinging. To his horror, he recognized Karamago's face.

He had spat out his tongue, and his arms and legs were stiff as a salted cod. There was a seagull perched on his head, pecking at him violently, trying to swallow in one gulp a choice morsel provided by the man: an eye, fresh that day. Edgardo stood petrified, unable to take his eyes off the horrible spectacle. They had hanged him. What about the trial, the judges, the evidence, the witnesses? They had executed an innocent Karamago and he had done nothing to stop it.

He heard a rustle behind him. A boatman with an oar over his shoulder was walking toward the dock.

"Did you see, Father, they got the eye murderer, and now look at this canker . . . Justice, finally."

"But . . . Has there already been a trial?" Edgardo stammered.

"Oh, yes, the trial," the man laughed smugly. "It was us who put him on trial, without wasting time . . . The judgment of the people is the judgment of God."

Edgardo could not take his eyes off poor Karamago, or the seagull enjoying its meal. He crossed himself and whispered a prayer.

"It's too late, Father, this fellow is already roasting in hell," the boatman said, heading for the dock. "Do you need a boat?"

Edgardo nodded and followed him, his head down.

Crossing the basin in front of San Marco, Edgardo saw in the stretch of deep, black water the reflection of his own soul, and for the first time he saw with clarity the truth about himself, the truth he had tried to hide and had never wanted to accept. That he was a coward—a coward of the worst kind. Fear was his queen and she ruled his heart and mind, shaping his every action and choice.

Suddenly, he remembered very clearly something that had happened when he was just a boy, something he had chosen to keep concealed in his heart.

Despite his crippled body, his father had trained him, alongside his brother Ruggero, to be a valiant knight. He was the eldest and that was his destiny. He had learned to ride even though it caused him unbearable pain. He had been taught to handle a sword and to shoot with a bow and arrow. With great effort, overcoming the limitations imposed by his body, the young Edgardo d'Arduino had adapted to military rules, to the principles of knighthood, to the rough, harsh life that was demanded by his rank.

Then the day of christening on the field had arrived—the rite of initiation. He was supposed to go with his brother and a group of soldiers to patrol the border of their county.

He did not sleep all night, thinking about the enterprise awaiting him. A languid tremor had seized his limbs, and he was sweating as though with a high fever.

They left the castle at dawn. The armor was wet with dew, the weapons glowed, and steam evaporated from the heat of the horses' backs. They rode in silence as far as the river. For a moment, Edgardo was even able to enjoy the excitement of feeling at one with the nature that surrounded him: the green expanses, the fog, the light wind, the icy brine on his face.

After patrolling the bank, they went as far as the edge of a forest of oaks. Everything seemed quiet. Suddenly, they heard shouts, the sound of broken branches and horses neighing, and found themselves faced with five figures wrapped in black rags, armed with clubs and burnished blades.

The figures galloped at them, with inhuman screams, attacking them without a reason, without even knowing who they were. Spiraling violence that came from the darkest shadows, overwhelming them. Even though the knights were larger in numbers, the strangers had a kind of furious, primitive wrath that increased their strength.

The battle flared in an instant. Bodies, animals, and blades merged and crossed in a pattern of primeval chaos. At first, Edgardo managed instinctively to strike a blow on the neck of an enemy. A spurt of blood hit him in the face and filled his mouth. He thought he was choking. The sickly sweet taste entered his heart and he felt all his energy, all his mental clarity, all the strength in his arms, ebb away. His body became limp, defenseless, numb. He tried to shake himself, turned his horse, and found himself on the margins of the fight. For a moment, he was able to gather his wits about him and saw his brother boxed in by two men who were attacking him viciously.

"I must run to Ruggero's aid," he thought, "or he'll die."

He heard his voice repeat that thought but his limbs did not obey his command. He was petrified, a knight without a soul, unable to act, unable to break the bond of fear that gripped him tight.

He did not move; he watched impotently as his brother struggled fiercely to save his own life. A few minutes later, one of his soldiers freed himself from the scrum and managed to intervene, saving Ruggero and forcing the remaining assailants to flee.

The return trip was for Edgardo an endless journey toward the undoing of his existence. Step by step, everything crumbled: dignity, honor, his rank, his self-respect, the right to live alongside his peers. He could never again look his brother in the eye or utter a word. He just felt like a crippled little creature without a future.

Back at the castle, in recounting for their father what had happened, Ruggero made no mention of Edgardo's cowardice.

The following day, after a tormented night, Edgardo announced to his father that he wished to enter an abbey as a cleric and to devote himself to studying. His deformed body did not allow him to carry with dignity the honor and responsibilities expected of a knight. His father willingly agreed, glad he would not be seeing his crippled firstborn around again.

And so his monastic life had begun. He had blotted out that incident for years, continuing to tell himself the lie that his choice had been dictated by the limitations of his body, while he knew only too well that he had decided to retire to a monastery because it was the only suitable refuge for a coward.

XXI.
ICE

"No, stop. It's my turn!"

"The canker on you. You've already had two throws."

"It's not true, shit-face!"

"Then get on with it, slowcoach."

A little boy picked up a stone from the ground and got ready to throw it. It whistled through the air and brushed the ear, missing its aim.

"Dirty pig. It's my turn now."

A group of urchins in ragged cloaks were bustling around the foot of the gallows where Karamago's body was still hanging.

That winter morning, the people of Venetia beheld an extraordinary sight. An icy *bora* wind had come down from the north during the night and, in a short space of time, had frozen the entire lagoon, as well as the merchant's wretched body. His long, windswept beard had frozen in midair, like the ribbon of a lady's headdress, forming a kind of embroidery suspended in the void. A crow that had landed on his shoulder to peck at what was left of his eyeballs had been caught in the blast of frost and remained wrapped in a skin of ice, like a stuffed animal placed as a decoration on an equestrian statue. That was what the little boys were using as a mark for their stones, like target shooting at a fair.

The Brolo outside San Marco was a single slate of thin ice, as transparent as the purest rock crystal. Galleys, chelandions, and *scaulas* stood stuck in the dock, trapped by thick slabs of ice. The entire city had been struck by a blinding, painful light that stabbed the eyes like the point of an arrow. The waters had been high over the previous days and had penetrated every gap and every corner, leaving a layer of damp everywhere. Consequently, the frost had infiltrated the oddest places: the brickwork of the basilica, the blades of grass and the branches of the trees, the folds of the sails, the hair and beards of the sailors, the assholes of birds, the thighs of whores, the open wounds of lepers, the toothless mouths, and the streams of piss between the *calli*, turning the latter, as though by magic, into glistening, pale yellow waterfalls.

Nobody could take a step without ending up ass over tip. Everywhere, you could see dramatic slipping and slow, quiet sliding. Women rolled cheerfully with their baskets of vegetables, fishermen slid while dragging their nets, boys pushed one another on the bank on improvised sleds, laughing at the sight of gondolas, loaded with people, being pulled by oxen and horses, gliding across the lagoon as though on a wide expanse of eel jelly.

Even though an icy wind had turned Venetia to stone, the city's daily activities, albeit a little slower, had not ground to a halt, and Zoto had returned to the Brolo to admire his work of art and claim the credit for having obtained justice for the wretches who had been so brutally murdered. The culprit had gotten what he deserved, and now the city was safe.

"We'll catch that foreign monk next!" he shouted smugly, boasting to the layabouts who were loitering by the hanging man, enjoying the spectacle of little boys target shooting.

A voice rose from the group. "Are you absolutely sure he was guilty?"

"Of course. We found the eyes in his shop."

"Karamago was just a merchant who thought he was clever, but he wouldn't have killed even a mouse." Maestro Tàtaro approached the hanging man. "Still, that crow on his shoulder gives him a princely air. Leave it there when you bury him."

People laughed.

"Who are you?" asked Tàtaro.

"Zoto, the crystal-maker."

"Was it you who hired out an oven to Segrado?"

"Yes—why, there's no law against it, is there?"

Tàtaro pressed his lips together, as though to stifle a curse, took him by the cloak, and pulled him aside. "Listen to me, you canker, do you know who I am?"

"Tàtaro, the glassmaker."

"Then you also know that I have many ovens in Amurianum, and that I often require the services of a good crystal-maker."

"Everybody knows Zoto is the best in town."

"Good. Come and see me in Amurianum, and we'll definitely find you something to do."

"Thank you, Maestro."

"I'm telling you now, I'm also interested in your oven. So if, one day, you decide to sell it, you could make good money."

"For the time being, I've hired it out to Segrado."

"Exactly. So keep me informed of how his business is going. It won't be hard for you to see if he's working on new glass, or if he's concocting some cock-and-bull formula." Tàtaro's expression turned nasty. "Take a peek every now and then—do you get my meaning?"

"Of course, I understand perfectly, Maestro, don't worry."

"You know, just out of curiosity . . . " Maestro Tàtaro added with a strained smile that made his lips almost disappear. "I'll expect you at the foundry, then."

He said goodbye and walked away, taking small, skating steps toward the basilica, where his workmen were arranging mosaic tesserae.

Zoto took a look at his own masterpiece. With a well-aimed shot, a little boy had just managed to knock down the frozen crow. Shame. Now the hanging man had lost some of his dignity.

To beg for forgiveness, to do penance, to purge his body and soul of all sin through prayer. Soon after Lauds, while it was still dark, Edgardo had retired to the herb garden cloisters to recite the psalms from the Psalter. He knew that an offense against God could not be erased with a few prayers, but it was the only way he could ease his tormented soul and regain some hope and clarity. He walked slowly around the portico, his head down and his eyes half-closed, whispering his litany.

The curve of her belly, the scent of her sex, the fold of her breast, the taste of her lips. He was persecuted by these images and recollections, so he raised his voice, prayed louder, walked faster. The roundness of her buttocks and that split that went down between her thighs, oozing with dew he wanted to drink. Her hoarse voice, those incomprehensible words, the narrow cut of her eyes brimming with desire . . .

Images of Kallis's body hurled against him like Barbarian armies invading his mind, sacking his thoughts, slaughtering his good intentions. Pray, pray, and pray more to banish the devil's temptation. Scream his repentance at the sky and ask God to forgive him.

What repentance? What forgiveness? Edgardo could not stop thinking about Kallis or wanting her, and was unable to cast her out of his mind. Her body had snaked into every corner of his brain and taken possession of it. He would have given anything to drink from her lips, to caress her skin, to stroke her hair. May God forgive me—is the power of the flesh that great? Is this what people call love? Is it this devastating force that capsizes everything, then stamps all over it?

Walk faster, Edgardo, and scream your prayer, so that Our Lord may hear your supplication and deliver you from this wondrous spell.

"I've found you at last." Ademaro had suddenly appeared out of the darkness behind him. "You're sweating . . . You're so pale . . . Stop—for the love of God, stop."

"I can't. I must keep walking, moving, otherwise temptations will have the advantage."

"What's happening to you, Brother?" Ademaro's voice was that of his old friend.

"I'm lost, Ademaro. Forever damned. I can't tell you everything, but events snowballed and I found myself caught up in an avalanche I don't have the power to stop."

Ademaro held him back by the arm. "You can confide in me."

For a moment, Edgardo hesitated, but the desire to bare his soul and free himself of the load that was afflicting him was too strong to resist.

"They hanged Karamago, the book merchant, because they think he was guilty of killing two men whose eyes were gouged. But I don't believe it was him. And, on top of that, they think I'm his accomplice."

"You, his accomplice? But why?" Ademaro asked, alarmed.

"Do you remember when I found the body of that young man near the mill? Someone saw me and now they're looking for me."

Ademaro stopped, his expression dark. "I'm telling you again, Edgardo, you must leave Venetia. The abbot is also very angry with you. Your presence has become inconvenient. There are rumors circulating among the brothers . . . that you're frequenting people of ill repute, that you're interested in alchemy, in magic stones, in crystals—"

"Yes, because of my eyes, and you know that."

"Yes, I do know, but what about the others? And then something strange has happened for the first time ever in the abbey. Carimanno has ordered Rainardo, the novice from Mantua, to guard the library, as though he's afraid of burglars and intruders."

Ademaro stared at his friend with pointed severity. Edgardo remained silent and cast down his eyes.

"Listen to my advice and go back to Bobbio. I'll take care of your eyes. I'll keep looking."

"My eyes . . . At this moment, my eyes seem like the least of my worries."

"Then don't delay any further," Ademaro pressed him. "Leave the city."

Day was dawning, and an opal light was caressing the tops of the cypresses.

"It's nearly Lauds. I'll wait for you in the church." Ademaro slipped away silently, vanishing behind the laurel bushes.

To abandon Venetia, leave Kallis, stay away from her forever. Edgardo felt he was being sucked into a vortex. He longed to rebel, to disobey, to think only of himself. Why should he give it all up? What did he care about all the rest? On the other hand, was he prepared to risk everything? Because if he stayed, his life would be in danger. He would have to move about with the constant fear of being ambushed, always ready to run away, hiding like a murderer. That was what awaited him.

On the one hand lay desire—could he call it love? On the other hand, there was the fear that paralyzed him. Now he had gotten to know the latter so intimately, he could no longer deny it. He had imagined for a moment that his love for Kallis would defeat his cowardice.

After leaving Edgardo in Venetia, Kallis had gone back to spend the night in Metaumaco, waiting for Segrado to return from Patavium. She felt charged with a new energy that enabled her to face and overcome any obstacle, almost as though she had just become aware of her powers. She was impregnated with the breath of knowledge she had stolen from Edgardo as they were making love.

When she came into the hut, she made herself a soup of oats and chickpeas, and swallowed it in one go, as if she had not eaten for days. Then she lay down on the bed, staring into space, thinking about herself and her destiny, and about what awaited her. Then, listening to the waves lapping against the shore, she fell asleep.

She was awoken at the dawn of the new day by Segrado's arrival. He looked tired but in the grip of an unusual excitement. When Kallis opened her eyes, she saw him filling a knapsack with little bags he was handling very carefully. He ordered her to get ready. They had to get to the foundry as soon as possible and, with the lagoon being frozen over, the crossing would be difficult.

For a long stretch, from Metamauco almost as far as Spinalunga, their *scaula* slipped between floating blocks of ice that had not yet joined. Segrado would frequently help with the oar, pushing the wood against the blanket of ice. Confused seabirds were skating on the crystal slates, and many boatmen, who had gotten stuck, were dragging their boats on foot with the aid of ropes. When they were near Luprio, the *scaula* got jammed and they had to walk the rest of the way, whipped by a *bora* wind that bent the tops of the cypresses down to the ground.

As soon as they had reached the foundry, Segrado began working at a brisk pace. Without uttering a word, he signaled the required tasks to Kallis, activities she had seen Niccolò perform on countless occasions.

She fueled the fire in the oven with sweet, dry wood, to ensure that the flames would be clear, smokeless, and not too high. Segrado started heating the molten glass, which he had already prepared with the Ticino pebbles. Then he took a tub of clean water and as soon as the molten glass had cooled he poured it into the receptacle and ordered Kallis to wash it several times, until the water was clear. Afterwards, he took the solidified molten glass, put it into a glass mortar, and pestled it finely before pouring it back into clear water to remove any residual salinity that would make the glass dark. After all these washes, Segrado put the vitreous paste back into the crucible and, checking that the flame was pale and smokeless, placed it in the oven to melt.

Every gesture, every move was made with extreme precision, in religious silence, like the celebration of a ritual. Just a look, a sign to Kallis, and she executed his orders immediately. There was an understanding, a synchronicity that surprised Segrado and, for the first time, he felt proud of the woman's qualities.

"Now we have to wait for it to melt," he finally said. "And then, God willing, we'll try to perform a miracle."

He took a full leather bag from the knapsack and placed it delicately on the bench. Kallis watched but chose not to ask questions. This time, it was the maestro who could not resist.

"It's my final attempt, and if I fail, I'll give up my dream forever."

He fell silent, unsure whether or not to reveal his secret to a woman, an inferior being, but in the end his excitement got the better of him.

"It's powder of manganese. Even the ancient Romans knew about it, and called it a 'magnetic stone' because it attracts the impurities in the glass and cleans it like soap. If my gut feeling is right, perhaps I'll succeed in creating totally pure glass."

Kallis said nothing. Her motionless face betrayed no emotion, but her heart was burning with joy, because the maestro had revealed the secret of his formula to her.

While waiting for the pestled glass to melt, they left the foundry to breathe some clean air.

The saltworks were at a standstill. The sails of the mill were covered in frost and the expanse of salt blended with ice crystals, reflecting a pale blue light. Two workmen were warming themselves by a makeshift fire. Kallis and Segrado approached to dry their waterlogged cloth boots. No sooner did they see steam rise from their feet than Zoto, the crystal-maker, appeared at their side. He was muffled in a threadbare fur that made him look even smaller and squarer, with a frozen wisp of hair standing up straight on his head.

"You should thank me," he said to Segrado. "I was the one who discovered Niccolò's murderer. If you walk past the basilica, you'll still see him hanging there. With this cold, he's likely to keep a long time." He burst into a whooping laugh, and spat into the fire.

Segrado did not as much as afford him a glance.

"And now it's the monk's turn. You know him well, don't you?" He gave Segrado a dirty look.

Kallis gave a start. Still silence, except for the crackling of branches devoured by the fire.

"How's work? These days, everybody's huddling in their homes. The nobles are thinking about crusades, the merchants are afraid of traveling because of the pirates, and there's not a penny to be made."

Segrado kicked a log without looking up from the fire, while Zoto continued his monologue.

"I saw smoke coming out of the oven. Are you preparing something? If you need a good crystal-maker, you know I'm the best, don't you?"

Maestro Segrado rubbed his hands over the fire one more time and, without replying, went back to the workshop with Kallis. Zoto followed him with his eyes, grumbling something or other, then turned his back to the fire, to warm his ass.

As soon as they were back inside, Segrado lifted the crucible out of the oven. The glass had melted, and he handed it to Kallis. He picked up the small leather bag from the bench, took a pinch of sifted manganese with the tip of a spoon, and cautiously poured it into the glass. Then he stirred the mixture slowly with an iron rod, until it had completely dissolved. As he worked, he watched the glass paste. Kallis watched as he rubbed his bald head thoughtfully and uncertainly before taking another pinch of manganese with two fingers and letting it slide onto the surface of the mixture. He stirred it once more, then waited breathlessly, murmuring a prayer: that God might grant him a miracle.

XXII

THE PERFECT CRYSTAL

The silence was so deep you could only hear the sizzling of the glass in the crucible. Kallis was trying to read the outcome of the experiment in the maestro's face. The paste, which still had a pale lilac tint, was transforming before his eyes. Segrado held his breath.

As it evaporated, the colored shade dissipated: the substance grew increasingly pale and transparent until it had reached a clarity and a light never before seen in ordinary glass. The maestro poured the substance into a mold. Kallis approached with trepidation. A piece of the purest crystal glowed before her eyes. Not a single impurity, not a shadow, not the slightest crack: glass that looked exactly like rock crystal. Segrado, his face red and his eyes moist, looked at Kallis.

"The perfect crystal," he said, overwhelmed. "I've been chasing after it my whole life, and now I have it."

Suddenly, a thought flashed through his mind and his face twisted into an angry grimace.

"Close the door securely—and the blinds," he ordered.

Kallis, frightened, obeyed immediately.

"Open your ears. You must never tell anyone what you've seen here. No detail, not even a hint. You've seen nothing. Swear it."

Kallis hesitated.

"Swear it—your life depends on it."

"I swear," she whispered.

"When the first crystalline glass objects start appearing in

Venetia, the news will spread like wildfire, and everybody will want to know. They'll use every possible means, and even all sorts of witchcraft, to find out every detail of how it's made and the formula. No matter what happens, you must keep quiet. If you let as much as a single word slip, I'll cut out your tongue—remember that."

Kallis nodded.

"This discovery will change the course of history for glass and glassmakers. Glass so pure, malleable, and inexpensive will quickly replace rock crystal, and will pave the way to other discoveries even I can't begin to imagine. That's why it's so important to keep this secret. We must be watchful and not leave anything in the foundry that could lead to the formula."

He took the empty little bag and shoved it into the knapsack.

"I'm going back to Metamauco. I need some more powder of manganese. I want to do more tests. You'll sleep here and guard the place. If anyone tries to enter, don't hesitate to cut his throat."

He wrapped the crystal cast in a piece of cloth and hid it in the trunk. Then he huddled in his cloak, covered his head, and left. Slipping on the ice as he struggled to reach the *scaula*, which was tied to a pole on the *rio* behind the mill, he noticed Zoto standing at the door of his workshop, spying on him.

When Edgardo walked into the scriptorium, the creaking of quills on parchment ceased, as though a blank line had suddenly been inserted into every page to be copied. The copyists imperceptibly raised their heads from their lecterns, and turned their eyes toward him.

"I wonder why my presence is causing so much amazement," Edgardo thought.

The only one to put on an act of sincerity and spontaneity was Ademaro. He stopped conversing with Ermanno di Carinzia and came to greet him with a smile.

"I'm happy you've come to visit us, Brother." His tone was formal and slightly false.

"I needed to breathe the scent of parchment," Edgardo lifted his mouth to his nose with a pointed expression, "but, in particular, I was looking for our most reverend Abbot, and they told me I'd find him here."

Carimanno was sitting on a high-backed chair at the end of the hall, consulting a manuscript, and had been the only one who had not paid the least attention to Edgardo's entrance. It was all too clear that he was ignoring it on purpose.

Ademaro approached him.

"Illustrious Father, allow me to interrupt your reading," he murmured respectfully. "Our brother Edgardo d'Arduino wishes to speak with you."

Carimanno lifted his head slowly and deliberately, as though his mind were struggling to emerge from a world of mystery, and looked at the guest. Edgardo knelt.

"I have come to ask Your Worship's permission to leave San Giorgio."

Ademaro could not hold back an expression of satisfaction.

"My health does not allow me to remain in this holy place any longer. I thank you for your kind hospitality. This visit has proved to be very rich in lessons for me, as well as a most enlightening stage on a path of discovery of the human spirit."

The abbot listened with his eyes closed, without betraying any feelings. "The path to holiness is twisted, full of suffering and hidden dangers we common mortals often find hard to understand. If this visit has helped you delve into the most secret parts of your soul, then I'm immensely happy . . . " Carimanno opened his eyes and stared at him with pity and a trace of melancholy. "I hope you find your way, Edgardo d'Arduino." He gave a deep sigh. "I give you permission to leave the abbey, and may God be with you."

Edgardo stood up, struck by the words of the abbot, who

seemed to know exactly the torments afflicting his heart. Then, walking from lectern to lectern, he took his leave of his fellow brothers. He would have liked to stop beside Rainardo and praise his progress in writing, but his eyesight no longer allowed him to make out words and the whole page was just an expanse of muddy gray. So he just smiled at him and walked on. When he had reached the door, he bowed in a gesture of thanks.

As they walked down the stairs that led to the library, Ademaro had slipped back into his old friendly tone. "You've made the right decision," he said.

Edgardo had a moment of doubt. "I don't know . . . I really wish things were different."

"This has been an important experience, Edgardo, but the time has come to return to the serenity of your past life. Back in Bobbio, you'll be with our fellow brothers again, you'll go back to your habits, prayer times, books—" Ademaro suddenly broke off, aware that he had said the wrong thing.

Edgardo pulled a funny face, and wrinkled his nose. "The only thing left for me to enjoy of books is their scent."

"Yes, I know, but don't despair. I'll still keep looking, I'll try everything. I'll find a remedy for your eyes, you'll see."

Edgardo shook his head doubtfully. In the cloisters, he breathed in the frosty air that smelled of snow.

"When do you plan to leave?" Ademaro asked.

"At dawn tomorrow."

"Then we'll meet again in Bobbio."

Edgardo smiled and bowed his head.

"I'm telling you again, you've made the right decision," Ademaro repeated before leaving him. "Go with a light heart. Don't take burdens with you that could weigh on your soul. Free yourself of all your loads, and leave all memories behind."

Edgardo had the impression that Ademaro wanted to convey one last message.

"Farewell, my friend."

Ademaro looked at him in surprise. "See you in Bobbio," he replied, hugging him.

Along the *rio* of the glassmakers in Amurianum, the freight boats were still stuck in slates of melting ice. Zoto's lame footsteps echoed eerily on the frosted *fondamenta*.* He stopped on the threshold of the foundry and immediately recognized Tàtaro among the workmen. Lean, his upper body naked, dark as a root blackened by smoke, he was blowing into a blowpipe. His cheeks were so inflated, they looked about to burst, and his face was like that of a toad. Zoto took a couple of hesitant steps forward. As soon as he saw him, Tàtaro handed the blowpipe to a *garzone* and signaled to Zoto to follow him to the back of the workshop.

"Do you have any news?" he asked abruptly, wiping his mouth with a rag.

"You said there was work for me," Zoto replied with an air of naivety.

"There's only work for those who deserve it."

Zoto swung his shorter leg, as though about to kick an invisible ball. "I've seen some activity at Segrado's."

"Don't try my patience. What have you seen?"

The crystal-maker spat green phlegm on the floor. It was a way of stalling. Finally, he made up his mind. "They've bolted the door and the windows. He rushed off on the boat and left the slave to sleep there."

"So?"

"He doesn't usually do that. Normally, he leaves everything open while he's working and nobody ever sleeps there . . . He's hiding something."

Tàtaro threw a coarse canvas cloth over his shoulders. "And have you seen the monk?"

"No, I haven't, but I'll get my hands on him sooner or

later . . . There's already a gallows waiting for him on the Brolo."

"Calm down. We need the monk alive. He's the only one who knows the contents of the Arabic book. If Segrado's discovered some new recipe, it's thanks to the monk and any information he will have given him. Segrado is nothing but a braggart. All he's capable of making on his own is beads."

Tàtaro laughed, and Zoto joined in with an unctuous gurgle.

"Stay vigilant. You'll see, sooner or later the monk will come out of the woodwork. And try and find out what Segrado's up to."

Zoto nodded.

"Come back when you have fresh news."

Zoto did not move. "You said you needed a good crystal-maker . . . "

On one of the shelves, a series of round vases were lined up in a row. Tàtaro picked one up and opened it. There was a handful of crimson glass chips of irregular shapes glowing inside.

"Can you make fakes?" Tàtaro asked.

Zoto swung his leg smugly. "I am the master of fakes."

"Then take these chips of colored glass, set them in quartz, and polish them properly."

"Leave it to me. In a few days you'll have a handful of Indian rubies that look so real, not even an expert jeweler will be able to tell the difference."

"We'll sell them to a merchant. In Alexandria, they can't tell an emerald from a piece of glass."

Zoto gulped contentedly, as though picturing the sumptuous meal that awaited him once he had completed the work.

"Now go, and come back soon with the stones and news."

Zoto skipped out of the foundry. Even his leg seemed happy.

He did not wait for the dawn. He had made his decision and perhaps that was the reason he felt strangely at one with the world. From under the plank, he removed the pages on optics he had copied out of the Alhazen and put them into the sack with his other belongings. They were his last hope. These theories seemed to him innovative and revolutionary, and perhaps they could help him find a solution for his ailing eyes. He clung to the sheets like a castaway to a raft. He moved slowly, with deliberate calm, to allow his mind to get used to the idea of what awaited him. When he closed the door of the cell behind him, Edgardo felt a dull pain in his chest, as though he had been kicked by a skittish horse.

There was an air of surreal peace hanging over the abbey. He paused in the cloister. The black outlines of the cypresses soaring into the sky like long spears seemed to have ceremoniously lined up to see him off. The tops bowed in the wind and Edgardo nodded his farewell in return.

As arranged, the boatman was waiting for him at the back of the island, at the far end of the wood.

"Have you found what I asked for?" Edgardo whispered.

"Yes, sir, I've got everything," the boatman replied, indicating a bundle in the bottom of the boat.

The ice had melted, leaving sodden streaks of muddy residue on the waters of the lagoon. With every stroke of the oar, a strange undertow seemed to drag the boat toward the abyss. As they moved farther away, it struck Edgardo that this would be his last journey from the island of Memmia.

As soon as they were in open water, almost in the middle of the Vigano canal, he ordered the boatman to stop. He stood up, making the gondola rock and slap the surface of the lagoon. He suddenly felt a moment of doubt, a sense of emptiness. He was hopeless, and afraid of the unknown world. Then he looked up at the sky, expecting a sign from heaven, absolving him of the sacrilegious act he was about to commit.

There was no comet with its luminous trail across the sky, no thunder or lightning, no divine voice. It was just him, alone, with his choice.

With a quick gesture, like the crack of a whip, he tore off his habit. He felt his skin burn and his heart swell. He was naked before the universe. Then he picked up from the bottom of the boat the bundle the boatman had brought him. Inside were a *garzone*'s clothes: a pair of large, torn breeches, a thick, coarse shirt, and a woolen cloak. He put on his new clothes with disgust. They stank of dried fish and were caked in mud. He completed his transformation with a woolen cap full of holes, which he pulled down on his forehead. With his fiery-red hair hidden under the hat and his fisherman's outfit, nobody would recognize him, not even Zoto. Dressed like that, he could walk around Venetia without running any danger.

He suddenly had an inexplicable feeling, as though his new identity had softened the deformities of his body. He touched the hump on his sternum. It was still there, cumbersome and knobbly.

The boatman was about to start rowing again.

"Wait," said Edgardo.

He bent down and picked up his old cleric's habit. The past, the mark of his life and faith. He lifted it up to the sky, then gently followed it down as he let it slide into the water, like a loving father teaching his offspring to swim.

The habit floated for a while, its color turning gradually dark as it soaked in water. The image of his life drifted away, undulating, then began to sink. Edgardo felt the water rise to his throat, a chill run down his limbs, and his belly stiffen with a painful cramp. He watched his past existence disappear beneath a pitch-black sea, dragged to the bottom by a demon's claws. The armor inside which he had hidden for so many years and the protection he had woven around himself—that of the learned cleric and expert scribe—had all ended up at the bottom of the lagoon.

Suddenly, he was a boy again, helplessly afraid, watching the strangers attacking his brother, once again tasting in his mouth the cowardice that froze his heart. He had made a choice and taken a step from which there was no turning back. He had abandoned his privileged position as copyist cleric, as the firstborn of a noble lineage. Now he was nothing. He had no protection and no family.

For a moment, he felt uneasy. Then the image of Kallis appeared before him, her mysterious eyes, her long fingers, and her body, thin as a thread of wool. A woman, a slave, had bewitched him with her magic arts and driven his soul to shake off the chain that had bound him for too long. He was afraid but, for the first time, he also felt free, ready to be born again. With Kallis near him? And Segrado? He did not have an answer to these questions but he felt that his soul was light, vibrating finely, and perhaps closer to God than before.

The boatman resumed his rowing, leaving the Vigano canal to the south and entering the mouth of Rivus Altus. The outlines of churches, monasteries, and rare stone buildings stood out like dark, eerie masses amid all the smaller and more fragile houses made of timber. The canal was deserted at that time of night. Edgardo noticed only a spot, far behind them, undulating in the night mist. Perhaps a small boat or a tree trunk adrift. They passed the church of San Samuele, where the bend of the canal was wider. Every so often, Edgardo would touch his clothes to become fully aware of his new identity.

They were approaching Rivoalto, where the boatman would leave him on the bank near the church. In the flicker of night shadows and his now uncertain, unfocused eyes, he saw a dark, imposing mass suddenly rise before them from the waters. It looked like a huge galley equipped with war machines, decks, and turrets. It stood sideways, touching both sides of the canal. Edgardo rose to his feet, and the gondola swerved to avoid it.

"Be careful, it's coming toward us!" he cried, alarmed.

The boatman laughed. "No, sir, it's we who are going toward it. It's the new bridge."

Edgardo blinked. Now even distant images seemed vague and without contours.

"The new bridge?"

"Wonderful, isn't it?"

He had seen construction start on it but could never have imagined such a magnificent piece of work. The dream of a future stretched between two islands to make them into a single piece of land, a united city.

Resting on raked piles that protruded from the shores, two sloping surfaces made of thick planks fixed snugly together and protected by parapets on the sides jutted into the center of the canal. The passage was as wide as a road, so as to enable a multitude of people, carts and horses to travel across it without risking falling into the water. In the middle, a space had been left, covered with walkways that opened and shut like a drawbridge, to allow ships with tall masts to pass.

Edgardo stopped to admire this wonderful work of ingenuity. At that moment, it seemed to him the symbol of a new beginning, the hope of the different life he was about to embark upon.

He paid the boatman, took his sack, and headed for the saltworks. He had no hope of finding anyone in the foundry, so would wait for Kallis to arrive. He had nothing now except her. He did not know where to seek shelter or sleep, and counted naively on her and Segrado's help.

He thought he heard a noise behind him. He looked around. In the labyrinth of alleys and *rios*, he did not see even the shadow of a bat. Fear creates ghosts and nonexistent voices. He had to remain calm. Not even Ademaro would recognize him dressed as he was. It was pleasant and comfortable to walk in those breeches; he felt more agile and relaxed. Even his bones seemed to appreciate the transformation.

He reached Segrado's foundry and was already about to

shelter in the mill warehouse when he noticed a glow filter through the beams of the wall. He approached. There was no sound. He walked around the foundry, looking for a chink so that he could see inside. Something creaked. Salt crystals that cracked with every step. The screech of an owl rippled the surface of the lagoon. The window was bolted and he pushed it, trying to move the shutter aside.

There was a hiss, like an arrow cutting through the wind, an arm around his neck, heavy panting, a hot breath on his cheek—and the tip of a blade pressing against his throat. Edgardo did not move.

D on't move or I'll cut your throat."
Edgardo held his breath. His muscles were petrified with fear.

"Who are you?" It was a thin, light voice he could not fail to recognize.

"It's me—Edgardo."

The grip loosened and the point of the blade was lowered. A hot smell of terror wafted from both bodies. Edgardo took off his cap. Kallis took a step back, panting.

"What happened? Why are you dressed like that?" She looked around suspiciously. "Let's go inside. It's safer."

The fire was still burning in the furnace and a weak light filtered through the mouth, projecting pale shadows on the walls. There were small spasms running across Kallis's face.

"I've left the abbey . . . forever."

Kallis looked at him in disbelief. "You've abandoned the habit? The library? Your books?"

"It's my books that abandoned me. And besides, nobody will recognize me dressed like this. I can walk around with no danger."

Kallis went to the furnace, shaking uncontrollably. "What will you do now? Where will you go?"

"I needed to see you. I couldn't wait any longer. My life as a cleric had no meaning anymore, my habit was just an unnecessary burden, and now I'm free . . . I left it all for you."

He put a hand on Kallis's face, which was ice-cold.

"Oh, no, please don't talk like that. I don't deserve your kindness. I'm nothing. Why did you do it?" Kallis was desperate. "There's nothing I can do for you. I'm not free . . . "

"We'll find a way, if you're willing."

"No, you don't understand, you don't know . . . my fate is sealed, while yours is linked to the abbey and to books. Go back, there's still time."

"God sent me a sign by taking away my eyesight. My life is at a crossroads and I must take a different path."

"It's not true. We'll find a remedy for your eyes. Segrado's made an extraordinary discovery . . . look."

Kallis took a knapsack out of the trunk and delicately unrolled the cloth with the oval sphere. It was limpid, transparent like springwater.

"It's crystalline glass. As pure as rock crystal but much more malleable and easy to work with."

Edgardo had never seen such perfect transparency. The crystal produced reflections so brilliant they were like painful darts in his eyes.

"It's as though it gives out its own light," Edgardo said in amazement.

"Do you still have the copy of the Arabic manuscript?" Kallis asked.

"Yes, I've brought it with me." He indicated the sack he had left lying by the door.

"I'm certain that with crystalline glass and the knowledge contained in the manuscript, Segrado will manage to create the eye stone you're looking for, then you'll be able to see again."

"Are you trying to get rid of me? Be honest. I understand. A poor cripple with no future and no trade . . . "

"You're wrong. It's not that. You don't understand . . . "

Kallis brushed his lips with the tips of her fingers. Edgardo took her hand and kissed it. She disengaged herself and, with growing agitation, ran out of the workshop.

The night air had frozen the sky into a mosaic of glittering tesserae. Everything looked false, like a mosaic background in the Basilica of San Marco: golden tesserae representing stars and a slice of yellow moon placed crookedly above the green expanse of the lagoon. Salt crystals were dancing, scattered in the basins. Edgardo joined Kallis, a thread of wool at the mercy of the forces of the universe.

"I didn't know it, and couldn't even picture it. I'd copied thousands of love poems by Greek and Latin poets, legends about lovers and men who'd lost their minds from missing their beloveds. And as I wrote, I tried to imagine these feelings, these emotions, the passion of the flesh. I'd fantasize but it never went any further than my quill. But now I know, because what I feel in my head and in my heart isn't just words. The yearning gnawing at my soul isn't made of ink, but is something much more powerful and at the same time simpler. It's a sudden blow of an ax on tender bark. A red-hot iron on the delicate skin of a newborn baby. An icy waterfall that makes your heart quiver. It's an explosion that spreads through your entire body, runs through your blood, muddles your mind, traverses your dreams, erases time, and blinds even those who, like me, have already been deprived of their eyesight. I don't want to give it a name because I'm afraid that if I discover its name, then it will go back to being just a word, just a sign on a sheet of parchment. Besides, it's not important that I know what it is because I'm so happy just to recognize it within me, to have every minute the proof that something exists—no matter what people choose to call it . . . So don't tell me anything, don't try to stop me, and don't chide me, because it was you that made this miracle explode and I cannot—I will not give up this supreme joy."

Edgardo put an arm around her waist. Kallis's chest shook with little starts: she was weeping. He gently wiped away her tears and brushed her lips.

The salt storehouse near the mill was full of hay for the horses. They took shelter there. Kallis took off her clothes, tearing them from her body as though time had suddenly broken into a run and at any moment their lives could speed out of control and end forever.

For the first time, Edgardo let his instinct guide him. His instinct—a force he did not know and which erased his thoughts, making him forget his fears and his hesitation, transporting him to a slow, never-ending fall into the void.

He saw Kallis's eyes widen and listened, bewitched, to the mysterious words she kept repeating in her incomprehensible language—words he imagined to be expressions of love for him.

When he reached supreme pleasure together with her, the climax broke apart, shattered into an illumination, an explosion of glowing slivers that carried body and mind to another world, other times, to a place of light where, for a moment, he thought he saw God.

He had never had such a mystical experience, not even during long nights at prayer in the cloister. Divine presence was manifesting itself through a woman's body, the very place where, he had always been taught, resided the origin of evil, sin, the devil. And now Kallis's body had become the house of God.

They were awakened by a relentless creaking and the sound of sails whipped by the wind. It was dawn and the mill was already in motion. They had fallen asleep, sunk in the hay, clasped in each other's arms. Kallis leapt to her feet and glanced at Edgardo. With that tousled red hair, white skin, and eyes so pale they were almost transparent, he looked like a mysterious forest creature from the Nordic moorlands.

She shook him. "Quick, let's go back to the foundry, the sun's up."

They sneaked out and ran to the workshop. The door was open.

"God have mercy!" Kallis exclaimed.

They approached cautiously. "Segrado is going to kill me," Kallis whispered.

They walked in. There was still a small fire burning in the furnace. Kallis rushed to the trunk. The knapsack was where she had left it, with the crystalline glass egg still inside.

"Thank you, God."

Edgardo looked around. Everything—tools and vases— seemed to be in its place. Only his sack was not where he remembered leaving it. He picked it up and untied it. The few things he had brought from the abbey, such as his clothes, were there. All that was missing was the copy of Alhazen's manuscript.

"The copy of the treatise on optics is gone," he said, agitated.

"You showed it to me last night," Kallis replied. "Perhaps it's outside."

"No, I put it back in the bag."

He rummaged again, halfheartedly. The copy had vanished. A strange, acidic smell came from the sack. It reminded him of someone, or perhaps of somewhere, but he could not form a concrete image.

"Nothing, nothing," he repeated, upset.

"Look among the tools, under the workbench," Kallis insisted.

Edgardo knelt on the floor and began moving planks, materials, and bags. There was a sheet—just one page. He picked it up and showed it to Kallis. "This is all that's left." It was the frontispiece, bearing the title of the book. "The rest is gone."

"How's that possible?" Kallis did not want to accept the truth.

"They stole it. Someone entered the foundry tonight . . . we left the door open." Edgardo's voice was cold and metallic, as though what had just happened did not concern him in the least.

"I don't understand," Kallis wondered. "They took your manuscript but left the glass behind."

"Whoever it was thought he'd found some secret formula. Who would be interested in that?" Edgardo was wracking his brain.

Kallis made a face. "The glassmakers all hate one another and steal secrets at every opportunity."

For a moment, they looked at each other like two strangers. Each was entertaining a secret thought. Then Kallis drew nearer.

"We mustn't tell Segrado anything. He left me here to guard the oven. The very thought that someone came in, even if nothing of his was stolen, and he'll lose his mind . . . When he gets like that, he doesn't think. He becomes crazy and very violent."

Kallis's eyes narrowed so much they practically disappeared, as though trying to set fire to an image from long, long ago.

"We won't say anything." Edgardo tried to calm her, while staring blankly at the only remaining page of the treatise. "This is absurd. Every time I seem to get close to the possibility of finding a remedy for my eyes, something happens to take it away. It's very clear. It's pointless to persist. The era of words, books, seclusion, libraries, and solitude is over." He looked at his scruffy clothes. "A new era awaits me, and I don't yet know where it will take me." He smiled at Kallis. "Do you know?"

She stroked his hair and held him in a tight, almost masculine hug. "You must go now. Segrado mustn't find you here when he comes. Nobody will recognize you in these clothes, not even Zoto."

Only then did Egardo realize that he had nowhere to take refuge, eat, or sleep. "I have nowhere to go," he said, naively.

She looked around, puzzled, then collected herself. "Go to

San Pietro, in Olivolo. In the courtyard of the archbishopric, there's a shelter for pilgrims and beggars. You can take refuge there for the time being, then we'll try to find you somewhere in Metamauco. I'll talk to Segrado."

"So you don't want me to leave?" Edgardo asked, hopefully.

She bowed her head. "I no longer know what's right. I can't read what's in my soul anymore . . . It's like there's fog everywhere around."

"Let's hope for a strong mistral wind to blow it away, so that the light can shine over us again."

"Now hurry, go!" Kallis held him back by the arm. "No, wait." She kissed him gently, with a light breath that had a hint of sadness in it. "I'll come and get you. Don't budge from there."

Edgardo picked up his sack, pulled the cap down on his forehead, and walked out into the blinding light of the saltworks.

The ice had melted and trade had fully resumed at the dock. Even so, a feeling of anxiety and uncertainty had spread among the people because of the extreme climatic changes and prodigious recent events—the feeling that some catastrophe or other could befall the city and its defenseless population at any moment, be it a famine, a sudden attack by pirates, or a plague epidemic. Nobody spoke about it openly, but rumors circulated from one district to another, playing on everyone's nerves.

Segrado left the *scaula* on Rio Bataro and walked purposefully toward the basilica. He had sworn it and now that he had achieved his dream, it was time to keep his promise. He walked into the narthex of Sant'Alipio. Inside, embellishment work was in full swing. The mosaic floors were not finished yet and painters were decorating the walls with frescoes representing episodes from the Bible. He approached the presbytery. In the apse, the mosaic artists were composing the figures of the patron saints of Venetia: Saint Nicholas, Saint Mark, and Saint Ermagora.

Maestro Segrado kneeled before the high altar and bowed his head.

"Thank you, Oh Lord, for allowing me back into Your flock. To You I dedicate the pure glass that I have created. Now I know You have forgiven me the terrible crime I committed. By removing all impurity from my glass, You've given me a sign that my soul is also pure and crystal-clear again, and that all the stains have been washed away. For that, I will never cease to give thanks."

He looked up at a corbel where a large, rudimentary cruet was displayed. It was made of green, opaque glass and contained a dark, thick substance.

"You know that, many years ago, I took a vow: that if I managed to create pure crystalline glass, I would dedicate my first piece of work to You, Lord. This second-rate cruet is not worthy to contain Your blood. I will make a cruet for You out of the purest, most transparent glass, so that all the faithful may honor and admire Your holy relic."

Segrado made the sign of the cross and stood up.

As he left the basilica, a gust of wind suddenly slapped him across the face, like a whip. Segrado smiled. God had forgiven him.

He got down to work as soon as he reached the workshop. He ordered Kallis to rekindle the fire in the furnace, and bolted the door and the windows. He felt full of creative energy. His head hurt and his temples throbbed, as though the form he was trying to give his new creation was pushing forth, trying to find a way to be born into this world. He had to find a design for the cruet that was worthy of the substance it would contain, and he wanted to create something unique and amazing. A specimen everybody would admire as the masterpiece of the most illustrious glassmaker in Venice: Angelo Segrado.

Kallis watched him, holding her breath, as he fussed around preparing the tools and measuring out the ingredients. She knew that when he was in that state, even one wrong gesture could unleash a violent burst of anger, so she kept to a corner, waiting for orders.

Segrado was like a lion in a cage. He took a piece of charcoal and began drawing sketches on the bench. A chalice with arabesques, a cup with spiral handles, a cruet adorned with a subtle filigree. Suddenly, he stopped, as though struck by a bolt of lightning.

"What a dumb animal, what a shit-eating birdbrain full of hot air and arrogance!" he exclaimed.

Kallis looked at him, surprised.

"I mustn't go shooting my mouth off to the world about how wonderful my art is!" he shouted. "It's not I but Jesus Christ, our Lord, who should be praised through His blood. No pilgrim should say, 'This is Maestro Segrado's splendid glass,' but 'This is the blood of Christ.' So no inscriptions, settings or floral patterns. None of that! I will make a receptacle that's simple, basic, and clean. Its uniqueness will lie in its purity, the transparency of the glass that'll be so fine and clear it will seem invisible. Everybody will have to reach out and touch it to make sure it's real. A plain cylinder, with a dome-shaped lid—like our basilica." He signaled to Kallis. "Come on, move, prepare the pebbles, get to work, I don't want to waste any time."

Kallis collected the already crushed pebbles and put them into the mortar, to pestle them finely. Segrado took Levantine soda ash—the best—that came directly from Syria, and threw it into water, which was ready and boiling on the fire. Kallis waited for the opportune moment, when Segrado looked calmer.

"The cleric—the copyist—came by." The maestro did not seem to hear her. "He almost can't see anymore, so he can't read or copy." Kallis sighed. "He's left the abbey, cast off his habit . . . and they stole the Arabic manuscript from him—the one he'd copied . . . "

The maestro stopped working. "Does this mean he has no more hope for his eye stones?"

Kallis nodded. "He's got nowhere to go. He's in San Pietro now. I was thinking perhaps we could find him shelter in Metamauco, maybe even work."

"And who'd want a blind man?" Segrado said.

"He can write . . . "

"A copyist with no eyes is like a glassmaker with no hands . . . Still, nobody's ever been refused a bowl of soup at Segrado's house."

Kallis blinked, satisfied. She was about to collect the powdered pebbles in the silk sieve when a muffled thud made her jump. Segrado darted to the door and flung it open. At first, he did not notice anything untoward, but then he heard footsteps and rushed to the back just in time to see Zoto walking away, dragging his short leg. Segrado caught up with him and fell on him from behind, pushing him to the ground.

"What were you doing, you evil creature?" he shouted. "Spying on me?"

"Let go of me, you stinking bear, I was spying the air from your ass."

Zoto was struggling on the ground like an overturned tortoise, but Segrado's bulk prevented him from moving.

"Talk! What did you see? Tell me the truth or I'll tear your eyes out!"

"I saw nothing, I swear. Only a toothless beast spitting in my face."

"Who told you to spy on me? Tàtaro? Confess, you son of a bitch."

"You're making a mistake. Let go of me."

"I'll make you swallow your tongue, you asshole!" He pressed down on Zoto's neck with all his strength, squeezing with his steely hands. Zoto started to cough.

"Let him go, Angelo, you're killing him!" Kallis was watching the scene but did not dare intervene.

"It's what he deserves."

Segrado kept squeezing. Zoto's face had turned purple, like the lagoon on a summer's evening.

"Think about the work you have to do. You'll get into trouble," Kallis shouted.

For a moment, Segrado hesitated, then released his grip. Zoto leaned on his side, vomiting violently.

"Thank the girl," he said. "And don't ever come back to my foundry."

Zoto was still coughing. "This is my foundry, or have you forgotten? Well, you can kiss it goodbye and go find yourself another one. I'm the one who doesn't want you around anymore."

"I don't believe you find my money repulsive."

"I don't need your charity. Tàtaro is willing to buy my oven even now." Zoto got unsteadily to his feet. "So what, cat got your tongue? You're full of shit, you old fool. You've ruined yourself with your own hands. Get out of my foundry. Out!" he shouted.

Kallis took Segrado by the arm and dragged him to the workshop. His anger had gotten the better of him and, once again, he had lost control. It was not a good thing. Now he risked being left without an oven just when he had to complete his most important piece of work.

XXIV
BLOOD GRASS

After he left Kallis, Edgardo felt terribly lost. His day, always punctuated by prayers, work, and religious tasks, suddenly felt like a useless desert.

It was Terce and he still had a lot of time before going to spend the night at the shelter in San Pietro. Trying to organize his thoughts, he roamed around the city without a specific destination, letting chance lead him. He ventured into districts he had never been to before, and felt as though the landscape was changing before his eyes, assuming twisted, surreal forms: increasingly dark, narrow *calli*, winding paths that stank like sewers, overrun by rats and all kinds of insects. The walls of the houses, corroded by mold and salt, leaned forward toward him, barring the way, while their crooked roofs protruded until they almost touched others across the path, stifling what little light came from the gray sky.

He felt as though these crumbling buildings, thus suspended, could come crashing down on him at any minute. And all around, like a crazy merry-go-round, *rios* flowed, canals intersected, merged and vanished amid shoals, into senseless labyrinths crossed by rickety bridges that also barely stayed up. Up above, the sky was smoky and so low, you could almost touch it with your finger.

"Mind those rafts, you stupid canker," a boatman cursed, threatening him with an oar.

Edgardo had unwittingly upset sacks of savoy cabbage stacked up on the bank of a canal.

"Shit-face, freak, fool . . . " The man kept insulting him without restraint.

Edgardo realized how uncertain and vulnerable his position now was. Since he was not wearing the clerical habit, even the humblest of people could get away with insulting him and perhaps even attacking him without risking any punishment. The habit he had chosen many years earlier to escape his own cowardice had been the knightly armor he had not had the courage to wear.

He was alone, naked, unprotected, hurled into an adverse world against which nobody had taught him to fight. He would not last long. Perhaps he still had time to go back, return to Bobbio, or retreat to his father's house where he would be received as a loser, a failure who had not been able to succeed even as a cleric.

And give up Kallis forever? The thought was unbearable. Was it for her sake that he had taken this drastic decision? For the love of her? Love: there, he had uttered the word softly to himself, in a whisper. Did he love Kallis to the point of renouncing everything? Was his desire powerful enough to erase all reason, all caution? He did not even know if his love was reciprocated. He had lain with her but perhaps that did not mean much . . . What then? Was he so sure of his love that it was enough per se?

The sun was already setting when he reached San Pietro on the island of Olivolo. He was hungry and his torn clothes did not shield him from the cold like the monk's habit. In the *campo* outside the patriarchal palace, there was a gathering of paupers, beggars, and lepers awaiting the distribution of food. Edgardo cautiously approached.

Given his simple clothes, his resigned demeanor, and the hump protruding beneath his jacket, his presence should not arouse suspicion here. Nonetheless, a few ragamuffins scowled at him, giving him surly looks. After all, he was another mouth to feed and would take food away from them.

Edgardo the Crooked. Never before had that nickname seemed so appropriate and even useful. His misshapen body certainly did not stick out in that multitude of outcasts.

He thought about the convenient abbey refectory, the safe refuge of the scriptorium, the silence of the cloisters, and felt a deep nostalgia.

A novice opened the gates of the archbishopric and invited them in. A shudder rippled through the crowd, which got up, shook itself, and rushed toward the entrance.

Ever since his eyesight had started to fail, he had noticed an increase in his ability to perceive smells and sounds, as though his other senses wished to compensate for the lack of the main one. As he joined the crowd, Edgardo realized that emaciated, infected human flesh gave off a putrid, revolting smell that enveloped everything in a deathly embrace.

Inside, there was a wide cloister with a grassy courtyard in the middle, surrounded by a portico. The beggars stood in line, waiting their turn. A cook, assisted by two *garzoni*, arrived with a huge pan and began dishing out the meal.

From the eldest son of a noble family, to a cleric, to a lowly beggar. It had been a ruinous, inexorable fall.

He took the bowl full of a soup that stank of fish guts probably stolen from the cats, and sat in a corner on the ground. He was hungry and, after a few mouthfuls, got used to the nauseating smell.

After the meal, everybody lay down on the ground, on top of heaps of reed leaves that had been scattered along the walls of the portico, huddling in the few rags they had brought with them. Edgardo found a niche near the front gate, and made himself as comfortable as he could. By now it was dark. There were laments, mumbled words, meaningless phrases, prayers: the polyphonic song of a wretched, suffering humanity resounded beneath the cloister vaults, mixed with the pungent smell of despair, the fight for survival, wounds that never healed, the regurgitations of insatiable hunger, and of death as a daily companion. He now had a place among men: those who were poor, lonely, and abandoned.

"Blood grass has sprung in the lagoon!" a little boy cried, running across the vegetable garden.

It was true. Overnight, a kind of grass nobody had ever seen before had grown on the water. It was slippery, limp, and of a dark-ruby color. Sailors said it had come from the sea, brought in by the tide, while fishermen claimed it originated from deeper in the lagoon, near the mouths of the rivers.

In any case, that blood-red cloak was advancing inexorably, covering the surface of the water in the bay of San Marco and in the Vigano canal, and was beginning to spread along the whole of the Rivus Altus. A gluey mush that stuck to keels, oars, and ropes, making it difficult for boats to move.

At other times, Venetians had seen their sea invaded by green algae, undulating beneath the surface, but never in such large quantities and of that dark red color that resembled coagulated blood. Some boatmen had even said that when they immersed their hands to free their oars from the strings of vegetation, they thought the water was much warmer than usual for the season. It was a strange kind of broth, like soup just taken off the fire.

Following the exceptional frost, this sudden appearance of grass in midwinter only contributed to the growth of people's fear of extraordinary events. Many were now talking openly of signs, omens of an imminent catastrophe that would strike the city. So much so that Doge Falier had considered it appropriate to pacify his people with a public declaration outside the basilica, promising to organize a procession as soon as possible to beg God's forgiveness for all their sins.

That morning, something else added to the deep anxiety that had crept into people's minds. It was the horror of another murder in a case considered closed.

Near the new bridge, lying on a bed of blood grass, floated the stocky, squat body of Zoto, the crystal-maker.

The boatmen who had found him at dawn had first assumed it was a drunk who had fallen in the water and drowned because of the slippery mass. However, when they pulled him out, they realized that his death had not just been a trick of fate. His eyes had been gouged out with a spoon, and the sockets filled with the usual glass castings.

What had made an even deeper impression on the onlookers was that there was an extremely pure light shining from the depths of the hollows, as though precious gemstones had been set instead of the eyeballs. A light that seemed to possess the power to read one's innermost thoughts.

The rumor had quickly spread and many had come running. One thing was certain: the eye murderer had claimed another victim.

Karamago, the merchant, considered guilty and executed, was innocent, and, by an absurd coincidence, the new victim was Zoto, his accuser.

The tribune, who in the meantime had suspended his inquiry, would have to start afresh, although everybody knew that a new culprit would never be found. Many believed that the eye murderer was protected by a devilish power that would safeguard him from any punishment. Thus, this terrible event drifted away from the human dimension and into the realm of the supernatural, and was added to other ill omens that had manifested themselves in Venetia in recent months.

Segrado seemed possessed by a kind of fever, an uncontrollable frenzy. He had to finish the crystalline glass cruet as soon as possible, as though his life was slipping away through his fingers.

Kallis had fallen asleep on a mat on the floor, behind the furnace. They had worked all night but the maestro was not satisfied. After many attempts, adding and subtracting the powder of manganese, he had not yet succeeded in achieving the limpidity the container of Christ's blood deserved.

He had blown a cylinder tapered at the top, a little dome-shaped lid, and another cylinder he would then weld to the base. Yet he was not satisfied. There was always an imperceptible imperfection. A bubble almost invisible to the naked eye had marred the piece. Also, the transparency was not as he had imagined it. He had to start from scratch.

He was exhausted. He lay down next to Kallis and closed his eyes. A vision penetrated his restless sleep. Rays of light, like incandescent swords, were coming down on him, piercing him through. Yet he felt no pain but, on the contrary, a sense of immense bliss.

A hard knock echoed through his head, and he shook himself. He had only slept for a few moments but it felt like days. Someone was knocking at the door. He staggered to his feet, shook his head to get rid of the fragments of light that were still vibrating before his eyes, and went to open the door automatically, forgetting all caution. In the opalescent morning light, blinded by the glare from the saltworks, he did not recognize the person at the door straight away.

"I want to talk with you." It was Tàtaro. His voice was hoarse, and his skin even drier and more wrinkled.

Segrado immediately closed the door behind him and carefully walked away from the foundry. "What do you want?"

"They've found Zoto, the crystal-maker, murdered." Tàtaro stared at him with a prying expression. Segrado grimaced.

"Don't feign surprise, Segrado. We know it was you who gouged out his eyes."

"What are you saying, you canker? I haven't gouged anybody's eyes out."

A kind of sob, like a gurgle, rose from Tàtaro's stomach. "Zoto threatened to take the oven away from you. You were seen attacking him."

"He was a Barabbas. He would have butchered his own mother for a handful of coins."

"I could tell everything to the tribune," Tàtaro hissed.

With a swipe of his paw, Segrado grabbed him by the cloak and pulled him toward him. He stank of spice and onions.

"It was you who killed Niccolò," Segrado growled. "If you want to denounce me, I'm ready to fight."

"Wait, let's say . . . that nobody saw anything."

Segrado relaxed his grip.

"I don't care about that cripple, his place is in hell. However, the situation has changed now. Zoto's foundry will go up for sale, and I could use it."

As he spoke, Tàtaro took a few steps toward the saltworks and, for a moment, remained silent, watching the men at work. Segrado was trying to read his intentions.

"It's time we stopped fighting," Tàtaro continued. "It doesn't serve either of us well. Together, we could reach the top. With our knowledge, working side by side, we'll become the richest and most powerful glassmakers in Venetia."

Segrado had never heard Tàtaro speak like that. "I've already told you, I'm not prepared to work under you."

Tàtaro leaned sideways, spread open his arms, and gave a small smile. "No, you don't understand!" he said. "We'll start a partnership. We'll go halves to buy this oven and join forces. We're the same, Segrado. You've always known that, ever since we were *garzoni.* We both want to rise to the top."

Segrado wondered what was happening. Why this sudden change? Was Tàtaro asking him to become a partner? Even yesterday, that would have been unthinkable.

Maybe he had heard something about the crystalline glass. Perhaps, before dying, Zoto had talked, and now Tàtaro was seeking an alliance in order to exploit his discovery. He saw that Tàtaro was breathing heavily, exhausted, as though what he had just said had cost him a huge effort. He had him in his hands. After enduring a thousand humiliations, Tàtaro was now proposing an alliance, begging him to work together as equals.

Segrado could not help emitting a smug growl. He picked a few salt crystals from the ground and rolled them in the palm of his hand.

"So, what do you think?"

"You see, Tàtaro, it's not true to say that we're the same." Segrado's tone was one of triumph. "It's true that we both want to rise to the top, but for you, the top represents power and wealth. For me, it's to go beyond what's imaginable, to achieve the impossible, to seek perfection. We could never work together. You've got your eyes on the ground, and I on the sky. I don't need you. I've achieved what I wanted." He stared into his eyes. "What I've discovered will change the course of glass-making history and nothing will ever be the same again . . . Just accept it. Your era is over."

Tàtaro bent forward, as though resisting a strong gust of wind, then wet his pale lips to gather his strength. "You're committing the sin of pride, Segrado. You're defying God. Remember that the punishment of the Almighty falls suddenly and unexpectedly on those who think they're above everybody else. Do you want to remain alone? It's your prerogative, but remember, death falls like an ax when you least expect it . . . and then what will become of your discovery? Nothing." Tàtaro regurgitated a hollow laugh from his stomach. "You haven't thought of that, Segrado, have you? It's death that decides everything. She is queen, while we're nothing. Think about it, Segrado, think."

Tàtaro peered into his chest with his tiny, snake eyes, then did a pirouette and, gurgling to himself, walked away with small, tired steps.

*

He was awoken by splatters of rain wetting his face, and by an unbearable stench of urine. An old man was pissing just inches away from his face. Edgardo jumped to his feet, wrapped himself in his cloak, and spat on the ground.

In the morning mist, he made out a heap of bodies, massed like worms under the portico, tight and jammed atop one another. Some were pushing, looking for a space, while others were standing and relieving themselves without any shame. A whiff of stench suddenly took his breath away and almost made him vomit.

His sense of smell had become so sharp, it exposed his body to violent transformation. He was growing sensitive to every exhalation, and was now able to recognize the most different varieties of hidden smells. Beneath the cloak which, like a blanket, enveloped this humanity made up of outcasts, mixed together in a nauseating eddy, he could smell the rancid sweat permanently embedded in the beggars' rags, the rot of the lepers' festering wounds, the steaming excrement laid in the laurel bushes, an imperceptible scent of incense escaping from the church, the burps smelling of fish digested the night before, and especially, overlaid on top of everything else, the sulphurous miasma carried by the winds from the lagoon.

He tried to shake himself and looked around for a well to get some fresh water. Many beggars had already formed a line for the food. He could not bear the thought of that disgusting soup again. He rummaged in his bag. He still had a little money. Perhaps he could buy a piece of goat cheese and some barley bread in the *campo*. He left the courtyard and headed toward the canal, in search of a shop. His hip bones were aching and a sharp pain shot through his back with every step he took.

He tried to organize his thoughts. What should he do next? He could not keep living like this. Kallis had told him to wait.

But what if she had forgotten about him? He had to make a decision.

He was thinking when someone knocked him violently to the ground. A body weighed on top of him, stinking of vomit. He was struck in the ear, in the nose. There was a sound of bones, and the taste of blood. Paralyzed with fear, he curled up, trying to shield himself from the increasingly hard blows on his back and head.

"Pull out the money . . . The money . . . Get it out."

He thought it was the end of him. A beggar murdered for a few coins. It happened every day. Then he heard screaming, the blows became less frequent until they stopped, and he heard footsteps hurrying away.

"He ran away . . . he ran away . . . There's no more danger."

A hand was placed on his aching shoulder. "Can you get up?"

Edgardo opened his eyes. Through his tears, he recognized a monk's habit. He slowly raised his head, thinking it was a vision, a miracle sent by God. "My friend . . . " he whispered.

Ademaro took a step back. At first, he did not recognize him, it couldn't be him: dressed like a beggar, his beard overgrown, and his tousled hair caked with salt.

"Merciful God . . . Edgardo."

Edgardo gave a crooked smile. The best he could do with a split lip.

"Go and fetch some water," Ademaro ordered the monk who was with him.

Edgardo recognized Rainardo, the young novice to whom he had given writing lessons. Ademaro helped him to his feet and supported him as far as a boat abandoned on the bank.

"Sit here." He began dabbing his wounds with the edge of his cowl. "How is this possible? In such a state . . . What happened to you, my friend?" He shook his head, an afflicted expression on his face. "Why are you here? I thought you were already in Bobbio."

Edgardo struggled to find the right words, since he was not sure why he was there either. "We shared a path for a while, Ademaro. We had moments of brotherhood and joyous spirituality. But now, my life has taken a different turn. I still don't know where I'm going, but I couldn't lie to myself any longer. The abbey was no more than a safe haven, and perhaps it has been the same for writing. The time has come for me to throw myself into the world."

Ademaro did not seem to understand. "What about the habit, the books, the monastery?"

"Away with it all. I must start from the beginning. I must confront myself and my fears."

"How will you manage on your own, without any support? As you can see, you could be attacked at any moment."

"I'll learn to defend myself."

Ademaro was not reassured. "Listen, my friend. I've just taken my leave of the Archbishop. We're returning to Bobbio. The novice is coming with me. Join us."

"I'm happy that he's taken my place. This way you won't be alone."

"I can't leave you like this."

"Don't worry about me. God will show me the way."

Rainardo came running back with a carafe full of water, and leaned toward Edgardo, offering him a drink. He took a long, restorative sip. He washed his face and wet his hair. The novice was about to step back.

"Wait. Another sip."

He took him by the sleeve, and Rainardo handed him the carafe once more. Edgardo sniffed it. It was a subtle thread of smells stirring memories and images. Where had he smelled that particular odor before? He breathed it in once again, as deeply as he could.

It came back in a flash. Cabbage and gum arabic. The boy stank of cabbage and gum arabic. It was the blend used for making ink. A common smell in scriptoriums, but Edgardo remembered smelling it somewhere else, recently.

"You have a familiar odor, boy."

"We all have this odor in the scriptorium. It's ink."

"Yes, I know it well. It's a unique smell, and, in fact, I was wondering how come I'd recently smelled it in the foundry of a master glassmaker, while I was bent over my sack, looking among my belongings." He stopped and stared at Ademaro. "Looking for the copy of a manuscript that had been stolen from me."

The novice got up abruptly and gave Ademaro an imploring look. The latter did not move.

"My friend, do you have an explanation for this strange coincidence?" Edgardo said.

Ademaro bowed his head, as though overwhelmed by deathly weariness.

Time froze like a marble bas-relief. Two stone figures, focused on their individual remorse, awaiting the truth, saw memories of their strong friendship flash before their eyes, with its struggles, its pains, its mutual joys, faith, and passion for writing and knowledge.

"No more obscure answers, tell me the truth, Ademaro."

Edgardo's voice sounded deeply afflicted. Ademaro looked up at the sky, searching for a gash of blue among the low, level clouds. Rainardo took a step back, as though to make room for a clash between the two friends.

"You're right. The time for lies has ended." He approached Edgardo and sat down next to him. He looked at the novice. "That night, Rainardo caught you in the library and tried to stop you. He didn't recognize you, so he started investigating and found that Alhazen's manuscript was in the wrong place, which meant that someone had secretly read it, and perhaps even copied it. He had a few suspicions about you but, not wishing to harm you, instead of telling the abbot immediately, he confided in me. I firmly denied your involvement, knowing you would never have committed an act against the rules of the abbey, and that you were perfectly aware that no book could leave the library without the abbot's permission. Rainardo wasn't so sure, and said that, if I agreed, he'd investigate on his own. I allowed him. The issue was so serious that no stone could be left unturned. He tried many times to discover if you were really involved, and if you were hiding a copy of the manuscript. He followed you to Venetia, to check if you frequented characters of ill repute. He searched the foundry of that master glassmaker to see if you had hidden the copy there, but found nothing. He also looked in your cell, but with no success. However, he did discover a quill, ink, and sheets of parchment, so his suspicion that somehow you were guilty grew stronger. The other night, when you announced that you were returning to Bobbio, Rainardo thought that if you'd made a copy, you'd take it away with you. So he followed you . . . " Ademaro tried to meet his friend's eye. "He was right. He said he found it in your sack, and that it wasn't difficult to get it back."

Edgardo had been listening with his head bowed, his blood dripping onto the dust. "Yes, it's true. I made a copy of the one chapter from Alhazen's book. It could have been of immense help in creating the eye stone. That's the only reason I did it. It was you yourself who brought me here to try to find a remedy for my ailment . . . " Edgardo raised his head with a sudden burst of energy. "But tell me, Ademaro, why was it so important to get back the copy of the manuscript? Why wasn't it supposed to leave the abbey?"

Ademaro stiffened, and assumed a cold, didactic expression. "A copy of *that* manuscript!"

"So then you knew the contents of Alhazen's treatise."

The flap of a seagull's wings cut through the silence that had descended between the two friends.

"I remember that when I asked you," Edgardo continued, "you said you knew nothing about books on optics."

"When we came to Venetia, I didn't know what Ermanno di Carinzia was translating. It's always like that. It's only after I arrive that I'm informed of the situation."

Edgardo could not understand his friend's logic, and some of his points seemed obscure. "What do you mean by 'I'm informed of the situation'?"

Ademaro sighed. He had gone too far.

"Explain it to me," Edgardo insisted.

Ademaro looked at his friend, reduced to a miserable state, bleeding and wearing torn clothes, seemingly a cause lost forever. "After we arrived, Abbot Carimanno showed me the manuscripts that, in his opinion, had to be protected. Alhazen's *De Aspectibus* was among them."

Edgardo's agitation grew with every word. "Protected from whom? Me?" he asked with involuntary defiance in his voice.

Ademaro leapt to his feet, annoyed. "Surely you don't think that we can circulate freely all the books that come from Greece and the Orient? We must make a selection, read them, evaluate them, and make a choice. Would you have humanity indiscriminately given dangerous theories and blasphemies that could subvert all the rules and undermine the foundations of Christianity?"

Edgardo looked at him, stunned. "And so you . . . "

"It's a task that carries heavy responsibilities. It's not easy to choose. You're often tormented by doubts. Fortunately, divine light shows you the way . . . I'm proud to have been chosen for this task, which I perform in all humility."

Edgardo closed his eyes, struggling to understand. "But these 'protected' manuscripts, as you call them—what happens to them?"

"Well, they're certainly not destroyed. Whatever else, knowledge is sacred. We collect them at Bobbio Abbey, store them apart, and shield them from prying eyes. If they were spread throughout the libraries of other abbeys, we would have no control over them, and knowledge would then circulate freely."

"But this way, you and a handful of others decide what it's right to allow people to read, and what to transmit to scholars and wise men?"

"It's natural that it should be so. It's the only way to safeguard knowledge." Ademaro was so certain, so decided. Edgardo almost envied him.

"So why is Alhazen's manuscript considered dangerous? I don't understand."

Ademaro exchanged glances with Rainardo, a look of complicity between two followers of the same sect. "All our certainties, the pillars of our faith, are based on the words of the Fathers. Our strength lies in transmitting a heritage that is immutable. Anything new could turn out to be dangerous and subversive to order. Everything we need to know has been passed on to us by Aristotle and Saint Augustine. Anyone who questions the knowledge of our Fathers is a threat to the social and political order. Anyone convinced that the horizons of our knowledge can be widened and that there are unexplored fields, new worlds to be discovered, is the incarnation of absolute evil. As Saint Augustine teaches us, the soul can reach the world of eternal truths only if it's 'enlightened' by God. Divine enlightenment creates a process of indirect enlightenment where the soul 'sees' eternal truths, and, through these, can judge everything else. In his treatise, however, Alhazen introduces the concept that the reading of empirical reality can happen only through experimentation. Our great Aristotle has already answered all possible questions, so there's no point in experimenting. *De Aspectibus* is a collection of observations from which the scholar draws a series of conclusions. According to Alhazen, only eyesight allows belief, so demonstration is fundamental. If one followed this path, one would end up subverting the primacy of the word, and of hearing. We'd then go from the primacy of the mind, of writing, to visual proof, which is deceptive and transient. According to his theories, God created a little-known, mysterious world that man can investigate. This way, Alhazen no longer relies on conceptual experiments, but on the observation of nature by means of instruments that can only create false knowledge, lies, and distortions—just like his experiments with refraction. So, Edgardo, do you understand what a danger such a book represents for our survival? The spreading of his principles would mean the end of knowledge."

Ademaro spoke so heatedly that his expression, and even his bearing, had altered beyond recognition. He looked possessed. Edgardo felt deeply sorry for him.

"And you didn't care if that meant sacrificing the possibility of saving the eyesight of a friend?"

"Edgardo, Edgardo . . . " Ademaro suddenly threw his arms around him. "Saving humanity is much more important than the small misfortune of an individual—surely you understand that."

"That's as it should be."

"Come back to Bobbio with us, I beg you. Now that you know everything, you'll live with greater awareness. Your life is in the library, among manuscripts . . . "

Edgardo disengaged himself from the hug. "I can't, Ademaro. Not because I harbor any resentment toward you. I know you've acted according to your conscience, thinking you were in the right. But, you see, I couldn't go back to the past. All those books I copied for years with great pain and love have been consigned to the library, and now I know that maybe nobody will ever read them, and they will be shut away forever . . . So my work has been useless. I wanted to divulge it, to spread it, while you want to hide it and keep it a secret. No, not even as a blind man could I ever again live by your side."

Clouds parted in the sky and the wind rippled the lagoon. A thousand years and many lifetimes passed by, and the shell that protected the souls of the two friends broke. A vortex swept away all memories, all hope, all illusion of a return. Their spirits were now irremediably divided.

"Now go," Edgardo said. He felt no resentment, only deep sadness.

Ademaro smiled benevolently. "One day you'll understand."

"No, I don't think so. I'm not that wise. I'm just a scribe . . . "

Ademaro raised his hand, as though about to bless him, but stopped himself. Edgardo followed him as he walked away with Rainardo. That boy had the same way of walking as Edgardo. Only he was less crooked.

XXVI

The Feast of Marys

They came from Luprio, Rivoalto, the Gemine islands, Dorsoduro, Canaleclo, the castle of Olivolo, Spinalunga, Amurianum, and even from Torcellus, Burianum, Majurbum, Aymanas, and Costanciacum. By gondola, *scaula*, or freight boat. On horseback or on foot. They had started off early in the morning in order to secure the best spots in Campo Santa Maria Formosa. It was the day after the February calends, the celebration of the Feast of Marys—for Venetians, the most important feast day outside the *Sposalizio*, the ceremony of marriage to the sea, on Ascension Day.

Edgardo had followed the crowd of beggars that had moved from San Pietro, determined to find Kallis at the foundry. A whole day had passed and he had not had news from her. She had said that she would come and get him. Instead, she had disappeared. Still, it was now very evident to him that his future was inextricably bound to hers.

Campo Santa Maria Formosa was heaving with people. The residents of all the districts, recognizable from the distinct colors of their garb, made up a colorful, joyous crowd bobbing like a storm-tossed sea.

Edgardo let himself be carried by the progression of celebrating citizens. It was how he felt in his heart—buffeted about by an unknown destiny. It was a sinister kind of pleasure to throw all caution to the wind and let himself drift toward an unforeseeable end.

When he heard his name shouted amid the confusion of

voices, children's shrieks and drunken racket, he thought he was hallucinating.

"Edgardo! Edgardo!"

He looked around, incredulous, not recognizing anybody's face in the out-of-focus mass fluctuating around him. He tried to push his way through. "Edgardo! Here!" It sounded like Kallis. Carried by the flow, he could not find anywhere to dock when a sudden wave threw him far out, sent him drifting out toward the edge of familiar waters.

Everything in his mind was a blur: childhood memories, the ambush in the forest, the taste of Kallis's lips, the smell of ink. A magma spinning at vertiginous speed. Then a hand seized him powerfully, and dragged him back to the shore. At first, the body seemed to him like a shadow with no contours, a projection of his desire.

"I looked for you in San Pietro but everyone had gone, so I thought perhaps you'd also gone to the Feast of Marys with the others."

Kallis was smiling at him. Edgardo caressed her face. She was real, she was flesh and blood.

"I've spoken with Segrado and he's willing to find you a place in Metamauco." She was happy. "Look, the twelve brides!" she said, pointing at the procession approaching the church. She was excited, inquisitive as a child.

Dressed in white, crowned by rose wreaths, adorned with gold, diamonds and pearls, long veils cascading from their heads down to their arms, wrapped in a cloud of incense, and lit by the rays of the dawn, the twelve young girls entered the church, which was decorated with myrtle and flower festoons.

Doge Falier arrived on horseback, followed by his court and by a group of children dressed as angels, who accompanied him to the sound of portative organs strapped to their waists with belts. He was greeted at the entrance by the parish priest, who welcomed him on behalf of the faithful. The Doge thanked him, walked through the church between two rows of kneeling crowds, and went to sit on the throne that had been placed at the high altar.

The scent from the thuribles blended with the fragrance of violets. The young women kneeled next to the bridegrooms who awaited them in the presbytery. A hydraulic organ intoned a concerto and the clergy sitting on high-backed chairs started chanting. Then the bishop stood up from the faldstool and the ceremony began.

Kallis followed every move attentively, engrossed, a child-like smile on her face. Fascinated, Edgardo could not help watching her. A new Kallis was standing next to him. A young, frail-looking girl the same age as those maidens, enchanted by all the ornaments, the gilding, the music, and the singing. Edgardo wanted to hug her, cover her with kisses, proclaim his love for her in front of all those present. He drew so close he brushed up against her, and she turned to look at him, almost surprised. "Do you know the story of the Feast of Marys?" she asked softly.

Edgardo shook his head.

"You don't? Everybody in Venetia knows it and foreigners come from afar to see it. You know everything and you don't know this beautiful story?"

"Tell it to me."

Kallis took a deep breath. "From the earliest days of Venetia, all the weddings used to be celebrated on the same day, the day after the February calends. The church devoted to this ceremony was San Pietro in Olivolo. They called it the Feast of Weddings then. The brides would head to the church, each carrying her dowry chest, and the bishop would bless their unions. Then the brides would hand over their dowry chests to their husbands before going back to their respective homes, escorted by a festive procession.

"Many years ago, it so happened that while the ceremony

was being held, shouts and commotion were heard in the *campo*. A group of pirates from Istria had disembarked on the island, armed with axes, sabers, and knives. They'd followed and slaughtered the residents, and reached the church where the weddings were taking place. Taking advantage of the fact that the men were unarmed, they abducted the brides and stole the dowry chests with all their possessions. They promptly returned to their ships and sped away from the island of San Pietro. As soon as the Venetians recovered from the ambush, they organized the chase. Many galleys went to hunt down the abducting pirates, who thought they were safe by now. They say that the wind suddenly changed direction, and that the pirates were forced to haul down their sails to avoid being pushed back toward their pursuers. So they decided that it would be more prudent to hide in a bay near Caorle. They landed, taking the women with them, and were about to divide up the loot when they heard shouts coming from the sea. Seeing the Venetians, the pirates tried to reach their ships to flee anew, but it was too late. The Venetians were ready to fight.

"It was a brief but bloody skirmish. The waves that spread over the beach drew back bloodred. Both Istrians and Venetians suffered heavy losses, but in the end, the Venetians had the upper hand, crying, 'Hail Venetia! Hail Saint Mark!' They managed to free the brides and recover the loot. They showed the pirates no pity, but slaughtered them all and threw them into the sea. When the triumphant galleys returned to Venetia, a crowd was waiting to welcome them like heroes. The Doge addressed the head of the chestmakers' guild—the guild had provided extra boats for the pursuit of the abductors— and asked him what he wanted as a reward. The latter replied that they had done no more than their duty, but if they really could claim a reward, then, since almost all of them were from Santa Maria Formosa, the only church dedicated to the Blessed

Virgin Mary, they would wish that, from then on, the Feast of Weddings might be celebrated at their church and renamed the Feast of Marys—partly because the majority of the abductees bore the name of our Lord's Mother. And that's why, ever since, the Feast of Marys has been celebrated at Santa Maria Formosa." Kallis looked at Edgardo, satisfied. "That's the end of the story. Did you like it?"

"You tell it well. Who taught you?"

Kallis's face tensed and her childlike expression gave way to a mask of affliction. "When I was very sad, my mother would comfort me by telling me the story of the Marys, and say that, someday, I too would be married. Me—a bride!"

She smiled strangely. Was it anger, nostalgia, or deep melancholy? Edgardo could not decipher the expression on Kallis's face.

Mass was over. Two by two, the married couples knelt before the bishop so that he would bless their unions.

The Doge left the church, got on his horse, and headed for the palace, preceded by his court and the crowd. Meanwhile, the Marys and their husbands got into richly-decorated gondolas and proceeded along the canal leading to the dock of San Marco, accompanied by freight boats, *sandolos*, and other small boats that formed a celebratory circle around them.

"Come, let's go too." Kallis took Edgardo by the hand, and dragged him along.

He had been deeply shaken by Tàtaro's words. In his delirium of omnipotence, it had not occurred to Segrado that the designs of God might be inscrutable. Death could suddenly come upon him and take him away together with his secret. And so nobody would be able to pass on the formula for crystalline glass. His discovery would be permanently lost, and who knows how many decades would pass before another glassmaker would achieve that kind of perfection.

He was haunted by this thought, which prevented him from working. He had to find a way of passing on the formula, of entrusting it to someone who would never betray him.

Whom could he trust? Who had no interest in divulging the secret for as long as Segrado was alive? He could not think of anyone. He got up from the stool, drank a ladle of water, and tried to muster the enthusiasm to resume his work.

The crystalline glass cruet could not wait. He had made a promise. He removed the crucible from the fire, lifted a ball of glass with the rod, and studied it attentively. It was pure. He raised the blowing pipe to his lips and began to blow slowly, softy, like a spring breeze. He felt the air rise from his lungs, slide into the pipe, reach the glass, and shape it into a cruet, the container for Christ's blood. His breath was like the supernatural breath that penetrates the world and, by means of a body as contemptible as his, creates the purity of divine light.

He used pincers to shape the upper part of the cylinder, so as to form an elegant spout. Then he took one of the small, round discs he had prepared in advance, and welded it to the base of the container.

The reliquary was taking shape. He put it on the work bench to cool and stopped to stare at it. He studied it carefully from every angle. The glass was clear, pure—this time, he had achieved perfection, and he was truly satisfied. He stroked his head.

"Segrado, you're the top master in Venetia," he said out loud. "The top!" He burst out laughing.

Then he went back to admiring his work. He could already picture it, filled with Christ's blood, in the tabernacle, displayed on the high altar of San Marco.

He paused in suspense, his head tilted to the side, as though something was escaping him: a flash, the rapid passage of a comet. Once again, he examined the cruet.

Impossible. He bent down. No, he was not imagining it, or hallucinating. He had seen it correctly.

The cruet stood on a sheet of parchment. He did not care how it had ended up there, but what he could not work out was what he saw beneath the cruet.

The base was right on the part where there was writing. Segrado could not tell what those words meant, but he could clearly see that the letters looked larger. As though by magic, the little crystalline glass disc had changed the shape of the letters, magnifying them.

He lifted the cylinder away from the writing. The words grew larger and swelled until their contours disappeared. It was amazing. Never would he have dreamed that such a weird contraption was possible.

He put the cylinder against his eye and looked around. Everything whirled and waved. Objects took on gigantic, monstrous proportions, losing their original shape. Contours melted, mixing colors and light in a confused world, in an absurd explosion where everything looked topsy-turvy.

He took another disc he had prepared and put it against the writing. This one magnified it differently. Every disc produced a different transformation.

He carefully examined them by lifting them to the light. One was thicker, the other thinner. This meant that their magic property varied according to their curvature.

Segrado giggled to himself with surprise and wonder. He did not quite know what use that chance discovery might have. Perhaps it was just a nice trick for cheating men and giving them nightmares and delirium without the use of drugs or other substances. Perhaps it was a tool of the devil for transforming reality and creating an illusory world that would lead man to perdition . . . Perhaps it was all those things, but for the time being he did not care.

That lentil-shaped piece of glass had an astonishing power. Nothing like it had ever been seen before. Somehow, or for someone, it would prove to be useful.

He remembered what Edgardo had said about the experiments of that Arab scholar, and he looked at the parchment on the workbench. Of course!

If that glass magnified letters, then maybe he could help that poor cleric who had lost his sight and could not read anymore. Once again, he burst out laughing.

The gondolas carrying the newlyweds navigated along the inner canals, greeted by a joyful crowd that escorted them along the banks. Aboard their miserable little *scaula*, Edgardo and Kallis had joined the tail of the procession. Standing in the bow, Kallis was maneuvering the oar. Edgardo had never seen her looking so beautiful or so luminous. It was as though she had broken out of a shell that enclosed and stifled her. He saw the whiteness of her teeth light up her face, her eyes open wide and full of wonder, her black hair shining like a starry night, her amber skin become like velvet. He would never grow weary of looking at her. At that moment, Edgardo knew that all he had left behind was nothing in comparison to what God had chosen to bestow upon him.

The procession reached the bay before San Marco, and the spectacle displayed before the triumphant crowd took everyone's breath away. The shouts, the singing, and the general racket stopped abruptly, unnaturally suspended, as though a gust of wind had swept everything away.

The entire lagoon, as far as San Giorgio and beyond, as far as the eye could see, was red. The blood grass had proliferated, covering the canals of the whole city. The surface had turned into an endless, undulating, ruby-red pasture, creating an eerie, unreal atmosphere.

After an initial moment of surprise, the singing and celebrations resumed, and the procession of boats carried on, slicing through the sea of grass, toward the Rivoalto Bridge.

Kallis followed the other boats for a while, then, with a

decisive stroke of the oar, turned south, away from the inhabited areas, threading her way through the beds of reeds behind Dorsoduro.

Once they were alone, apart from the world, she pulled out the oar, allowing the boat to drift, and went to sit next to Edgardo. She was so proud and attractive, her features so noble, that Edgardo felt a pang in his chest, thinking it was nothing short of a miracle that such a beautiful woman had chosen a cripple as a lover.

He acted on impulse, obeying an ancient instinct, recreating an image he had often seen in manuscript miniatures.

He kneeled before her, took her hand, and looked at her, bewildered. Kallis expressed surprise.

"I'll never find the right words to say exactly what my heart feels for you," he said. "I wish I were a poet, but I am only a lowly scribe, so accept what my lips can humbly express. You are the greatest gift God could have given me. You are divine light manifested on earth. You are a balm for my eyes. You are the transparency of a pure soul."

Floods of tears began running down Kallis's cheeks. Edgardo bowed his head and pressed his forehead against her hand.

"Will you do me the honor of becoming my wife? You would make me the happiest of men."

Kallis quickly pulled her hand away.

"I know full well that there are obstacles to our union," he continued. "I'll speak with Segrado. I'll explain. I'll try to buy your freedom. I'm sure he won't refuse."

Kallis leapt to her feet. The boat rocked violently. She looked around as though searching for an escape route. Surrounding them were only reeds and algae. She rushed to the bow and began rowing with an energy full of anger, her face still streaked with tears.

"Wait—perhaps I've offended you. If so, forgive me, I didn't mean to."

"Quiet! Stop!" A desperate cry flew out of Kallis's mouth. "I beg you. Do you want me to die of a broken heart?"

"Why do you say this, tell me, please . . . "

Not a word. Only the swish of the oar.

"Speak, Kallis, I beg you."

But Kallis carried on pushing the small boat through the rushes, her face rigid, like a mask of pain.

XXVII.
EYE DISCS

He wished he could be inside those tears, throw himself at her feet, hug her knees, and beg her to say something, to open up her heart to him. Kallis was pushing the *scaula* across a ruby sea without a word, head erect, sniffing the wind. Edgardo would have given his life to penetrate the reason for this silent weeping.

What secrets, what bonds and torments were agitating her soul? Did she perhaps not return his love? If so, why not say it openly and stifle any hope of his at birth? Or did her attachment to Segrado go far beyond what he imagined a relationship between a master and a slave to be? He remembered the noises he had heard that night at their home. What had really happened? Had it been a dream, a nightmare, or a truth he was refusing to admit? Kallis was Segrado's slave, as well as his concubine: a woman he used as he pleased, a piece of property he would never relinquish. And that was something Kallis could never confess.

If he were a man worthy of the name—a knight, like his brother—he would abduct her by force without asking Segrado's permission, and take her with him without the least concern for rules or etiquette. However, he was Edgardo the Crooked, a blind scribe now useless to the world, with no clothes, nowhere to sleep, and no friend to confide in.

The boat advanced slowly, impaired by the threads of algae wrapped around the keel.

The algae that had reached the basins had colored the

saltworks bloodred. Kallis tied the boat to a pole on the *rio* behind the mill. She walked slowly, as though bearing the weight of a cross she was tired of carrying. Edgardo stopped her on the threshold to the foundry.

"I'll talk with Segrado, and ask for your ransom," he said decisively, waiting for her to react.

The response he thought he saw in her eyes was a flash of hatred mixed with despair. As they walked in, he was deeply confused.

They found Segrado in full swing, prey to feverish agitation. His torso bare, his skull glistening, his hands dancing in the air as he handled tools: pincers, rods, forks, shovels. He seemed pleased to see them.

"Oh, good—you brought the scribe." He took Edgardo by the arm and pulled him toward him. "I have a wonderful surprise for you."

Edgardo was not expecting this welcome. All his resolve suddenly melted away.

"Thank God—He has granted you to be born again . . . " Segrado spoke like a possessed man. "Can you feel that fire in your chest? The ray of divine light, enlightenment . . . Our Lord has chosen to bestow His grace upon you."

Edgardo still did not understand, carried along by the master's frenzy. Kallis had approached the furnace in disbelief.

"Come and look at the miracle . . . "

Segrado went up to the workbench. There was a strange contraption on top of the parchment. Two little planks of light-colored wood—perhaps soft cherrywood—shaped like a spoon, inside which Segrado had carved two large eyelets the size of shriveled lemons. In the widest section, he had set two circles of crystalline glass, clear and transparent, thick as the bottom of a bottle. On the edge of the handles, he had drilled two tiny holes, and linked together the two spoons with the lenses, almost like a fork you could lengthen or tighten.

Segrado lifted the contraption with two fingers, as though he were handling the wings of a butterfly.

"Here, it's for you."

He handed it to Edgardo who, surprised and embarrassed, at first could not even bring himself to touch it.

"It's for your sick eyes . . . Go on, try it."

Kallis approached, staring.

"Weren't you looking for *lapides at legendum*?" the master said. "Well, these are much better—they're eye discs."

Edgardo picked up the object, tried its weight, and studied it carefully, turning it in his hands.

"Be careful, it's still very delicate and not very precise. I worked with whatever materials I had at my disposal."

"How does it work?" Edgardo asked naively.

Segrado burst into laughter. "Well, since it's supposed to be for your eyes, it certainly doesn't go on your behind." Once again, he laughed heartily. "Bring the lenses close to your eyes by holding them by the two handles. You can adapt them to your face by widening or tightening them at will. But mind you don't drop them—the glass is extremely precious."

Edgardo followed his instructions.

"So, what do you think?"

He opened his eyes, closed them, then opened them wide again, and the world around him melted. Objects, bodies, and faces dematerialized, colors blended into a drunken rainbow, the floor undulated, and the ceiling came crashing down on him.

"Everything's upside down," Edgardo exclaimed, confused. "I can't see anything,"

"No, not like that, it's not for seeing from a distance . . . it's for up close. Take that piece of parchment."

Edgardo tentatively lifted the sheet, which he immediately recognized as the copy of the frontispiece of Book VIII of *De Aspectibus*, and brought it slowly closer to his eyes. At first, the writing was huge and illegible, then, as he gradually moved it closer to the glass discs, he noticed that the outlines grew clearer and sharper. He stopped, astounded. He brought the sheet even closer and the words lost their consistency.

"You need to find the right distance for your eyes," Segrado explained.

Edgardo moved the sheet and the writing became perfectly clear, as though his eyes had suddenly been cured.

"It's amazing."

A wave of heat spread through his chest, and he felt his skin burning. He thought it was a miracle, that he could see once again. He turned to Kallis.

"It's incredible! I can read again!"

She closed her eyes calmly, as though she had always known it.

"The contraption needs perfecting," Segrado said. "You shouldn't have to move the sheet. I've noticed that the discs act differently depending on their thickness and curvature. Maybe it's the crystals that need to be adapted to your eyes. We must try things out and adjust the glasses."

Edgardo still could not believe it. He brought the parchment closer again. He could recognize every letter, the inclinations and flourishes, even the lines traced on the sheet.

Kallis burst out laughing. "You look funny with that thing in front of your eyes—you look like an owl."

"Better an owl than a mole," Edgardo replied. Then he turned to Master Segrado. "I can never thank you enough. How did you do it?"

"I'm working on a cruet and I noticed that the disc I'd blown to make the bottom had this miraculous property."

Edgardo caressed the contraption thoughtfully. "Sometimes, life is really strange," he said. "I spent so much time chasing after glassmakers, crystal-makers, and Arabic manuscripts, hoping to discover the eye stone, and it was all for nothing . . . And then, by pure chance, while working on a cruet, you find what I was desperately seeking elsewhere."

Segrado's face lit up with a candid, almost boyish expression. "You of all people talk of chance? You, a man of the cloth? Can't you see the divine plan?" he said, raising his voice like a preacher. "God filled me with the light that guided my hand, so that I might create a pure, transparent glass in His image, to His praise and glory. An image of purity that every Christian should seek. If I hadn't discovered crystalline glass, you wouldn't have your discs, and you would be wandering blindly, aimlessly, without a purpose. In His immense generosity, God chose to give us new possibilities and show us the way." He paused thoughtfully. "To you and to me. Now, with this contraption, you can go back to performing the task for which you were chosen: copying manuscripts."

"I envy your faith, Maestro. You manage to see a divine plan in every event, and in every object around us."

"But it's so obvious," Segrado added with an ineffable smile.

Edgardo felt ashamed of his shortcomings and looked at Kallis, hoping for a sign of encouragement from her. He noticed, however, that a veil of deep melancholy had fallen over her face again.

He plucked up his courage. "Maestro, I wish to ask you a favor—"

"No, wait," Segrado interrupted, "it's I who have something to ask you."

"Tell me. I'll do anything for you."

"Now that you've regained your eyesight, and are able to use a quill again, I'd like you to write something down for me."

Kallis listened, alert.

"But first you must swear on your honor that you will never disclose to anyone, or for any reason, what I'm about to reveal."

Oaths, honor, solemn undertakings . . . Edgardo remembered

the words he always heard his father repeat before the knights lined up in the castle courtyard when he was a child. Although this was just a poor promise to a glassmaker, he felt that, for the first time, he was being asked to carry out a responsibility to the very end, even if it involved putting his own life at risk.

"I swear," he said resolutely.

"Good, I thank you." Segrado grew very stern. "I'd like you to transcribe the crystalline glass formula. Nobody knows the secret of the formula, and if I suddenly died, this discovery would be lost forever. And who knows if any other glassmakers would ever discover a way of creating such pure glass?" He paused, thoughtfully. "Do you think you could do this for me?"

There was a sudden crash. A terra-cotta mold had fallen to the floor, and broken into a thousand pieces. Kallis was watching him, stunned. Segrado gave her a piercing, burning look.

"The canker on you—be careful!"

"Forgive me." Kallis was pale, her lips drained of their color, her eyes full of fear. She stood there, motionless, by the furnace, staring blankly at the fragments of mold. Then she bent down to pick them up, casting terrified glances at Edgardo.

"So, then," Segrado said. "Are you willing, yes or no, to transcribe for me the formula for making perfect crystal?"

"Of course, Maestro," Edgardo replied.

Kallis bowed her head.

"In that case, I'll expect you tomorrow in Metamauco, away from prying eyes and ears. I'll find all that you'll need to do the writing. Meanwhile, if you've nowhere to go, you can spend the night here in the foundry."

"I gladly accept. Thank you for your hospitality." Edgardo tried to resume what he was saying. "As I was about to tell you, Maestro, I too have a favor to ask you." He turned to Kallis, who was still bent over, collecting the last fragments.

"Tomorrow," Segrado replied hurriedly. "We'll talk about everything tomorrow. I must rush to the basilica now. He is waiting for me. I must keep a promise."

Having said that, he wrapped the cruet in various rags and put it into a knapsack.

"Mind you," Segrado insisted, pausing on the threshold, "don't forget the eye discs." He indicated the miraculous contraption Edgardo had placed on the workbench, and left.

Kallis was still kneeling on the floor, cleaning up slowly, as though concentrating on a ghostly image only she could see.

When he was sure Segrado had gone, Edgardo approached her and reached out a hand to help her up. It struck him that perhaps she was angry with him because of his lack of decisiveness.

"I promise you, tomorrow—" He did not have a chance to finish his sentence. Kallis leapt to her feet and held him in a stifling embrace.

"You mustn't go, you mustn't, please, I beg you . . . I beg you," she kept repeating in a restrained voice. Her eyes were bloodshot, and her hands shaking. "Don't go to him, don't do what he asks, don't write down that formula."

How sweet it was to hold that thread of wool in his arms, to feel her body trembling and hear her voice imploring him in that heartfelt tone.

"Calm down, calm down." Edgardo kissed her velvet forehead, her hair, and the corners of her mouth, which tasted of salt. "Nothing's going to happen. I'll explain everything, I'll tell him that I love you, and that I want to take you as my wife. I'll ask him to set you free. He can't deny me this favor. He needs me now."

"But, Edgardo, don't you see? Once you've written down the formula, you'll no longer be of any use to him . . . and he'll kill you."

It was like a gash, an explosion. Edgardo pulled away from

her as though he had been stabbed in the back with a sword. "What do you mean? Why would he kill me?"

"Nobody must know the crystal secret besides him. You'd be a constant threat. You could talk, report it, even if you didn't want to, under torture or drugs. No, he'd never allow that."

"But I've sworn."

"Do you know what your oath is worth to Segrado? It's like dust you can blow away. You don't know him. He's a man capable of anything. He's violent, implacable. He doesn't allow anyone to interfere with his plans. For that he's ready to kill— he's already killed once . . . "

Edgardo could not believe it. Impossible to think that the master he knew and even imagined as a father could turn into a murderer.

"I don't believe it."

"It's true. Trust me." Kallis hugged him again and took his face in her hands. "Don't come to Metamauco. It's death that awaits you there." She let go of him and picked up the contraption for the eyes. "Take the glasses, it's what you came for, after all. Go back to your abbey. Now you can see again, return to your manuscripts and your quiet life. Flee Venetia. This city is sick. There are monsters lurking beneath the waters of the lagoon, and the people here are afflicted with a terrible disease that transforms and destroys their souls. The miasma, the fog, the winds—they all eat away at the mind, crush feelings, and wither the heart. Go away, Edgardo, forget everything. If you want to live, then I beg you, leave Venetia."

Edgardo felt as though he was being tossed by the currents, hurled against the rocks by a huge wave, his flesh torn, and a splinter of basalt stuck through his chest. Everything was breaking into pieces. His dream of a life with Kallis, freedom. It was as though all he had lived through over the past few days had been nothing but an endless nightmare.

"What about us, Kallis? I can't leave you."

Kallis shook her head and walked away, turning her back. "Do you believe in a divine plan for everything?"

"I'd like to."

"Then perhaps we'll meet again." She took a bead streaked with a thousand colors from her pocket and placed it in Edgardo's hand. "My mother gave me this when I was a child. Hold onto it, and give it back to me when we meet again."

Edgardo held it tight in his fist. At that moment, they heard Segrado's voice, calling Kallis from the boat.

"Don't come to Metamauco. He'll kill you," she whispered and ran away.

And so, in the end, he had to confront his ghosts. It was pointless hiding, disguising himself as a copyist. The day of battle had come and he could no longer run away. He had to make a decision. To go to Metamauco and risk his life, or return to Bobbio and give up Kallis forever? To face his fear or, once again, flee?

His heart was telling him to go forth, to meet Segrado and fight for the woman he loved, but his cowardly soul stopped him from acting. Fear is a subtle disease that worms its way into the depths of your soul, attacking your mind and limbs, forcing them to capitulate to its sneaky ways. It is easy for those who possess courage within, but when cowardice takes root inside you, it takes away all hope, willpower, and strength.

Overwhelmed by uncontrollable torment, Edgardo left the foundry and started roaming aimlessly through the district, meditating on himself and his destiny.

The city was immersed in a pale sunset that cast ghostly indigo shadows on the banks and houses. In just a few hours, the bloodred algae, swept by the tide, had all but disappeared and, although it was still February, the water temperature was unusually mild, as during the summer months. A *scirocco* wind was blowing from the sea, its heat draining humans of energy, and making animals by turns lethargic and anxious, as they sensed the approach of some extraordinary phenomenon. In the *calli*, the timber walls of the houses were unusually damp, and a smell like that of rotten eggs was coming from the lagoon.

Without realizing it, he found himself on the edge of a dense forest of alders and oaks, where there was a church with a large portico surrounded by fishermen's houses. Just beyond the village, it was possible to glimpse a wide canal navigated by galleys, freight boats, and *sandoli* with sails. The place inspired a sense of peace. Simple houses, gathered around the church, fishing nets spread out to dry, boats pulled ashore. An idyllic landscape which, for a moment, made him forget his torments. He sat down on a low wall next to the portico.

There was a woman huddled near the entrance to the church, totally covered by a black cloak, muttering a short prayer and stretching out her hand.

"Excuse me," Edgardo asked. "Can you tell me where I am? I'm lost."

The cloak quivered, the hand pulled back, and a head covered in crusts with but a few locks of yellowed hair popped out of one of the folds. "You're in San Nicolò dei Mendigoli. It's called that because this tiny stretch of land is inhabited only by very poor fishermen and beggars who live off kind folks' charity."

Edgardo could not restrain a horrified grimace. Most of the woman's face had been eaten away by leprosy. Her nose had been reduced to a growth of shapeless flesh, she had bluish gums instead of lips, and her ears had disappeared, as had her eyelids, which could no longer conceal two protruding, blood-shot eyeballs. Around the mouth that had been corroded by the disease, the gnawed flesh exposed the jawbone in which teeth were set. Half skeleton and half body, as though death itself were performing its task day by day, with the patience of a skilled craftsman.

"Thank you, my good woman," Edgardo stuttered. "God be with you."

He would have liked to give her a coin, but lacked the courage.

"Come closer, let me get a look at you." Her voice echoed as though in a cave, suggesting an empty chest. Edgardo did not move.

"Come on, don't be scared, I'm not dangerous." A laugh crackled through her few remaining teeth. "Come on, boy, let me show you something, have no fear . . . "

Fear, fear, fear . . . The word echoed in his ears, flooded his mind, throbbed in his heart. Once again, his brother's astounded face, when he had seen him flee from the enemy, flashed before his eyes.

"Come on, be brave," the old woman insisted.

He could turn and run once again. It was possible, and it would free him. Always run away. He resisted his first impulse and took a step forward.

"Well done. You see, you can be brave if you want to. Let me give you a hand."

Once again, she laughed and stretched out a shred of blood-streaked flesh, a ridge of bones and tendons at the tip of which hung long yellow nails. Edgardo took another step forward, bewitched by this monstrosity.

"There we go . . . Now you can finally look your fear in the face."

As she spoke, the leper woman took off her hood, uncovering the whole of her head. Edgardo immediately recognized the features, the shape of the head, and the eyes. He saw his own reflection in a puddle of muddy water, rippled by the wind. He recognized his hump, his deformed bones, the remaining locks of hair, the shreds of transparent skin hanging from the cheeks. A picture of horror, a crooked demon. He was his own fear. Fear was inside him and he could not escape it.

He made another effort, reached his hand out, and had almost managed to touch himself when his tunic grew suddenly limp and he felt his chest being pierced through by a red-hot blade.

For a moment, he was stunned, unable to move. The leper woman had disappeared. He looked around. He was alone. His wound was still burning.

In a field almost clear of blood, Kallis was pushing the *scaula* amid the shoals that surrounded the islands of Aymanas and Costanciacum.

When they had reached Metamauco, she had used the pretext of going to find food to keep the boat, and had gone to the abandoned convent of San Lorenzo.

The *scirocco* wind had brought a humid, sticky blanket that made it hard to breathe and move about. White bubbles full of vapor had appeared around some of the small islands, and were gushing out from the bottom, bursting on the surface, filling the air with a nauseating smell of rotting flesh. Inexplicable phenomena she did not remember ever seeing before. The *scaula* passed the monasteries of Sant'Agata, then San Filippo and San Giacomo. When she reached San Lorenzo, she realized that, since she had last been here with Edgardo, the water had risen further, submerging portions of the shore and flooding fields and woodland.

Walking through the ruins of the convent, she saw frightened snakes hide under stones or in the cracks of walls. The air was unbreathable, swarms of insects whirred about aimlessly, as though driven crazy, while seagulls and redshanks circled overhead, shrieking relentlessly.

She passed the tower she had made her secret refuge and walked across the cloister as far as the dilapidated church, behind which, on a tiny plot of land, a few headstones stuck out, some lying on the ground in pieces.

Kallis snapped a laurel branch from a bush, then rummaged in the grass until she found a tiny, rusty iron cross. She knelt, pulled out a few clusters of grass, and stuck the laurel branch into the soil, as though it were a flower.

"Rest in peace, Mother. I know that you're finally free and happy, but I miss you so much . . . I really need your advice. You know every one of my thoughts, my most intimate feelings, even those I'm not aware of. Please tell me—what should I do?"

Kallis bent toward the cross, as though afraid not to be heard.

"I made you a promise, I know, I swore it on your grave, but so much has happened now . . . I don't understand anything anymore . . . I'm confused. Please tell me, what path should I follow? I don't want to betray you, and up to now, I've always followed the preordained path, step by step. But now my heart is hesitating and I'm full of doubts."

Kallis prostrated herself on the grave and hugged the piece of land marked with the cross. "Time is running out. Help me, Mother dearest. Tell me what to do."

XXVIII

THE FORMULA

He spent the night praying, just as he had seen his father do before a battle. He had always wondered if prayers were for asking God to keep your life safe, or a need, through invocations, to feel Him at your side before going to face death.

Kneeling in a corner of the foundry, Edgardo had listened to the words coming out of his mouth: the word of God. Words and set phrases he had learned by heart but of which he had forgotten the meaning, and which filled his heart and his head until he was in a daze. Was this their meaning? Was it to be drugged with litanies, with invocations, until you stopped thinking and forgot your fear? Filled with vacuous, truthless faith, he prepared to face his enemy: a ghost created by his mind.

They were ringing Lauds in the nearby church of San Giacomo di Luprio. Edgardo left the foundry and went to the well by the mill. He stripped himself bare and began to wash, rubbing himself with a wet cloth. He wished he could wear clothes worthier of his first battle, but all he had were his *garzone* rags. The *scirocco* wind dried his wet skin, leaving a layer of steam around his body.

Segrado was waiting for him in Metamauco. He pictured the meeting, the danger, the possibility that he might be killed, and tried to read the deep motivations of the soul.

He drank a sip of water, got dressed again, and returned to the foundry. He felt purer, ready to face whatever event God had chosen in order to put him to the test.

He took the eye disc contraption from the workbench, wrapped it in a rag to protect it from any knocks, and put it at the bottom of his sack. He would shortly start writing again and that made him nervous.

Before going out, he thought of his brother. He wished he had him at his side, heard their horses' gallop blend into a deafening thud, and his voice, so full of assurance, inciting them to victory. Since he could not go back in time, Edgardo decided to dedicate his small, insignificant act of courage to Ruggero. He looked at himself: he was a decidedly lowly knight.

He was already at the door when he heard a creak bite into the deep silence of the night. Broken salt crystals, crushed by heavy footsteps coming from behind the mill. An uncontrollable shudder ran down his skin. He tried to restrain it. The footsteps grew louder in the dark, approaching. Edgardo knew that there was a time when he would have gone back in and bolted the door. Now, instead, he remained on the threshold, waiting motionlessly. The sound of footsteps ceased and silence returned. The mill sail moved imperceptibly, squeaking, pushed by the wind.

A shadow appeared before him. Edgardo thought he recognized his brother. Perhaps the latter had heard his call.

"Ruggero, brother," he murmured with a broken voice. "It's me—don't be afraid."

The shadow materialized into Segrado's bearlike body.

The unexpected apparition made him take a step back and put him on the defensive.

"Maestro," he said, "I was about to join you in Metamauco. That's what we'd agreed."

Segrado breathed out heavily. The steam turned white, like a cloud of smoke.

"I decided to come to you, instead. It's safer." He walked into the foundry.

This unexpected change of plan threw Edgardo. He tried to put his thoughts in order. Why had Segrado come to him? Was it so that he could be alone and act undisturbed? In Metamauco, he would have had to take Kallis into account, whereas here, after he had finished dictating, it would be easy for Segrado to eliminate him and then throw him into the canal, just like he had done with Zoto. Or else he could leave him to soak in the saltworks, like Niccolò. Where was Kallis? Did she know he was here?

Without paying attention to Edgardo, the master moved calmly and naturally. He had put the leather knapsack on the high-backed chair, and was in the process of rekindling the fire.

"I've brought everything we need."

On the workbench, he lined up a sheet of parchment, a horn filled with ink, and a goose quill.

"I hope I haven't forgotten anything."

Edgardo glanced distractedly at the tools, and asked, "Did Kallis stay in Metamauco?"

"Yes," Segrado replied abruptly. "It's better if it's just the two of us." His reply did not reassure Edgardo. "So, are you ready? Do you have your eye glasses?"

"Maestro, I'd like to make a request before we start."

Segrado turned abruptly. "What kind of request?"

"I'd like to talk to you about Kallis."

Segrado emitted a kind of animal grunt from the depths of his bear soul. Then he shook himself and swelled his chest as though to sweep the world away with a powerful growl. Edgardo expected to see anger in his eyes but, instead, there was just an expression of deep sadness.

"What are you imagining? You know nothing." Segrado stopped, not sure if he should continue. "It's all such a muddle. Don't think of Kallis now. There'll be time later. Let's get down to work now."

He brought the stool close to the workbench and handed

Edgardo the goose quill. Edgardo approached and prepared to write again, perhaps for the last time.

Confused, violent feelings shook his chest. Two contrasting passions clashed within him. On one hand, the joy and exaltation of being able, once again, to guide the subtle quill on the page, and to see the formation of those miraculous signs that could inspire thoughts, images, emotions, dreams, and logic. On the other hand, the awareness that the success of his writing could mean his death.

He picked up the quill and held it tight. His fingers were shaking. He opened the horn with the ink and put it on the table. The clean, untouched parchment awaited him like an expanse of sand swept by the wind, never dented by human footsteps.

"Are you ready?" Segrado asked solemnly.

"Yes . . . No, just a moment."

He had forgotten the most important step. The one that had allowed him to return to life. He pulled the parcel out of his sack and unwrapped it. The glasses gave off an unreal light, like the glow of a comet cutting through the night. The transparency and purity was like that of crystal. Segrado looked at them with satisfaction, proud of his work. Edgardo slowly brought them up to his nose, supporting them with his free hand. Then he drew his face close to the parchment, bending toward the table until he had found the right distance that allowed him to see the lines marked on the sheet clearly and precisely.

"Now I'm ready," he said.

Segrado sat on the bench beside him. "I'll dictate slowly, so you have time to write. I'll try and find the right words, so that everything is as clear as possible. Whoever reads this formula mustn't have any doubts. Let's start with the title: 'Formula for Making Perfect Crystal.'"

After dipping the quill in ink, Edgardo drew close to the parchment, and prepared to trace his first letters. For a moment, he had the impression that the ink was melting and that the signs on the sheet were running, like waves on the water's edge. He bowed his head, squinted a little, and at last, new, clear, precise writing appeared through the glasses. Maybe he was a bit slower, but he could read what he was writing.

His eyes shut, focusing, as though revisiting the various stages of preparation, Segrado continued:

"First of all, you must make sure that the furnace is set to a light-colored flame, without smoke—not like when you use fresh, green wood, or when you don't stoke the fire and the flame fails. Equally, you mustn't stoke the fire too much or carelessly, because that can cause great damage to glass and, in particular, to crystal. Instead, you should stoke it little and often, so that the oven remains light, smokeless, and also uses up less wood. Now take the proper quantity of crystal pieces, coarsely pestled, put them into the oven in a crucible, and leave them there for twelve hours without stirring. Keep a tub of fresh water ready, where you'll pour the crystal from the crucible. After it has cooled down, wash the crystal several times, until the water runs nice and clear. Then pestle the glass in a stone mortar and wash it once again. You do this in order to remove some of the salt that would otherwise damage the crystal and make it dark. After washing, put it back into the crucible, always making sure that the flame is light-colored and smokeless. Allow it to melt for a maximum of four days, then stir with a rod."

Segrado stopped, uncertain whether or not to continue. Edgardo lifted his hand from the page, and studied his work. It was as perfect as the filigree of a leaf, rich as a miniature, sweet as honey, fragrant as a field of lavender. It was his handwriting once again. He felt a flush in his chest. He forgot his fear and the danger of death. It was as though he was proudly and resolutely galloping toward the enemy.

Kallis woke with a start to find Segrado's bed empty. She leapt to her feet. She was too agitated to think or act. The master had left in the middle of the night, secretly, without waking her. She could well imagine why, and where he had gone. He had never meant to wait for Edgardo in Metamauco. He had planned something quite different: to find him at the foundry in order to have a free hand and dictate the formula without her being present.

A powerful anger went to her head. She had thought herself cunning, she had thought she had studied every move of his, but she had been wrong. It had happened before, when she had trusted him and he, in return, had ruined her life. A treacherous, violent man.

She had to catch up with him and stop him before he started dictating. Maybe she was still in time. Perhaps he had not been gone long. She slipped on her tunic, wrapped herself in her cloak, and ran out to a *sandolo* that was moored at a nearby *rio*. A *scirocco* wind was still blowing and its close heat drained you of strength and made your mind obtuse and idle. A gloomy darkness spread across the sky, and in the first pale light of day an army of low clouds scurried, lapping at the waters.

Kallis started to row, trying to reach Venetia as quickly as possible. Although the wind was not strong, breakers rose tall, forming long, wide waves. An acid, metallic smell rose from the waters, and crackling sparks spread over the surface, like sea lightning.

It was an enormous effort trying to keep the boat on the right course, and several times Kallis thought she would not make it. Sudden currents tossed her about, shifting the bow like the tip of a needle and making the keel slide as though it was on a sheet of ice. A deep roar rose from the depths of the lagoon, and the waters quivered with a muffled sound. The birds were squawking and fluttering restlessly, while eels darted out of the water.

Kallis did not remember ever seeing anything like this, not even before a storm. There was the breath of something suspended in the air, as though awaiting imminent catastrophe. She had never felt so anxious, as if she were shut up in a well, deprived of air and unable to move. With every stroke of the oar, she felt weaker, her mind uncontrollably numb. She struggled to advance just a few fathoms at a time.

It was pointless fighting. She would never get there in time. Edgardo was lost.

A favorable current tossed her toward Spinalunga and she finally saw the shores of Dorsoduro. The cumulus clouds were so low they concealed the tops of belfries and towers, and it was barely possible to make out the outlines of the churches. The galleys, chelandions, and warships moored in front of the dock of San Marco were rocking so violently that the tips of their masts touched.

With a final effort, she managed to take shelter inside the Rivus Altus, where the waves were not as powerful and the currents gentler. Drenched in sweat, her muscles aching, she rowed mechanically, refusing to think that she might be too late.

"And now we come to the most important part," Segrado continued. "Write it down exactly as I say it. 'Then take a little finely-sifted manganese, pour some into the glass, and let it dissolve. You must know that all glass naturally tends to be green, but manganese lightens it. However, be careful not to put too much in, or the glass will turn purple, in which case you'll need to add as many crushed and sifted crystal pieces as it takes to make the crystal light, white, and beautiful again. But it's much better to add manganese a little at a time. There isn't any determined rule or quantity, so you have to keep checking as you go along that your crystal is becoming light and as transparent as water, and then you'll have reached the right moment. Until you see that the glass is clear, keep adding manganese little by little, as I said, to avoid it turning purple. However, bear in mind that this kind of crystal needs to be worked very carefully, on a low flame (it doesn't require a large flame, like ordinary glass) and always on a light-colored, smokeless fire, stoking it little and often. Moreover, it has to be worked in a clean environment, with no dust, because it can easily get dirty if you're not careful.'" Segrado paused, his eyes drifting over the tools, the furnace, as though looking for confirmation, then added, "There. I've finished. This is my formula for making perfect crystal."

Edgardo raised his head from the parchment and examined his work. He was still a modest copyist, despite that heavy contraption in front of his nose.

Segrado approached and bent over the page. "These are the words I dictated to you . . . ?"

"Yes, Maestro."

He shook his head, incredulous. "The canker take me. Did I really say all that?"

Edgardo nodded with satisfaction.

"You're a talented copyist," Segrado exclaimed. "Listen, could you add my name at the bottom of the formula? My name is Angelo Segrado, glassmaker."

Edgardo was about to transcribe the signature, but stopped. "Would you like to do it yourself, Maestro?"

"What do you mean? You know I can't write." He sounded vexed.

"I'll guide your hand."

Segrado was suddenly agitated, and anxiously looked at his hand, almost as though he had been asked to lay it on the fire. "Really? Could you do that?" He had the same childlike tone Kallis sometimes had.

Edgardo stood up and gestured to Segrado to sit in his place. He placed the quill in his hand, put his own hand over it, and started guiding it. He noticed with surprise that the large bear paw could move with the delicacy and lightness of glass itself.

"Angelo Segrado," the scribe spelled out.

As by a miracle, a black arabesque appeared on the parchment. A subtle, refined miniature. Segrado's toothless mouth opened into a great big smile he had never seen before. He was so happy, admiring his work with an entranced expression, that at that moment it struck Edgardo that he did not care if Segrado killed him. He removed the discs from his nose and placed them delicately on the workbench.

"And now, Maestro, may I ask you a favor?"

Segrado seemed taken aback.

"I'm asking you to set Kallis free. I want to make her my bride."

Segrado's face tensed. He seemed wounded, at a loss. "Kallis . . . your bride? Dear God, what are you saying? Kallis is very different than how she appears. It would be a serious mistake. You don't know anything about her . . . Wait, it's time to reveal the truth to you."

At that moment, the door was flung open, and the *scirocco* wind enveloped the furnace, blowing on the fire. At the door, barely lit by the gray hues of a dawn stifled by the storm, Kallis stood motionless, staring at them.

She was shaking and her eyes were wild, her face moist with sweat. Her body, wrapped in a cloak swelled by the wind, seemed gigantic. The door kept slamming and the flames undulated in the furnace, casting sinister shadows on the walls.

Edgardo looked at her, puzzled.

"Have you already transcribed the formula?" Kallis asked, panting.

Edgardo lifted the sheet of parchment.

"No!" she screamed. "No . . . Why did you do it? Merciful God. Why?" She covered her face with her hands.

XXIX.
THE BATTLE

A powerful gust of wind shook the roof. The walls creaked and the fire in the furnace went out, leaving just two dark shadows in the room. Their bodies gave off the wild smell of animals shut in a cage. The cage of their faults, their fears, their regrets.

As though she had suddenly regained her sense of balance in the dark, Kallis slowly closed the door behind her, took a small step to the side and, with an artificially calm voice, said, "I'd asked you not to write down that formula. Why did you do it?"

Her words resounded in the dark like arrows shot by invisible bows.

Instinctively, to avoid being hit, Edgardo took a step back and, still clutching the parchment, moved away from Segrado, who remained rooted to the ground—a mass of heavy, shiny granite, which nobody could dent.

"In exchange for this favor, I've asked the maestro to set you free, to let you go." Edgardo was surprised by the calmness and steadiness of his own voice. He turned to Segrado. "You mustn't fear. I've sworn I will never divulge this formula to anyone. I've already forgotten it. There's no point in killing me. Let us go. I only want to take Kallis away."

There was a clanging of irons rolling on the floor. Segrado's huge shadow had moved back, as though he had lost his balance.

"Kill you?" His voice was broken, filled with sadness. "Why would I kill you?"

Edgardo desperately sought Kallis's face in the darkness, hoping for a sign, a word. He sensed a quiver through the air, the flapping wings of a lost illusion.

"Edgardo, I beg you, destroy that parchment. Throw it into the fire." Kallis's voice was metallic. The tone of request concealed an order that admitted no refusal. "Now he doesn't need you anymore, you're just a witness, and he'll kill you."

"What are you saying? You're lying!" Segrado's voice rose, powerful, and echoed across the room, above the noise of the wind. "I never thought of getting rid of him."

Edgardo stopped, seized by a realization. His body shook, giving off a scent of deep sadness. He took a step toward Kallis.

"It's you who doesn't want there to be a written-down formula, isn't it? You don't want the formula to end up in somebody else's hands. It's true, isn't it? Confess . . . "

A long silence stifled the illusion of a reply. In the dark, Edgardo tried to find the features of her face, the beating of her heart. He moved toward her, seeking the warmth of her body, yearning for a confirmation that would bring some peace and hope to his tormented thoughts.

"Is that true, Kallis? Is this formula really so important to you?" Edgardo lifted the parchment. "I don't understand. Why?"

"He'll kill you, he'll kill you," Kallis repeated.

Segrado approached Edgardo. "All right . . . Let's make a deal. Take her away . . . Leave me the parchment, take Kallis and go away together, far away. Isn't that what you wanted, scribe? There. You're free. Free!" His tone grew more intense, filling the foundry. "You're free, Kallis, finally free. Go away. Go away with your scribe."

There! Destiny had been fulfilled and nothing else mattered. The battle was won. Edgardo went up to Kallis and took her hand. It was stiff and cold.

"Did you hear? Let's leave. He won't stop you. He won't kill me. We're free." He put the parchment on the workbench.

"Stop!" Kallis screamed. "This parchment belongs to me!"

"So now you understand," Segrado said in a deep, ailing voice. "You heard her with your own ears. She doesn't care about you. She doesn't want her freedom. She's always been free. What matters to her is the formula, the secret, power . . . Isn't that true, Kallis?"

"Deny it, I beg you, dispel all my doubts, look into my eyes, and give me hope," Edgardo whispered a final prayer to himself. Enclosed in her armor, Kallis was preparing for battle. Her nerves were tense, ready to spring, her features like threads of iron.

"Segrado, you know this parchment belongs to me, just as all this belongs to me." She indicated everything in the foundry. "It's mine by right—a right you refuse to acknowledge. I've learned your art by living at your side all these years, by spying on your every move, your every attempt. I've suffered your failures with you and rejoiced in your discovery of crystalline glass, but always in silence, obeying, working like a mule, enduring beatings, bearing your insults . . . " Kallis's eyes were filled with sadness. "And, in return, you have always favored others over me. You raised *garzoni* as your disciples, treating them like your sons, while I have never been anything to you. You see, even now, you chose to have the formula written down so it can be passed on to some learned glassmaker who can also read, and you didn't even spare a thought for me. For you I don't exist. I am nothing. Just a bastard slave with no rights, no soul, and no heart. I'm taking all that's mine."

"You're wrong," Segrado replied. "Nothing belongs to you. You have no rights."

"I'm telling the truth." Kallis's tone was so calm, her voice so gentle, it sounded unreal. "Have the courage to admit it, Segrado. At least once, utter that word before an innocent bystander, utter it for the love of God."

Segrado huffed and grunted, expelling air from his nostrils as though with bellows, but said nothing.

"You're a coward. I'll tell the truth, then."

Kallis approached Edgardo so that their faces were almost touching. He could hear her raucous breathing.

"I'm his daughter . . . his daughter . . . his daughter!" she screamed. "Isn't that true, Segrado? Have you got the courage to deny it? I'm the heir to your art—me, the repository of your secrets. I'm your family, your blood, your name . . . whether you like it or not."

The master's voice tore through the air like an arrow, and stuck into Kallis's heart. "You're not my family. You're nothing to me . . . You're just a slave, the daughter of a slave."

"It's the truth!" Kallis shouted. "A slave, the daughter of a slave you got pregnant without any compassion. After using her and exploiting her, you beat her to death, like a dog, because she was no longer any use to you. She was old and tired, so you replaced her with a fresh young slave. You didn't care that she was your daughter."

Segrado swayed. A gust of wind whistled through the reeds.

"He killed her without pity." Kallis brushed Edgardo's arm. "Just because she didn't obey an order."

"I didn't want to kill her, I swear." For the first time, Edgardo heard genuine pain in Segrado's voice. "Anger betrayed me and took over my mind. I lost all sense of reason. But I really didn't want to. I've been oppressed with guilt for years. I've atoned . . . Only now has God sent me a sign of His forgiveness. When I obtained crystalline glass, I had the proof that my soul had become pure again. The cruet containing Christ's blood is already displayed on the altar in the basilica. I've paid . . . and now I'm setting you free. Go with your scribe. Go on your way. But this," he indicated the parchment, "cannot belong to a slave, to a woman."

Kallis took a step toward the workbench and stretched out her hand.

Something glistened. Edgardo saw a flash of steel at his side. Kallis's hand was clutching a long, thin dagger, the point aimed at her father.

"Do you want to kill me?" Segrado asked calmly. "See this, scribe, now who is ready to kill? That's right, you must kill me if you want to be the only one to know the secret of crystalline glass. You must kill me—like you killed the others . . . " He put out his hands, as though searching for Kallis in the dark. "It's true, isn't it? It's clear to me now. You eliminated Balbo, my first *garzone*, then Niccolò, because they both knew too much, they stood between you and me, they knew my secrets, they'd seen everything . . . That's why you gouged their eyes out and replaced them with glass ones, so skillfully crafted. It was a message for me, to show me how expert you'd become."

"All children want to show their parents how good they've become." There was a note of yearning love in Kallis's words. "But you didn't see me. You didn't consider me, not just as a daughter, but even as a *garzone* . . . I was less than nothing . . . and I knew that sooner or later Balbo, then Niccolò would take your place, they would become your disciples, your heirs, and you would pass your knowledge and secrets to them alone . . . "

"And Zoto? Why did you kill him?"

"I punished him. He'd spied on us. He'd told Tàtaro about the glass. I did it for you."

Segrado laughed. "For me? What are you saying? Didn't you plan that one day my turn would come? By then you knew everything about crystalline glass, so if you'd killed me you would have been the only one to know the secret. But the copy of the formula upset your plans. Isn't that true, Kallis?"

"My God, how is this possible?" Edgardo thought. "Everything is crashing down . . . The angels are falling . . . Their wings are burning . . . They are turning into demons . . . Kallis, a murderess, responsible for those horrible deaths . . . God, take pity on me and wake me from this nightmare!"

"I swore on my mother's grave that I would avenge her," Kallis said. "I was waiting for the right time but then there was a moment, when the two of us were left alone, when I almost started to believe, to hope that you would accept me as your daughter, that you would recognize me as your disciple, your heir. I prayed so much that this would happen. But then I realized that nothing had changed . . . That I was still Kallis the slave and bastard . . . And you were still the same, there was no hope, so . . . "

The remaining words remained stuck in her throat, trapped by sudden breathlessness. She reached out toward the workbench where Edgardo had put the formula.

Segrado leapt on her, trying to take the dagger from her hand. A thread of wool in the paws of a bear. Despite her father's powerful build, Kallis managed to resist him. She freed herself by pushing him to the side. Segrado lost his balance and went crashing against the door.

"I can feel it snaking under my skin," Edgardo thought, "twisting my guts, turning my blood to water. I can feel the all-enveloping fear that clouds the mind and paralyzes the limbs. Motionless, I am watching this fight without doing anything, without intervening, just like when I saw my brother's blood flowing out. Edgardo the Crooked. Edgardo the Coward . . . "

He suddenly felt overwhelmed by a mysterious force. A light exploded in his chest and he saw his body stirring after a long sleep. He threw himself into the fray between the two fighting bodies without thinking. He tried to stop Segrado and remove the dagger from Kallis's hand. He smelt the rotting odor of the fight, and saw the two bodies bend and break apart, and Kallis's eyes, full of hatred.

Then, like a gift from the sky, a hot flash pierced through his chest and something sweetly squirted all over his face. He swayed and realized he was slowly sliding down to the floor.

With a final effort, he tried to hold onto the workbench, which he pulled down, along with glass, tools, and cruets.

The eye discs slid off the table, circled in the air for a moment, as though held up by an invisible force. Finally, dragged down by a destructive hand, they fell heavily to the floor, but the glasses, protected by their wooden frame, did not break. Edgardo saw them sway, immersed in a rain of light, then heard the door fly open and glimpsed Segrado's shadow running out, clutching the parchment in his hands, followed by Kallis.

A gust of wind caressed his face. Then he closed his eyes and lost consciousness.

XXX.
CALAMITY

Time stood still. He was shut in a dark, cold, silent cave, suspended between the earth and the sky. He felt no pain, had no thoughts, no feelings. Nothing but a simple, useless void. Except that he was waiting for something to happen. Years—or perhaps only a few moments—later, he was struck by a vortex that threw him out of the darkness. A light flashed through his mind, forcing him to half-close his eyes. Where was he?

He was lying on the floor, not far from the overturned workbench. The foundry door was wide open. He remembered everything. He tried to get up, but the wound in his chest squirted blood and made him rock back in pain. He gathered all his strength, took the eye discs, held them in his fist like a talisman, slipped them into his pocket, and dragged himself outside. The landscape before him alarmed him.

The world was upside down. Clusters of dark, swollen clouds were drifting across the sky, pushed by a strong wind, twisting like breakers, feeding off one another in a crescendo of power and intensity.

The surface of the lagoon was strangely calm, flat and smooth, of a purple no sailor had ever seen before, even on long journeys to the Orient. The water level, driven by the wind, had risen rapidly, flooding a large part of the lower-lying lands. The saltworks were totally submerged, and an unnatural glow rose from under the surface like the light of a sunken volcano.

Edgardo took a few steps forward and let his eyes wander, hoping to see a trace of Kallis and Segrado. He did not know how much time had passed, or how long he had been unconscious.

He managed to reach the mill. It was deserted. The water reached up to his ankles and grass and algae twisted around his feet. He walked behind the foundry toward the shoals that separated the built-up area from the tangle of canals, and saw something amid the logs tossed by the tide. He approached and saw two wooden statues floating in the water, the effigies of saints carried during a procession.

Kallis was kneeling before a prostrate body wrapped in a watery shroud. He drew closer, held back by the mud and his wound.

"She's alive," he thought. "Kallis is alive."

Segrado was lying in the water that lapped at his body. His face was uncovered, as was his side, where the dagger was sticking out.

The blood was pouring out of the wound and dyeing the cloak of the surrounding sea scarlet. His eyes were open, expressive, like those of a man deep in thought, mulling over his future and the decisions that awaited him.

When she noticed Edgardo, Kallis turned and looked at him as if he were a ghost. Segrado was still clutching the parchment in his hand. The ink was dissolving, producing light swirls in the water, like the squirts of small cuttlefish.

The formula was now illegible.

The master seemed to recognize Edgardo. His lips parted in a thin breath, like a wind instrument. His limbs suddenly shuddered, stirring the water, like the last flap of a fish's fin, and his life force exited his body.

The master closed his eyes and, just then, a bolt of lightning flashed low across the horizon, illuminating the surface of the lagoon with a white, moonlike light. Segrado seemed to lift himself, as though pushed by a subterranean glow. Then the gloomy darkness of the storm returned. Horrendous lightning and deep thunderclaps tore through the sky, and the body fell back down, enveloped by the waves. Edgardo made the sign of the cross.

Kallis got up. She was unrecognizable. Her face was deeply lined, her eyes empty, glassy, as though in just a few moments she had aged many years. A thread of wool that had been twisted and broken. She reached out to Edgardo and touched his wound, as though she wished she could heal it with a miraculous gesture.

God almighty, how could he love her so much . . . He loved her even though she was a murderess, a slave, and a traitor. She had killed her own father. She had tricked Edgardo, lied to him. And yet he loved her above everything else, above any right, any reason, any divine laws.

She gently touched his eyelids with her finger.

"Forgive me, I'm just a slave," she whispered. "I thought I could redeem myself, be born again. I defied God and lost the light of reason. Slaves have no right to another destiny except being slaves forever. Forgive me, I didn't want to hurt you . . . "

Edgardo held her in a desperate embrace. "Kill me too," he whispered. "I beg you, kill me. My life has no more meaning. I've lost everything and now I've also lost you. Kill me and make me happy. Set my soul free . . . "

A light flutter of the eyelids and the vanishing memory of a happy moment flashed across Kallis's face.

"It will be a release for me. Kill me," Edgardo repeated. "I'm a danger to you. I know the formula. Kill me and you'll be the only one who knows the secret."

Kallis pressed her lips to his face, covering him with kisses. "No, my love. I'm in no danger with you because I know you will never reveal the secret. You've sworn. You're a knight, and a knight never goes back on his word."

She cast a final glance at her father and walked away, toward the canal where the *scaula* was tied.

"Kill me, please!" Edgardo shouted again. "I'm already dead, so free me from this useless body."

His cry was swept away by a gust of wind that suddenly came from the north, upsetting the waters.

Kallis ran to the boat and, with a few strokes, rowed away from the shore, southward toward Metamauco.

The world had turned over again. The sky stood still and the waves in the lagoon had risen, tall and raging. Edgardo collapsed in the water, which was still rising. For a while, he managed to follow the course of the boat shaken by the waves, and watched it being lifted on the crests of the breakers before tumbling down into the eddies. Then he saw Kallis disappear in a mass of foam and vapor. A thread of wool swallowed by the muddy sea.

The rain fell abundantly and produced tiny sparks as it hit the water. The line of the horizon, torn by flashes of fire that lit up the vault of the sky like the northern lights, turned blood-red. The sea roared and a hollow rumble shook houses, land, and the water all around.

Suddenly, shaken from its depths, as though by magic, the lagoon drew back and vanished, leaving *rios*, canals, basins, and even the Rivus Altus, dry.

Seeing the wonder, the citizens of Venetia thought the end of days had come, and knelt down to pray.

Then an almighty rumble, like an army of a thousand men galloping across a plain, shook the earth, and a wall of water as tall as two towers, and as imposing as a mountain, came crashing angrily down on the city, penetrating all the harbors, passing the beaches, flooding everything with its might, leaving in its wake smashed galleys, collapsed houses, demolished banks, uprooted bridges. Even the new bridge was swept away, stone walls and dams ripped open and pulled off, the vineyards and vegetable gardens destroyed.

All the lands of the lagoon were flooded and an entire island, Metamauco, vanished, swallowed by the billow, totally razed to the ground by the gigantic wave. The harbor, the palaces, the fishermen's houses . . . Everything was erased by the power of nature, sunk to the bottom of the muddy sea. Nothing remained of that wonderful, blooming island.

I have seen thick, black rivers rise from the ruins of derelict churches and stifle the city in a deadly embrace. I have seen broken slabs of marble, uprooted bridges, collapsed towers, and galleys, *scaulas*, gondolas, and chelandions all piled up in a heap in a mountain of sails, timber, and stays, in the dock before the basilica of San Marco. I have seen corpses floating all over the lagoon still tinged with blood. And fishermen's huts razed to the ground, and fishing boats hurled into the branches of oak trees, like birds waiting to take flight. And herds of cows and horses roaming around the shoals in search of grass to nibble, where everything was water and destruction. And the people, bewildered and terrified, wandering in what was once the city of Venetia, searching for the bodies of missing relatives. I have seen death and destruction, but also strong minds already working to rebuild bridges and houses. I have seen the skies open, the clouds turn pink, and the lagoon become clear like springwater.

And I have seen a knight, dressed in rags, his body deformed, his eyes wild as a madman's, roaming on a *scaula* in the lagoon, near the vanished island once called Metamauco, peering into the depths of the water, amid the ruins, in search of an illusion, a dream, a ghost named Kallis.

GLOSSARY

Ca': Short for "Casa" (house). In Venetian, it stands before the name of the house.

calle: Venetian word for a narrow street.

campo: Venetian word for a city square, which in the early days often had vegetation on it.

fondamenta: In Venice, a stretch of road along a canal or *rio.*

garzone (**plural** *garzoni*): Shop boy.

junctorio: A stretch of land outside houses that allowed passengers to disembark.

Luprio: In 1106 Venice was divided into districts that corresponded to groups of islands. For example, Rivoalto was the current Rialto, Luprio is now Santa Croce and San Polo, the island of Scopula is now Dorsoduro, the island of Canaleclo (where reeds grow) is now Cannareggio, Gemini is now San Marco, while Castello di Olivolo, with the Island of San Pietro, is now Castello.

patera: Circular ornamental bas-relief inserted into the façades of Venetian buildings.

Popilia: Known nowadays as Poveglia.

quartarolo: Ancient Venetian currency of little value.

rio: Internal canal in the city.

Rivoalto: Ancient name for the modern Rialto.

Rivus Altus: The ancient name for Canal Grande.

sandolo: A light, flat-bottomed fishing boat widely used in the Venice Lagoon.

scaula: A light boat, like a gondola, used internally in Venice.

Schiavonia: Friuli valleys, in Northwest Italy, inhabited by Slavs.

zoto: inVenetian dialect, a man with a limp.